ICED TEA AND IGNORANCE

Also by Howard Lewis Russell

Rush to Nowhere

ICED TEA
AND
IGNORANCE

BY

HOWARD LEWIS RUSSELL

DONALD I. FINE, INC.
NEW YORK

Copyright © 1989 by Howard Lewis Russell
All rights reserved, including the right of reproduction in whole
or in part in any form. Published in the United States of America
by Donald I. Fine, Inc., and in Canada by General Publishing Company Limited.

Library of Congress Cataloging-in-Publication Data

Russell, Howard Lewis.
Iced tea and ignorance.

I. Title.
PS3568.U7666I25   1989   813'.54   88-45384
ISBN 1-55611-094-4

Manufactured in the United States of America

10 9 8 7 6 5 4 3 2 1

Designed by Irving Perkins Associates

TO NOVA LENORE LACEFIELD.

Yes, Mom,

this one's for you.

Sloth, iced tea and ignorance
Are the sustenance of
Southern heritage.
The sloth is at least
Climatically excusable,
But the only difference
Between iced tea and ignorance
Is that one of them requires
Some preparation.

After all, there *is* such a thing
as life-saturation: the point
when everything is pure effort
and total repetition.

TRUMAN CAPOTE
The Dogs Will Bark

It was hard to know which was
more important: the garden's
surface or the graveyard from
which it grew and into which
it was constantly lapsing.

JERZY KOSINSKI
Being There

Chapter One

RAINE, 1983

I'M TWENTY YEARS OLD this winter, the winter my life begins, so it feels like everybody ought to be twenty. Actually though, Sheba Eagles, who's flopped in the sun next to me, just turned twenty-nine, which I don't suppose is *that* old. But Sheba's one of these southern girls raised to believe that fornication is a first-class ticket to Hell, and so she managed to hold onto her virginity until she was twenty-five (until she finally realized her parents had lied, that frustration doesn't have to be a lifestyle). So now, like all people making up for lost time, Sheba doesn't look or act anything like her real age.

On my other side, greasing his stomach with sunscreen and stabbing a finger into his bellybutton to make it splash, is Brent Brantley. Brent's twenty-three, but me and Sheba both agree that mentally he must have stopped developing somewhere around seventeen. This doesn't bother anyone though, least of all Brent, who seems perfectly happy mired in permanent adolescence. Besides, at twenty, I guess I'm more or less still an innocent myself. So all three of our ages even out kind of nicely.

Today, two days after Christmas, the temperature must be in the eighties. The radio this morning said it was a record high, even for Alabama, which just supports Mom's theory that the world is quickly incinerating itself. Mom claims the destruction of all the rain forests has caused some kind of awful imbalance in the carbon dioxide-oxygen ratio, the carbon dioxide winning out, which supposedly aggravates the greenhouse effect. Mom's up on this sort of global disaster stuff. Also, all the hairspray everybody uses doesn't help much either—you know, chlorofluorocarbons.

But damned if it doesn't make for good skin color. I tan pretty easily anyway, even for a blond. Well actually, I guess my hair borders on brown, which explains it. But Sheba tans well, too. In fact, she *always* has a tan and her hair's almost white. But it's sort of frazzly, like cotton candy, and Brent sometimes calls her Miss Poodle Puss. Brent's hardly one to talk, though. He has swimmer's hair, real flossy, which he helps along with peroxide and lemon juice. Why, in the sunlight you can almost see a rainbow around his head. At least I have the upper hand in the eye department. Mine are real aqua-blue, whereas Sheba's are pushing gray, and Brent's, well, his are probably closer to black than blue. You can tell there's just nothing behind them either. But again things average out because Brent has a real classic-looking face, a *GQ* face, and the best I can be called is "cute." As for Sheba, she looks *exactly* like a grown-up version of the old Sunshine Bread girl. Yeah, seen together I guess we're all so Aryan it's petrifying.

Our laying-out spot today is the same place it always is—the big grass triangle out front of The Dakota. The Dakota used to be fashionable back in the twenties, and it's located on the good part of Southside, the artsy part, even if it is a little run-down. Sheba lives on the eighth floor (my lucky number), and Brent lives next door to her. We helped him move in just last week, right after final exams were over. By the way, the building isn't *really* called The Dakota. It's really called The Claridge, but Sheba, who's been renting here for over five years now, has always fantasized about living in New York City. (I know she never will though. She's too lazy.)

Anyway, this triangle, which is about the size of a baseball diamond, is surrounded on all sides by street. There's no privacy whatsoever—the whole building looks out over us—but Sheba treats the triangle like her own private country club. She's always holding court here naked with her friends, her size forty tits hanging all over the place. Each of them has a name—Isabelle and Annabelle, although it doesn't necessarily matter that you get it straight which is which; Sheba switches the names around all the time. It's just that when you're talking about both of them together you have to call them The Belle Sisters.

And speaking of nicknames, Sheba's you-know-what used to be called The Tookie Bird, God knows why. But last night Sheba threw her annual Christmas party—the one where everyone has to show up wearing his clothes backwards; again the reason escapes me—and one of the guests, a crasher actually, commented that Sheba didn't have an angel for the top of her tree. I think the crasher was just trying to make party conversation (everybody had been ignoring her all night; she looked weird). But Sheba *hates* other women anyway, and only invites a few token ugly ones to her parties, and those that she does know better than to risk small talk with her, especially about something as important to her as her Christmas tree. After all, every year Sheba uses a different theme. This year it was Christmas at the Betty Ford Clinic, so of course the tree was decorated with glass vials of baby powder (cocaine), gold spray-painted syringes, silver spoons, miniature liquor bottles with ribbons tied around their necks, and reflector sunglasses with palm trees on them. There are no angels at Betty Ford.

Well, Sheba must have been higher than a Georgia pine, because she got a razor from the bathroom and went over to the tree, and in a loud voice said, "Luckily one of my dear guests has been kind enough to point out that as a traditionalist I have failed, for I'm lacking an angel on the tree this year," and there in front of everybody Sheba threw off her bathrobe and slowly shaved off every curl of her pubic hair. I swear to God she did. And then very ceremoniously she tossed all the white hairs into the tree and said, "So instead I give you angel hair!" Well, everybody at the party thought it was just great. They all gave her a standing ovation, except for the crasher, who left. So now, whenever you talk about Sheba's you-know-what, you have to call it The Bald Eagle.

So today we're just nursing hangovers and hanging out, taking advantage of this freak weather; not that we couldn't be found out here most days short of a snowstorm anyhow. Don't ask me why, but in our case laziness always seems to take precedence over the more important things in life. For instance, I should probably be at the registrar's office this very moment, trying to figure out what I'm going to take next quarter, not that I'm at all interested, but on the surface I should at lease *pretend* that I care about my future. I'm sure though that I'll just procrastinate until the very last second, until the day classes actually begin. And as usual, I'll end up taking whatever isn't full-up. And as usual, I won't study. And as usual, I'll make straight A's. It's like boredom is my middle name.

And speaking of boredom, I turn my head to look at Sheba who, with a great sigh, tosses down her *Cosmo* only to pick up her Tab and suck at it slowly while picking lint from her toenails. Then she sets her Tab back down and pinches at the flesh on her waist. Finally, with her left hand she cups Isabelle, and with her right hand she begins poking it with her fingers like kids love to do with a bag of marshmallows. "Honeys, can you tell me why I hate women so much?" she asks. "Southern women especially?"

" 'Cause most of them are *so* boring," says Brent, smearing oil on the insides of his legs.

Sheba, with a thoughtful look on her face and squeezing the bottom side of Isabelle extra hard, ponders this a moment. "You think that's it?"

"Well take a look around. You don't see any of the others tanning *their* twats, do you? No, they've all skipped off to nursing school in their pink grasshoppers to snag wealthy doctors."

Sheba says, "But I didn't make too much of a spectacle of myself in front of that Yankee girl last night, did I?"

"How do you know she was a Yankee?" I say to Sheba. "She didn't sound like one to me."

"Well honey," Sheba huffs, turning to me with a look on her face that says if anyone could spot a Yankee a mile away, she could. "Didn't you see how she was done up? What with wearin' that straight blunted hairdo and bein' dressed all in black like she was the elf of death or somethin.' Now I ask you, have you ever seen a girl wearin' black outside New York? It's not even fashionable at funerals anymore." She switches hands to Annabelle, and a few moments later cups both The Belle Sisters and says, "Healthy as usual," yet then laments, "Oh but honeys, the worst part is the elf of death probably has a date tonight, while I'm just gonna be stuck home wasting a perfect tan picking divinity out of the carpet."

Neither Brent nor me say anything to this. Dates and boyfriends are a touchy subject with Sheba, who's never been able to keep one too long. It's probably because she's overweight. Well actually, she's downright fat, but at least she seems to get away with it better than most fat women. Personally, I can't even imagine her thin. To me, there's nothing wrong with her, but I can see how it might bother a potential boyfriend. Nobody wants to date a cow. Just ask my sister Cyra.

"So I take it you're off tonight?" says Brent, the hint in his voice being that if Sheba would care to work, she's more than welcome to take his place.

"Well, not completely," she says, taking another sip of her Tab, "but you know how it is. I'll probably fall ill. I mean *nobody* eats out two days after Christmas, nobody decent, and tonight I really just don't feel up to serving another well-done sirloin with ketchup. How about you boys?"

"I'm working," I say.

"Ditto," says Brent.

"Then that settles it," Sheba says. "We'll all just call in sick together and go to Atlanta. Doesn't that sound nice?" and she flutters her lashes and pretends to fan herself with a palmetto. "Of course though, I still haven't paid this month's rent, but fiddle dee dee."

"December's rent?" I say.

"Uh-huh," she nods. "Scandalous, isn't it, but it's not late until the tenth."

"But Sheba, this is the twenty-seventh."

"Well honey, they know how I am. Why I've been livin' here forever. I'm good for it."

"What about Christmas money?" Brent asks. "Didn't you get any?"

"From *my* parents? Honey, you know they gave up on me once I passed marrying age. The most I get now is a new add-a-bead every year."

"But don't they like you?" Brent says, a little confused, and he pulls down on the elastic of his Speedo, which has started to crawl up his butt.

"Of course honey, but they just have a difficult time understanding the type of personality who'd spend rent money on a bottle of perfume, especially a girl like me who has to work for a living. Why my mother's never worked a day in her life. She got married a week after college graduation. And now she wanders around from room to room in that great big house up in Huntspatch, wearing her Laura Ashley dresses, and when she's bored she sorts her jewelry. To her, that's what a girl's life ought to be—ivory tower entrapment."

"It's so sad," I say, thinking about my own mother. She's not quite as materialistic as Sheba's mother sounds, but God knows she's just as befuddled as to what her niche is in the great scheme of things. This is a woman who planted trees on the days me and my sister were born, my fat sister Cyra, and on more than one occasion I swear I've caught Mom talking to them. Now I don't mean the normal way people speak to plants, mind you, nothing like, "How are we feeling today? Do we need some water?" No, Mom actually treats these trees like they're human or something. She carries on *conversations* with them!

"Sad," agrees Sheba, "but safe. And sometimes I do envy her. I mean let's face it, I'm not exactly Christie Brinkley at the beach. I have been known to dip into second helpings from the salt and vinegar potato chips bag. But it's not like I haven't tried. Jesus knows I've tried. Why I spent the first twenty-five years of my life trying to catch a husband. I lacquered my hair, nobody had bigger pageant hair than I did, and I joined the Tri-Delts at Tuscaloosa, I gushed over those drunken oaf football players, I was even bulemic . . . why I did everything a good girl was supposed to do, and honeys, I absolutely *hated* it."

"Well, at least your grandfather was governor of Arkansas," I say, "which must count for *something.*"

"That's right, and even Mother was second alternate to Miss Georgia, so it's not like I don't come from good stock or anything." And on this note, Sheba fluffs her pillow, turns her face to the sun, and puts on her shades.

Brent and I take this to mean the subject of Sheba's spinsterhood has been dropped, so for the next few minutes we all just sort of stretch out and close our eyes and feel the melanin in our skin grow darker. I pick up *How the Grinch Stole Christmas* and flip lazily through it. It's about my favorite book, but one I only feel comfortable reading in December. I chuckle softly over the scene where Max doesn't realize he's supposed to be the reindeer. Instead, he's perched on the sleigh, smiling and wagging his tail, anticipating the ride down Mt. Crumpit. Poor Max. "What time is it anyway?" I say.

Brent takes a swig from Sheba's Tab and glances at his watch. It's a new watch, a Christmas watch, a Rolex no less—a gift from Ampersand, the owner of the restaurant we all work for. Nobody else got a watch of course. Nobody else got anything. Ostensibly, the watch was Brent's reward for being chosen as Employee of the Month. Strangely though, no one had even heard of this "Employee of the Month" deal until Brent won it; Brent, who looks nice in a tuxedo, but who doesn't know the difference between an aperitif and an appetizer. It'll be interesting to see if Ampersand continues this little work incentive program into January. I wouldn't mind a Rolex myself. "It's eleven o'clock," Brent says.

"Is that all?" I say, and for some reason I'm thinking it ought to be midnight. I don't know what it is with me lately, but I just feel so anxious . . . so nervous . . . so convinced Fate is brewing something wicked to tempt me with, something out of the ordinary, something extraordinary. I mean, I keep thinking something, *anything,* ought to happen every once in a while, but just *nothing* ever does. If anyone's due some excitement it's me, 'cause at the moment, monotony is like the most prevailing force in my life.

Finally, about half an hour later, I just can't take anymore. So as I stand and pull on my jeans, Sheba says, "Where are you going?"

"I don't know, but I'm sick of laying around here getting cancer."

"Can you see if my back's red?" Brent asks, twisting his head around to peer over his shoulder.

So I bend down and punch a finger into one of his shoulder blades. "It's leaving a white spot behind," I say. "Oh shit," and Brent grabs for his shirt. "I'm gonna be stuck in that damned monkey suit all night, too. Why I might as well douse myself with gas and light a match, as hot as I'll be."

"Oh honeys, I've got an idea," says Sheba, screwing the lid back on the suntan lotion. "Why don't we all go see a movie? *Terms of Endearment* is supposed to be good."

"I've seen it twice already," I say. "Besides, I don't feel like crying."

"Then let's go shopping. We can return presents. My grandmother gave me a beautiful Japanese kimono this year, it's all embroidered and everything. I know it's expensive, too, because she only shops at Lillie Rubin. So, if we returned it, I could make at least a couple hundred, which would be more than enough for us to go to Atlanta on."

"You and Brent go on ahead," I say. "I'm really not in the mood. Besides, I need to work tonight. I'm trying to save up enough to move into my own apartment."

Brent says, "But I thought you were going to move into that room over the garage out back of your mom's place."

"Well I was, but my sister beat me to it."

"Honey, is she still fat as me?" Sheba asks.

"Fatter," I say. "You know, I don't know what her problem is, but she's becoming like some kind of recluse. I mean, she won't go to college but she won't get a job either. Lately, she won't even leave her room. All she does is sit around getting fatter and fatter and fatter."

Brent adds, "Well, she never has liked me, and I've always tried to be nice to her. She thinks I'm some kind of flake or something. Hey, why don't we all just go to California?"

"Oh no, honey," says Sheba, accepting Brent's idiot suggestion at face value. "If I'm going to make a radical upheaval in my life, I'd rather go to New York."

17

"It's so cold there, though."

"I know, honey, but Jackie Onassis lives there, so it couldn't be that bad. Besides, in New York we might be more exotic-looking. I mean, *everybody* has blond hair in LA." Brent says, "Listen, Miss Poodle Puss, I'd never have a chance of becoming *anything* in New York. I'm too shallow and too dumb. In LA at least, those things aren't a handicap. And don't forget, you're not exactly Marie Curie yourself."

"Well fine," says Sheba, throwing up her arms, obviously having had her fill of the male sex for today. "We'll all just rot slowly here in Birmingham then, and grow old and die having never even stepped foot in Van Cleef and Arpels." She stands and glances around the grass. "Honeys, do you see my swimsuit? I know it's around here somewhere. It's that white one, you know, with the ladybug design in mother-of-pearl."

"I don't see it," Brent says, slipping into his clothes.

Sheba rests her hands on her hips with a scowl on her face. I button my shirt and roll my head around until the bones finally crack. Sheba says, "I bet that damned dog ran off with it. I hate that thing. Whose is it anyhow?" and she jerks a towel angrily around her shoulders.

Sheba's talking about Beowulf of course—just some stray mutt that hangs around The Dakota. It eats anything—mice, squirrels, cats, Big Macs, plastic cups, swimsuits—anything. I'm the one who named him Beowulf—me and my friend Jack Roe, who nobody likes—for no particular reason.

So Sheba's mad and Brent's burned and I'm bored, and we all slowly begin sauntering back toward The Dakota. I guess we'll just end up lounging around on Sheba's bed the rest of the afternoon, watching MTV or "I Love Lucy" reruns and eating chips and dip with Tab until it's time to go to work. Sheba starts grumbling about how much that suit cost her, that even at Loehmann's it was eighty-five dollars. But nobody's listening, and

ICED TEA AND IGNORANCE

Brent's doing his impression of Lucy when she's sunburned at the Don Loper fashion show. As for myself, I'm trying to resist the temptation to just vomit up my guts, 'cause right as we get to the steps of the building, here comes Beowulf bounding around the corner with a dead baby in its mouth.

Chapter Two

CYRA

"DEAR GOD! Please tell me my eyes are deceiving me. I'm not seeing what I think I see!"

"What? What is it?"

"Chocolate candy and a nightgown novel in your lap? Cyra, it's eleven in the morning."

"Mom . . ."

"I don't want to hear it," she says, holding up her hands in front of her shoulders, and she comes over to my window and snatches open the drapes. I pull a quilt over my face to block out the sun.

"Now Cyra, it's a beautiful day outside. The weatherman said it's going up to eighty-two degrees. You should be enjoying it. Raine was up hours ago."

"But he's always up early. You know I'm a late sleeper."

"Honey," she says, sitting on the edge of the bed next to me, "you haven't been out of this room in two days. The last time we saw you was at Christmas dinner."

"Well I don't feel good . . . I've got a stomachache."

Mom grabs the Godivas out of my lap and rattles the box. "Empty," she says. "Two pounds of chocolate and the box is empty. It's a wonder a stomachache is all you've got."

I don't try to argue with her. Instead, I open my book to a random page and pretend to read, but I can feel her eyes boring into my forehead, wondering how she ever produced such a shiftless bitch. Finally she asks, "Couldn't you at least read something educational?"

"You used to say *all* books are educational." I say this without even looking up. "You told us no matter what we read we'll still learn *something.*"

"And you will the *first* time. But honey, these nightgown books are just the same thing over and over again." (Mom calls them "nightgown" books because the cover invariably shows a woman running terrified across the moors at midnight wearing nothing but her silk nightgown. Behind her you always see the silhouette of a castle with one light burning in the tower.)

"They're not always alike . . . the names are different. Besides, you never say a word to Raine when he's holed up in his lair reading *Winnie the Pooh* and *The Jungle Book* and that Dr. Seuss shit. It's kind of sick if you ask me."

"Well I don't. And in any case, those books are children's classics. They're ageless."

"Always defending him, aren't you? . . . Why Raine's so smart. Raine's on the Dean's List. Raine's never had a pimple, he never needed braces, he sleeps seven and one half hours a night, he laughs at weddings, cries at funerals . . . wind him up and he'll entertain you!" Now I hurl my book against the wall and with my hands over my ears I howl, "Raine, Raine, go awaaaaaay!"

"Cyra," Mom says, "honey, calm down," and she brushes back my hair with a worried look on her face. "Sometimes I just have so much trouble understanding you. You're eighteen years old. This should be the best time of your life. Why you're pretty, you're bright—not many people finish high school a year early—yet all this past summer and fall you've barely left the house."

She looks at me now as though waiting for my explanation but I don't bother with one, choosing instead to cross my arms and press my face into the pillow, hoping she'll leave. Mom sighs and lifts the lid on my Godiva box. She eats the last one—a macadamia cream, my very favorite. I don't think she even realizes what she's doing.

"Mom, we've been through this before. I told you I just need a break for a year. I've been in school since I was four years old. Just give me until I'm nineteen to think about college. Is there anything wrong with that?"

"Nothing at all. Why I think every person should have a year just to sit back and figure out what he wants from life. But you know that's not my point."

"Then what is?"

She begins picking at the gold foil on the box. "Sweetheart, have you weighed yourself lately?"

"I knew it! This whole lovey-dovey routine is just an excuse to bitch about my weight. You know, you're not exactly Karen Carpenter yourself!"

"There you go again," she says. "All I'm trying to do is find out if you're happy. That's all. I'm not asking you to lose any weight if you don't want to."

"Well good, because I don't. I'm *very* happy with my weight."

"Cyra," she says sternly, getting up and pacing around my bed, "I'm doing my damnedest to hold this family together. It would be nice if you'd participate."

"The family? The family? You mean you and Raine?"

"Yes," she says. "Me and Raine and you. We are a family, you know."

"Huh! Keep reminding me. Maybe it'll stick." And before I know it, Mom has reached over the bed and slapped me across the face. It happens so quickly we're both too stunned to do anything but stare at each other in horror. Mom's never slapped me before. It didn't hurt really, but I don't suppose that's the point. For a second or two I debate whether this deserves tears, but then Mom wraps her arms around my shoulders and starts crying herself.

"Honey, I'm so sorry," she says.

"Oh Mom, don't cry."

"No, I'm all right," and wiping her eyes she gets up from the bed. She walks to the door and manages to regain some composure. "Would you like an elixir? The blue quartz is wonderful for stomachaches."

I start to say something, but luckily I catch myself before smarting off about her "Aquarian remedies." Mom has a greenhouse built onto the back porch. She uses it to make her "gem elixirs"—glasses of tap water with rocks in the bottom—malachite, amethyst, jade, rose and blue quartz, onyx, lapis, obsidian, beryl—glamorous-sounding rocks, but rocks just the same. According to Mom, the longer you leave the elixirs in the sun, the more energy they absorb. She's been "energizing" the diamond from her wedding ring for over seven years now, ever since Dad died. It gets special treatment—in a bottle of Evian on the top shelf of the greenhouse. God only knows what she's planning to cure with that one.

"Sure," I tell her, trying to sound pleasant, "the quartz would be super."

So when she returns, I drink it down like a good little girl. But of course the rock has no flavor. All it really tastes like is stale water; yet Mom says, "Delicious, huh?" and I agree with her.

After I'm finished, she takes the rock and quickly wraps it in a black cloth, which then has to sit in a drawer for at least twice as long as it had been exposed to sunlight for. Supposedly, this total darkness deal recharges it, and Mom's a big believer in recycling. "Well," she says, accepting my glass, "if you'd like to go shopping in a few minutes, or . . ."

I shake my head. "Maybe later."

"Are you sure you're okay, Cyra?" And she gives me a long, intense look—one that says "Mothers know more than you think they know."

"I'm fine. I told you I've just got a little bit of a stomachache. That's all."

She nods. "All right then, well I'm going to go to the nursery and pick up some plant food and things. That Japanese pear I planted from seeds last year looks like it has rust; and that damned stray dog, whoever he belongs to, chewed to death my wandering jew, not to mention knocking over the birdbath and breaking it. He must have gotten a bird, too—there's blood all over the base. I just don't understand it, suddenly everything's dying," and she gives me another of those looks as she closes the door behind her.

I listen to her footsteps as she goes down the stairs. Then I watch through the window while she crosses the yard to go back into the house. It's so nice living out here over the old garage— you can always tell when someone's coming. I like my privacy anyhow, and Mom, after I begged her forever, finally let me fix up this place as my own apartment. Just so long as I don't throw any wild parties or such. Yeah, like I'm really a partying kind of animal. Anyhow, I moved out here a little over six months ago, right after graduation—just about the time I began to suspect things.

But I can't stand to get into that now. It's all I've been worrying over these last two days, ever since I got up from the table at Christmas with stomach cramps. Really, it's too hideous to even think about anymore. So I just lie in bed and stare blankly at the mirror across from me. My room is always the prettiest this time of morning because the windows face east, and morning light is always the nicest light. Most of the stuff in here came from the house, like the bed and the chest of drawers and junk like that. (I made Raine move it all.) But of course I've added my own personal touches here and there—the wallpaper with big yellow roses, the wicker baskets full of sweet potpourri, the blue ceiling (I made Raine paint the clouds on it), and the Battenburg lace bedspread that I stole from Grandmother's cedar chest—you know, feminine stuff.

Looking at myself in the mirror, I really don't like that bloated creature staring back at me. But then that's just the way it is. So I sort of roll my tongue around the inside of my teeth, getting the last bit of chocolatey after-flavor, and then I begin pulling a comb through my hair. *Mom's right, you really are pretty . . . well, you could be.* I squeeze a blackhead lodged on the side of my chin. *In fact, you could be beautiful.* Examining all the angles I discover that if I turn my head slightly upwards and stretch up my chin, and if I don't look at anything in the mirror below my face, and if I sort of squint my eyes until the reflection is blurred, then I can almost look anorexic. Beauty and anorexia—what more could a healthy girl want?

Some coconut macaroons I guess. So I reach into my secret stash beneath a layer of potpourri in the basket on the end table. Only two are left, but not to panic—I stole Raine's box of choc-olate-covered cherries that Grandmother gives us every year, and in case of an emergency there's that giant Hershey's Kiss and a big tin of fried peach pies under the bed. The pies really belong to that crone next door, the Lemurian or the Shaman or whatever she calls herself; the one who claims she moved to Birmingham because it's going to be one of the few "safe areas" when the earth's axis shifts next decade. She really is a doomster, and what's worse, she's slowly hooking Mom on all this shit too—Zen, astral travel, homeopathic healing, I Ching, automatic writing, gem elixirs—good God!

Actually, I would have probably given the bitch her package of pies the other day if only the UPS man hadn't been so cute; but since he was, and since he personally asked if *I* would be kind enough to deliver them to her, well, it practically seemed like a gift from him to me. Anyhow, the damage is done now, so I pry the lid off the tin and swipe three of the delicious pastries from their paper nest (one still has a little shred of oily napkin stuck to it) and I just start gorging. Across from me, I can see I'm eating so quickly that some of the sugary brine is oozing down my chins and slopping onto the pretty lace bedspread. I start laughing. I rub my swollen belly like Buddha, open my mouth, stare at the mush inside, and just howl.

It really is rather comic if you think about it . . . well it would be, if it weren't so sick. Mom's hardly dumb though, and I'm sure that little performance of hers was designed to snare me into a confession. But she won't get one. Not in a million years she won't. I bet it just blows her mind, too, what with her wondering how on God's earth this could ever happen to *me,* of all people. I mean she's never seen me with any kind of boyfriend to speak of. Nobody, after all, wants to date a girl fifty pounds overweight. (Just ask that fat bitch friend of Raine's.) So I can practically hear Mom thinking out loud, "Well if she *is* pregnant, who's the father?"

I don't know why, but abortion never once crossed my mind. Not once. Then again, we're talking about someone so dumb it took her half a year to even realize she was missing her period. I guess I just refused to let myself think about it. Instead, I began eating everything in sight; not because I was hungry actually, but because . . . because . . . well, to keep my mind busy I suppose. And by August I'd gained sixty extra pounds on top of my extra fifty! By that point though I began to admit to myself that something wasn't quite normal, but I was too embarrassed to see a doctor. Besides, how would I have explained the bills to Mom? So I just tried to keep pretending nothing was wrong. I don't know who I thought I was fooling.

It's horrible when you let something go by for so long, knowing you should be doing something, but being just too scared to even do anything. And looking back, I think I could have handled admitting I was pregnant, if that's all I'd had to admit to. But unfortunately, I would also have had to name the father, which is just something I could never have done in a million years. So as I saw it, only one course of action was left available to me, and by Christmas I was spending a lot of time at the library reading books on natural childbirth—yes, I was going to have the baby all by myself without anyone ever finding out. And I did . . . sort of.

The first labor pains began at the dinner table Christmas night, but I was well-prepared. Laid out on the end tables next to my bed were extra towels, sheets, rubber gloves, scissors, gauze, bandages, compresses, feminine pads—everything. So I excused myself and went out to my apartment, where I stripped and turned up the stereo as loud as it would go, and with my knees up I laid on the bed and waited. I figured it wouldn't be too long, because Mom and me both were born shamefully fast. Sure enough, my water broke within ten minutes of my first contractions. The pain wasn't even that bad. I had a little in my back and some in my stomach, and then came this uncontrollable urge to push down, which I did. Oh, I do remember vomiting a little—I guess because I'd just eaten—but it was all over in less than half an hour.

And I know this is going to sound like the most cruel thing in the world, but I couldn't look at my baby. I just couldn't. I was afraid I'd fall in love with it if I did, and no way was I going to let that happen, not after the nightmare of its conception. I mean there's just no telling what it might have looked like. So I closed my eyes and reached under me with the scissors and snipped the cord. After that I fell asleep, only to wake up a few hours later feeling sort of like I'd been hit by a train. The music was still blaring like hell, but I turned it down and then switched off the lamp. (I figured it would be easier to do what I had to do if I did it in the dark.) I got up from the bed despite the pain, and by the light of the moon I folded up the corners of my blanket into a big sack. Luckily, nothing had soaked through to the mattress cover. Then I slipped on my robe and snuck down the stairs outside to the old garage underneath, which is now just a place to store junk, and there I hid the bundle in a wood soda crate and flipped it upside down. The plan was that I'd haul it all off in the car somewhere the next day, yesterday, and dump it.

But I guess all plans go awry, or at least perverted ones do, because Mom and Raine were home all day yesterday, so I didn't get a single chance to slip away unnoticed, and I didn't feel like having to make up some lie about where I'd be. Also, I was still kind of dragged out, so I figured it wouldn't hurt to wait one more day. Besides, neither of them ever set foot into the garage (Mom says it's haunted, and Raine saw a cottonmouth there last summer), and I'm not exactly psychic or anything, so how was I supposed to predict what would happen this morning?

I have to admit, too, it's a damned insensitive person who can calmly watch what I saw. I was so nervous I'd barely slept anyway. So just imagine my terror when I woke up at dawn to the sounds of things being knocked over in the garage. Shivering, I pulled the covers around my chin and tried to remember if I might have left the garage door ajar in my haste to complete my mission the other night. Suddenly though, the sound stopped. Just stopped, making me wonder if I had been imagining things; but then from the corner of my eye, right as the sun was peeking through the treetops, I saw the birdbath out behind the patio smash over.

And that, let history record, was the exact moment in my life (just a few short hours ago) that I realized I have a heart colder than a corner of Hell. I mean what other eighteen-year-old girl could watch emotionless, absolutely emotionless, while some stray mutt totes her baby away in its mouth?

Chapter Three

RAINE

"HONEY, ARE YOU SURE it's dead?"

"Sheba, of course I'm sure. Look at it."

"I don't want to look at it. I hate those things. Stomp on it again, would you, just one more time? Please, Raine?"

"Let me do it," Brent says. He presses down his foot and grinds his shoe into the floor. "Oooooh," he grimaces, "just listen to it squish."

"Honey," Sheba snaps from her ottoman, "don't smush it up too much or we'll never get the carpet clean. Now throw it out the window or something."

So Brent rips a page from a *House Beautiful* and begins folding it into an airplane. I'm sitting in the windowsill, cracking my toes and gazing down at the triangle eight floors below. The wind has picked up some. It feels like the temperature might be dropping, too. My feet are cold.

"Here we are," Brent says. He holds the airplane against the floor like a dust pan and flicks the roach into the groove on the back of it. "Bombs away!" Brent says, then he propels the plane out the window. About five feet away it hesitates briefly, then nosedives down to the street. I'm reminded of the old Saturday morning Road Runner cartoons, where Wiley Coyote inevitably races beyond the cliff's edge, pauses in midair, shrugs, and plummets. Brent, squatting on the floor like an Indian, begins folding another airplane.

I stand up and close the window, then sit back down again, watching a car below roll over the roach transporter. Unconsciously, I pick up a candle from the windowsill and begin scratching at it nervously. It's shaped like Santa Claus, and his face starts peeling away under my fingernails. "So . . . so what are we going to do here, y'all?"

"We?" says Brent, folding a crease down the middle of his Boeing. "Wait just a minute here. *You're* the one who decided to be the good samaritan."

"And just what was I supposed to do? Leave it for the dog's lunch?" Santa's nose breaks off under my thumb.

"Now honeys," says Sheba, her face pallid and contorted. She swallows hard and steals a glance toward the pillowcase resting on her bed. Sheba's naked, naturally, except for a big floppy red bow tied around her head. The ends of the ribbon wrap under her chin, and she's pulling alternately on each end, making the bow slide over the top of her head from one ear to the other and back again.

Looking at her and Brent makes me almost burst out laughing. This situation, after all, is just too weird. We aren't the type of people who can cope with anything that deviates from the totally superficial. I mean it's *so* bizarre it doesn't feel real. I even have to turn my head when I pass a dead dog in the road. So just what am I supposed to do about a dead baby?

"Hey," I say, "shouldn't we call the police in on this?"

"Well don't look at me," Brent says, licking the tip of his plane. "I'm the one who had to wrap it up in the pillowcase."

"And I hope nobody saw that," Sheba says. "They'll probably think *we* murdered it."

"Maybe it was an accident," I propose. "Maybe the mother had put it down to play and then . . ."

"Oh honey, it wasn't an accident. This baby's a newborn. Why, it couldn't be more than a day old."

"How would you know?" asks Brent.

"Because honey, my brother and his wife breed like rabbits and I've been at the hospital every time. I know what new babies look like."

"Well it couldn't be *that* newborn," I say. "It wasn't bleeding or anything. So Beowulf must not have dragged it off until after the blood had had time to coagulate. That *is* what happens after you die, isn't it? The blood gels? Damn, I wish I'd taken an anatomy class."

"Well personally," Sheba postulates, throwing the bow off her head and under the tree, "I'll bet you nobody even knows about this baby except its mother. And I'll bet you she murdered it, too—either smothered it or let it die of exposure—I'll bet you she did it and then fed it to that dog thinking he'd eat it all, and that would be that."

"How perverted," Brent says. He flicks his plane into the air and it soars up, does a loop, circles around the room twice, and crashes into the tree. A glitter-encrusted hypodermic syringe falls and spears the floor. "You know, we should've just left it alone in the first place and let somebody else have found it."

I scratch harder at Santa's face, plowing my thumbnail into his eyes. "Well we didn't," I say, "and now we've got to do *something.*"

Brent says, "Well let's just bury it somewhere then. If we call the cops there's no tellin' what they'll think. Besides, last year I got a speeding ticket which I never did pay. Not even to mention my tag expired a good three months ago. I can't risk a rundown on my files."

I turn to Sheba, an amazed look on my face. "Is that how you feel, too?"

"Oh, honey," she stammers, getting up and putting on her robe. "I don't know what I feel. On the one hand, all my maternal hormones are revolting and want to see justice served, but on the other hand, I'm thinking, how many parking tickets have I not paid this year? Sixty or seventy at least."

"What?" Brent says. "Seventy tickets!"

"Well honey, it's not my fault they don't provide enough parking for all the tenants here, and it's like if you don't find a space before five o'clock you're out like Flynt. The only place left is in front of the fire hydrant. Just what am I supposed to do? Walk two blocks and risk getting raped seven ways from Sunday? Thank you, no. That's probably what happened to the poor mother of this child."

Nobody says anything for a few minutes after this. I imagine we're all busy wrestling with our personal demons and attempting to salve our consciences. I keep telling myself that it's definitely for the best that we don't go to the police. I mean, the mother is probably just some innocent victim of an unspeakable crime of passion, just like Sheba said. In doing nothing, we're probably giving her the chance to start over again and erase her past. Otherwise, the publicity would surely drive her to suicide. God knows there'd be no end to it, too, especially during Christmas time, when dead children make such wonderful headlines. Yes, it's a good thing we're the ones who found her baby and not some yule-spirited do-gooder. A good thing indeed.

Sheba walks to the tree, makes a cross with her right hand in front of the Belle Sisters, and starts examining all the vials of baby powder. She says, "I'm going to have a breakdown if I don't get something to take my mind off this. One of these is real. My last date left it behind—about five or six months ago I guess. Boy did we have a fun time that night. He's the one I told y'all about who has muscular dystrophy, you remember, and when he came his legs locked. Honey, you never heard such a scream in your life. Eight to eighty—blind, crippled, or crazy. It don't matter to me."

"Amen," says Brent.

Sheba takes a vial down and unscrews the cap. I notice her back is to the bed, that she's trying to avoid looking in that direction at all. "Maybe it's this one. It was gonna be a prize for the person who gave me the best kiss under the mistletoe, but then that Yankee girl made me so mad I forgot all about it. Here Brent, you test it," and she hands it behind her without turning around.

He dabs a pinch of powder to his tongue. "Nope, wrong one."

"Damn," says Sheba, reexamining the tree. "You know honeys, it *is* the right thing. If we did call them we'd never get rid of them, even if they didn't check our files. I mean the police in this town are so stupid they can't tell the difference between a cow's tail and a pump handle. Why we'd be answering their dumb questions for the rest of our lives, just like my friend Jason Wyndham. Y'all remember Jason, don't you? He's the one who had that girlfriend who worked for the bank— Etoile, I think her name was—the one who embezzled half a million, then disappeared. Well, the police were so dumb it took them almost a week to check if Etoile's car was parked at the airport. Sure enough, that's exactly where it was. Anyhow, they've never left poor Jason alone since. They're just convinced he knows where the money is. Why they bug his phone and everything."

"Oooh," shudders Brent, but his curiosity overpowers him and he asks, "Well, *does* he know where the money is?"

"Honey, of course. It's with Etoile on the beach in Rio. Where else would it be?"

I stand up again and place the noseless wax Santa back in the window. Then I slip on my shoes and say to the two of them, "Well if we're not going to go to the police, then we're going to have to destroy the body or bury it somewhere where nobody will ever find it. Any suggestions, guys?"

Suddenly, there's a knock at the door from the rabbit hole in the kitchen. "Is anyone home?" comes a muffled voice.

"Oh my God!" hisses Sheba. "Somebody saw us take the baby. They're coming to arrest us!"

Brent and I both jump about a foot into the air. For a split second all eyes turn with terror to the bundle wrapped in a pillowcase on the bed. My mind races with scenes of a vice squad bursting through the walls. From somewhere a tiny voice squeaks, "But you've done nothing wrong," yet from somewhere else thunder the words, "Tell that to the dead baby!"

"Hide it! Hide it!" I say.

Brent leaps to the bed and jerks up the ends of the pillowcase . . . but they're the wrong ends. Sheba sucks in a long, rasping breath, and Brent, turning his face away, stuffs the baby back into the case, gasping, "Now what?"

I glance around the room desperately, as though the stacks of junk and crud piled around everywhere might supply me with an answer. I never gave much thought to Sheba's packrat habits before, but she throws nothing away. You name it and it's here — magazines, newspapers, throw pillows, incense lanterns, spilled jewelry, overturned fish tanks, stuffed animals, perfume bottles, iron furniture, photographs, carnival glass, dead plants, old boxes . . . *boxes!*

"Wrapping paper," I bark. "Where is it?"

"I know somebody's in there," says the voice. "I hear you."

"Here's a roll," Brent says, throwing me a long cylinder of green foil emblazoned with poinsettias, candy canes, and holly berries. I snatch a big box from atop a mannequin's head and order Brent to put the baby in it. "The tape," I say.

"Over here," says Sheba, throwing it at me. "Hurry, Raine."

Deftly, I fold the lids over the box and unroll the paper around it, thankful for the first time that Mom once made me take a job as a gift-wrapper the Christmas I was a sophomore in high school. It was my punishment for opening all my sister's presents the year before. I'm sure she'd done something to make me mad. She's such a bitch sometimes, but I can't even remember what she did now. "Scissors? Are there any scissors?"

"Catch," Sheba shouts, tossing a pair at me, and a second later a stack of old magazines goes scattering across the kitchen floor, as Jack Roe pushes his head in through the rabbit hole.

"I knew you guys were in here," he says, as he stands up and dusts off his jeans. "Why didn't you answer me?" he asks, looking down at the tiny door he's just scuttled through—the rabbit hole. It's only about eighteen inches high and connects Sheba's kitchen to The Dakota's hallway. I'm sure it must have served some real purpose back when The Dakota was a real apartment building (maybe the milkman put milk through it), but the last time Sheba lost her front door key the management said enough was enough and refused to give her another one, saying she could just call a locksmith and have her own made if she couldn't be any more responsible than a five-year-old. So now, anyone entering Sheba's apartment has to do so by way of the rabbit hole.

"Are you guys still wrapping Christmas presents?" Jack asks. No one says a word, but three chalky heads turn toward him with hateful looks on their faces.

"Well what does it look like we're doing?" I say, and as a final camouflage, I grab up Sheba's discarded bow and ribbon from under the tree and tie it around the box gaily. Then I kick the bright package beneath the limbs.

"I was only asking," Jack says. "What's wrong with y'all anyhow? You act as though you've never seen me before."

I tell him, "Well what do you expect, busting in here like white on rice."

I don't have to be particularly nice to Jack if I don't feel like it. We're too close to bother being kind. We've known each

36

other since fifth grade, and ever since then we've been friends, although God knows why. You see, Jack's very secretive and basically antisocial, which is why he never sunbathes with us or goes to the movies with us or even comes to Sheba's parties—and he lives in the apartment right above hers. But I guess Sheba's willing to make allowances for a genius, which, despite Jack's failing grades all through high school, is what his IQ supposedly makes him. I think Jack's main problem is that his scope of interest is extremely limited. In fact, I can only think of one thing he's really enthusiastic about—death. I mean, if he knew there was a dead baby under the Christmas tree, he'd be absolutely delighted.

"Well," Jack says, "if you're going to be huffy I'll just leave and you won't ever get to find out why I came by." He walks over to the bed and flops down, crossing his hands behind his neck as he leans against the headboard. The sunlight catches his hair, which is all colorless and thin and clotted, like a diseased camel's. Jack never has been very good-looking, although he couldn't really be called ugly either. He's just sort of there. His most distinctive characteristics are bad skin and a protruding neck, which juts forward instead of up, making him look kind of like a human candy cane. "Now," he says, "I'm not going any-where until you all tell me what's going on. I haven't seen faces like yours since I was at my granddaddy's funeral. Who died?"

"Died?" shrieks Sheba. "Who said anybody died?"

"We didn't kill anybody," blurts Brent.

Jack gives Brent a peculiar look. "It wasn't meant to be taken literally," he says. "As long as we're on the subject though, I might as well tell you why I'm here."

"We can hardly wait to find out," I say.

Jack ignores me. He pulls a sheet of paper from his pocket. "I've written down a preliminary list. Now mind you, this is in no way definitive. I'm always open for suggestions and argu-ments, but considering how there's only four more days left in the year, the winner will probably be one of these." He reads off the list. "Gloria Swanson, Jack Dempsey, Tennessee Williams, George Cukor, Lillian Carter, Bear Bryant, Jessica Savitch, Karen Carpenter, Carolyn Jones, Buster Crabbe, and David Niven. So, who will it be?"

Brent squeezes his brows together. A look of puzzlement comes over his face. "But didn't all those people die this year?"

"Bravo, Sherlock," and Jack gives Brent a look that asks, "How did the world ever produce such a class-A moron?"

"Yes," he says patiently, "that's what I'm doing here. Didn't Raine tell you I'd be by today for the vote? Haven't you heard? It's time to select our 'Death of the Year.'"

Chapter Four

CYRA

WELL, YES, I'VE decided to commit suicide. It's just that the more I think about it, the more I realize there's something terribly wrong with me. It's more than just being an amoral bitch . . . a fat amoral bitch. Lots of people are those things. It's more like I'm finding out for the first time that I really do have a soul—not much of one, thank God, but enough to realize that normal people don't kill their own children.

Maybe if I came from an unhappy environment I could justify it some. But there's no precedent anywhere. Mom is perfectly sane, for all her weirdness. Dad was, too, and God knows Raine is as compliant as ditch water. In fact, the only trace of family scandal anywhere is some vague rumor that my great-great-grandfather was run out of England by the sheriff for apparently doing something so bad that no one even found out what it was. I always assumed sheriffs existed only in bad westerns. But even if it is true, whatever he did couldn't begin to approach the sickness of my mind. So before I get any worse, I should destroy myself. Maybe I'll come back as something better next time, something capable of emotion. Something with feelings. A kitten, maybe.

I guess my main dilemma boils down to: "What is the easiest, most painless way?" Pills would be nice—tranquilizers—Valium, let's say; but occasionally I've read horror stories in magazines about people who take pills and don't die. They just turn into brain-dead vegetables instead. And who's to say for sure that brain-dead is the same as heart-dead? A doctor? Please. How does *anyone* know for sure that those people can't think? It sends a shiver down my back. Besides, it would just wreck Mom permanently if she had to spend the rest of her life visiting a breathing slab of dead meat in a hospital. Raine too. So pills are out.

Maybe the old crank-up-the-car-in-the-garage routine? The trouble is, I'd need the place to myself for several hours. Otherwise, Mom or Raine would be sure to come out and check what's going on. ("Oh, not much. I'm just killing myself.") Also, sitting in the car would give me too much time to think— to talk myself out of it. I sure don't want that. And even if I didn't back out, there's the matter of who would find the body first. More than likely, it would be either Mom or Raine. That wouldn't be good. Finding out I'm dead will be shock enough to them. There's no point in having them discover the body too. That settles it then; however I do it, I'm going to have to go where they won't be the first ones to find me.

I could jump off a building, I guess. I've always wanted to experience the sensation of falling. It happens so often in my dreams, but Birmingham just doesn't have that many tall buildings—oh, certainly tall enough to kill a person, but who wants to settle for just a ten- or twelve-floor drop? Besides, they're all closed off at night anyhow, so I'd have to do it in broad daylight. I don't want a public death, though. It's none of the public's business. It's only mine.

So what's left? Not razors or knives or guns. Mutilation just makes me cringe. I'll never forget how sick to my stomach I got that time after Billy Netherland's cat had six kittens. Billy Netherland lived next door to us until I was ten years old. I remember him having greenish red hair, too many freckles, and when he walked his left foot stuck out to the side. Fortunately, he was hit by a garbage truck and died on the first day of school back in fifth grade. His parents moved back to Mobile about two weeks later, and that's when that crazy witch moved in, the one who came to Birmingham because it's safe from the coming apocalypse. There must be something about that house that just attracts demented people.

Anyhow, nobody knew Billy's Siamese cat was pregnant. But she had six kittens on the foot of his bed one morning that summer before Billy died, and they were just the most adorable things you'd ever seen. Nobody knew who the father was. It could have been any old tom. Each kitten was a different color, and not one of them Siamese-looking, but my favorite was solid white with blue eyes that I named Sugar Ball. I asked Billy to let me have Sugar Ball when it was old enough to be weaned away, and Billy promised he would.

Well, I went next door and checked on Sugar Ball every single day for about six weeks. The whole litter was so playful, and I could sit for hours dangling a piece of yarn or string in front of them and never get bored. One day though, the day before Billy said I could take Sugar Ball home with me, I went over there and they weren't in their box in the basement. I remember it being so hot that day. It was just so unbelievably hot. I checked upstairs, but Billy's grandmother, who stayed with him during the day, was asleep on the sofa. (Both Billy's parents worked.) I went to Billy's room, but he wasn't in there. Then I heard the lawn mower being cranked out back.

It was when I went out onto the deck that I got sick. Down below, the kittens were planted all in a row, like they were cabbages or something. Billy had buried them up to their necks and was pushing the lawn mower toward them. When he saw me he waved, just like anybody does who's mowing the yard. The kittens looked like they were screaming, but you couldn't hear anything over the sound of the mower. The mother cat, Bonsai, was running all around frantic. I don't remember whether I screamed at Billy to stop or not. All I remember is the sound the lawn mower made when it ran over Sugar Ball's head, and the color of the grass that came spitting out with Sugar Ball's brains. The same thing happened with the other five kittens. Then Billy turned off the lawn mower and flipped it on its side to see what it looked like underneath. Vomiting on the deck, I saw Bonsai in a raging fit gnash her teeth into Billy's ankles. She just wouldn't let go, so Billy picked her up with both hands and drop-kicked her just as hard as he could. Then he walked into the basement and came out with a baseball bat. He picked Bonsai up off the lawn, whimpering, and tossed her into the air and swung at her like he was Hank Aaron. If Bonsai had been a baseball, Billy would have hit a home run.

Billy Netherland is the reason I can't stand mutilation. He's also the reason I had to turn my radio up full blast and have my baby in the dark . . . so I wouldn't have to look at it or hear it scream. Every time I see blood I think about poor Sugar Ball and that hot, hot day. That whole summer, whenever I heard a lawn mower cranking up, I didn't know whether somebody was trimming a lawn or butchering the pets. It was a very formative season in my life.

I think drowning would be easiest. I've heard say it isn't painful at all, that it's real peaceful and you see all the wonderful things in life flash before you as the water fills your lungs. A girl I knew from school drowned last year when she went river rafting on the Colorado. She wasn't really a friend of mine, but in driver's ed we were paired off together in the same car because our birthdays matched. On her driving test I remember she scored the all-time school low of eight points out of a possible hundred. I think it's because she slammed on the brakes to keep from hitting a squirrel and broke the instructor's collarbone. She was such a shy, nervous thing that it's hard to believe she ever mustered up the courage to go river rafting, but it's perfectly believable she drowned doing it. Now that I'm thinking about it, I don't even know how to swim myself. Drowning, then, it is.

But where? Not the bathtub. Bathroom deaths are just the worst. Besides, like I said before, Mom or Raine would more than likely find me first if I did it there. Besides, a bathtub's not deep enough. Knowing me, I'd probably make some half-assed attempt to hold my head under, but then I'd end up just pouring in some Mr. Bubble and enjoying myself. No, I need something so deep that when I hit the water I'll just sink like a boulder. Something so deep I'll just go down, down, down until the pressure crushes me. Mom could just as easily call it an accident. I'll use my car. That's what I'll do . . . I'll drive over the edge of the quarry!

The only quarry I know of is down in Pelham. I guess they used to mine limestone from it a long time ago, back in the seventies maybe, and even though it's the biggest hole I've ever seen, with these high sheer cliffs all around it, you still can't see it from the road because the cliffs drop away so steep. It's like a giant pit, with the water level beginning about two hundred feet down. The pit is supposed to be practically bottomless, but the surface is very still and smooth and blue, and somehow they managed to graze a slope along one piece of the wall so that a beach could be installed. Lots of high schoolers go there during the summer and on senior skip day. A local band sometimes plays on weekends, and you can rent inner tubes to float around on if you like. You're not supposed to drink beer there, but people do anyway. Occasionally you hear a story about so-and-so who floated out into the middle to sneak a six-pack, fell asleep in the sun, and slid through the hole of his inner tube never to be seen again.

So, as long as Raine's gone off and Mom's at the nursery, I decide I might as well get it over with. This way I don't have to make up some excuse about where I'm going—you know, ask me no questions and I'll tell you no lies. But it's kind of hard figuring out what I should wear. I guess the water's going to be cold, so I'll need something warm, yet I want to look nice too. That's the problem with being fat, though. Nothing looks good on you no matter how carefully you dress.

Jeans would be more comfortable than anything, but you can't die in jeans. You have to die in a dress—which presents a problem. The only dress I have is this tent-looking thing made out of white taffeta that Mom forced me to wear at senior graduation last May. It has fairy-tale princess puffed sleeves and an ecru lace bodice, and stuffed into it I look like some sow hog let loose at the Redstone debutante ball. You know, more than anything in the world I'd like to have been thin just once in my life. If I were, I could probably win a beauty contest. I'm sure I could be a Miss Alabama, maybe even a Miss America. God knows it couldn't take much: a little poise and makeup and the ability to hammer out "Feelings" on the piano without sheet music, which even a monkey could be trained to do.

It's going to be a shame to have to ruin my car—well, actually it's a Jeep, but it'll be a shame nevertheless. I'm sure it won't set too well with Mom either—once she finds out the environmental hazards a submerged vehicle presents, what with the scummy film of oil and gasoline it's bound to leave on the water. That'll probably upset her more than the fact that I'm dead. Mom's so weird that way. She keeps threatening we're going to all have to move to Brazil and stand in front of bulldozers so there will be something left after the year 2000. Apparently, if the current rate of consumption continues unabated, then everything is scheduled to give out about the turn of the century—all the plants and endangered animals and petroleum products. In fact, Mom thinks suicide is a wonderful concept— anything to keep the population under control. If not happy I'm dead, she'll at least look at the bright side—one less human to squander the earth's resources. Mom's kind of cool if the truth be known.

As much as I dislike it, I've put on my taffeta graduation dress, white pumps, and a string of pearls that aren't real but look it, and staring into my dresser mirror I'm wondering if I'll even look this angelic when I'm strolling through the pearly gates of Heaven about an hour from now. Of course, it could be the fiery gates of Hell I go strolling through. They say suicide is the only unforgivable taboo, that no matter how holy you've lived your life, you won't get into Heaven if you kill yourself; and being my child's murderess isn't exactly a point in my favor either, although on the other hand, I don't know how seriously I should take religion. I believe in God I suppose. Nature's balance is too well set up not to believe in Him, but for the most part, I think when you're dead you're just dead.

With a final glance in the mirror I check my hair. It's wonderful hair, very lush and brown, tinged with the tiniest hint of auburn. Mom's used to be my color, but premature grayness runs in our family and now hers is white. I don't know where Raine got his blond hair from, and it's wavy, too. Mine's straight as a gate, and I have to roll it every other day just to add a soft cascade to it, but I've absolutely refused to have it permed. I don't care what stylists say, there's never been a permed head of hair that wasn't a frazzly head of hair. And I'm never going to get it streaked either, like every other girl in the South seems to do. They all turn nineteen, gain twenty-five pounds, and streak their hair. *Mine* will always be natural, thank you.

45

Luckily, just like Mom said, it's a beautiful summerlike day. At least I won't have to feel like a fool driving around in a white debutante's dress. Maybe the water at the quarry won't be that cold either. It's kind of sad leaving this house for the last time, because it's a lovely place. Dad had it built in the sixties, before he caught the flu, and like most of the homes on Argyle Road, it's all russet brick with a blue-slate mansard roof, and the windows are paned with leaded glass, and each window has a big fleur-de-lis below it. It's like a little piece of England here in Alabama, and the view is just unbelievable. Argyle Road runs along the crest of Red Mountain, and so all of the city is laid out in the valley directly beneath us. Also, I'm sure it's because of our location that the witch next door moved here. As she says, "When the earth's axis shifts in ninety-nine, all of us up here will be the lucky ones. Everybody down below us will drown as the ocean rushes in."

It took me about half an hour to get to the quarry, but here I am now, parked at the edge of the abyss. There's lots of scrubby pine trees growing around up here, so I'm having to stand up in my seat with my hands clutching the safety bar just to get a clear view of the lake. I figure I picked the steepest point to drive off of, because it looks like if I turned a football field up vertically it still wouldn't reach from the top of the cliff to the linoleum-smooth surface of the water. Even if I could swim, it seems like the impact alone would do the job.

So I sit back down and back up my Jeep a few hundred yards. Then I put it in park and check my hair while I race the engine. It's so weird how there's nothing growing around here but these mangy pine trees. I mean, I'd kind of like my last view of landscape to be something prettier, but there's not even any grass growing between them. It's like the dirt up here is so awful only the cheapest things can live, and God knows if there's anything Alabama doesn't need it's more pine trees.

46

At least it won't matter a minute from now, and I jerk my Jeep into drive and slam my foot on the gas and all these ugly pine trees get sucked up under the front, just like Sugar Ball under Billy Netherland's lawn mower. The edge is coming closer and faster. You can't imagine such exhilaration. And the lake below, why it's starting to spread into view. It's just a big blue pancake spreading wider and wider. *I could have been Miss Alabama if I wanted to.* The wind feels so good. I'm going to be flying. In just two seconds I'm going to be sailing over the edge of this pit, sailing down toward that pancake...here I go... here I go...Oh God...it's like I'm a bird! Wait, the Jeep's slipping away. It's going off in another direction! I'm all alone ...I'm falling all alone. All alone—a two-hundred-pound killer debutante plunging all alone into a limestone pit. Where's my Jeep? Is the water cold? Am I insane? *I could have been Miss America!*

Chapter Five

R A I N E

"DEATH OF THE YEAR?" says Brent. "What kind of morbid thing is that?"

Jack, who I can tell is in all his glory, says, "Well, one Sunday afternoon back in 1979—it was during the summer—me and Raine were bored as usual. We'd already played 'The Gods' —you know, The Gods say if you murder your mother you get to have eternal youth, but if you don't murder her, you'll die a gory death sometime before the month is over—which do you choose? It's always a no-win situation like that. They're vicious creatures, those gods are. Anyway, we were bored with 'The Gods,' so we decided to call Alice Roosevelt Longworth.

"You know, amazingly enough, most former presidents' children have listed phone numbers, and somewhere I'd read that Alice was living out her twilight years on Massachusetts Avenue in Washington D.C. It's not that I had this great admiration for her or anything. What, after all, did she ever do? But a celebrity *is* a celebrity, and it would have been the awfulest shame for her to die before we got to say hello. That's all we wanted to do really . . . just hear her voice—the sound of American antiquity, of history books and hoary anecdotes. What must it be like to be that old?"

"Well, what did she say?" Brent asks.

"Nothing. We didn't get past the maid, who said that even if Alice had once known us, she wouldn't remember us now. She was just that old. It's really a shame, too, because she died not long after that, right after the first of the year. And in loving memory of her, me and Raine began our Death of the Year Award, honoring her as the hands-down winner of 1980. And against stiff competition, too—Hitchcock and Lennon. Later of course, we decided that Lennon was really *too* big to completely be shut out like he was. I mean he *was* a Beatle after all, so the following year we established The Natalie Wood Award—for the most unexpected and untimely death—and gave it to John retroactively for 1980."

"Well honey, did Natalie Wood win Death of the Year in eighty-one?" Sheba asks, really seeming to be getting into it. "I'm confused here. Are there two awards or just one?"

Jack sighs heavily. "Two—The Natalie Wood Award and The Death of the Year Award. I admit it can be confusing at times, especially since Natalie won a grand slam in eighty-one, only because we had such a pitiful showing that year. William Holden was the only real contender for Death of the Year, but somehow he just didn't seem big enough. Luckily, however, eighty-two made up for it. We had a real bumper crop that year. Princess Grace won The Natalie Wood Award—it was a tough decision between her and John Belushi—and Bess Truman was awarded Death of the Year. Again, Bess was a sort of sentimental choice. I'd been expecting her death for years and had tried to find her phone number before she kicked, but I guess she was still too famous to be listed. In any case, she would have been a hard one to beat, regardless. First ladies always take precedence

49

over movie stars, and former presidents take precedence over first ladies."

Brent asks, "But does anyone take precedence over presidents?"

"Only one of *us,*" says Jack. "For instance, Brent, if you die next year I'll promise you'll get Death of the Year."

"And Natalie Wood, too?"

"Don't push it." Now, turning to the three of us, Jack says, "So who will it be for eighty-three?"

"I cast my vote for Tennessee," Sheba says lazily. "He's the only one of the bunch who's really left anything worthwhile behind. And honeys, that is the most important criterion, isn't it—immortality?"

Brent says, "But what about Karen Carpenter? I mean, who could ever forget a song like 'Muskrat Love'?"

Jack says, "You idiot, that wasn't the Carpenters. It was The Captain and Tenille."

"Well, same difference," says Brent, as he begins singing. "Muskrat Suzie, Muskrat Sam, do the jitterbug in muskrat land . . ."

Jack says, "I suppose in a pinch we could give the Natalie Wood to Ms. Carpenter, but I agree with Sheba about Tennessee. Is everyone happy with that?"

"Well I, for one, am ecstatic," I say, and staring at Jack, and then at the package under the Christmas tree, I realize that if anyone should be told about this, Jack should. Nobody loves death more than him. I'm thinking of when we took advanced biology together in high school. I hate science and only signed up for the damn course because it could be substituted for physics, which I couldn't have done to save my soul. Jack hates science as much as I do, but he took advanced biology for an entirely different reason—dead animals.

I'll never forget when we had to skin a cat. The shark fetus had been bad enough, what with having to reach down into a barrel and pull one out like a pickle, but at least sharks are remorseless creatures. I didn't feel guilty about the aborted shark at all. A cat on the other hand is, well, human somehow. And though I'd been preparing myself for weeks, repeating over and over that it's all in the name of science, I still didn't expect to see a *real* cat—a big stiff yellow tomcat—and in a pickle barrel, too. And that smile on Mrs. White's face, that Hitlerian leer, as she slapped down the cat onto a square of plywood, stabbed a pair of scissors into its gut, and said, "There's only one way to skin a cat, Raine, and since you're the last through the door, I'm going to guide you through it step by step for the class's demonstration." How Jack howled afterwards—Jack, who saved his cat's skin and tacked it to the wall above his bed.

For six miserable weeks we had to pick and snip at that rotten, formaldehyde-reeking carcass. We had to learn every muscle, every bone, we had to pin back its arms and legs, pry open its skull, cut out its tongue. My cat had seven little BB's in it. One was in its eye. Mrs. White swore the cats had been humanely "put to sleep," but I could just see some grinning white-smocked lab student bringing in his little brother's BB-gun to pass the time. It didn't help any either that I'd grown up with my fat sister's secondhand horror stories about Billy Netherland, the bloodless next-door neighbor, and his kittens—although you never can be too sure what Cyra makes up and what she doesn't. She loves shock value, and it is strange how she was the only witness to Billy's escapades with a lawn mower. Billy was a weird one, though. I'll grant that. I remember at school how he used to carry around a cigar box that he'd dare anyone to lift the lid of. He claimed it had a hundred-dollar bill in it . . . and something else, too. Billy said you could keep the money if you'd lift the lid. But no one ever dared.

"Let's play 'The Gods,'" I say suddenly, noticing that Brent and Sheba seem to have completely forgotten about the baby. Sheba has wandered into the kitchen, where she's scrounging through the cabinets for something to eat, and Brent is twisting and wrenching some stupid mind puzzle, the object of which is to contort a bunch of little cubes into one big cube. To make it even more disgusting, the sides of the little cubes are different colors, six colors altogether, and when you make the big cube the colors have to line up. Maybe it wouldn't be so difficult if the little cubes weren't attached to one another. I'm not opposed to games or anything, but they should at least be solvable.

Jack is the only one who seems interested in *my* game. "Well, go ahead," he says. "I hope it's a good one."

"It is. The Gods say you've just found a body—I look to Brent, and then into the kitchen at Sheba, but they aren't catching on—you've just found a body, the body of a baby—they're catching on—and The Gods warn you that if you go to the police, an incompetent and suspicious lot, you'll be arrested for murder. But if you don't go to the police, if you simply hide the body, no one will ever in a million years find out where it is, although the guilt will gnaw at you until it drives you insane. Which do you choose?"

"But why would you have a guilty conscience if you're not the murderer?" Jack asks.

"Well, because justice has gone unserved. Because you're a decent, God-fearing soul."

"Oh right, yeah we're all such pillars of respectability here—Sheba, the nymphomaniac exhibitionist. Brent, the insouciant homosexual. You, the impassive stoic. And me, the twisted genius."

"I am neither impassive nor stoic."

"Of course not," says Jack. "That's why if a gang of machine gun-toting guerrillas burst in here this very second and asked how you'd feel if they murdered everyone in the room but you, you'd say, 'Well go right ahead, just so long as I don't have to watch.' Besides, it's either-or and neither-nor. In the future, try to keep your conjunctions in order, would you please?"

"What's insouciant? What does that mean?"

"Honey, there may be sequins on the floor, but I am not a nymphomaniac. I hail from the first family of Arkansas, thank you, and my great-granddaddy owned a hundred and fifty slaves in Jonesboro."

"Let's just get back to the point," I say, and I turn back to Jack. "The point is you've just found a dead baby and you don't know how to handle it."

A slow grin spreads across Jack's face. "Well naturally I'd hide it," he says. "Maybe I'd burn it, actually—drop it into a hospital's incinerator. Or maybe I'd put it in an aquarium tank, which I'd fill with vinegar and charge people two dollars to guess what it is at the State Fair." Then he looks to Sheba's Christmas tree. "Or I might just wrap it up in a pretty little package with a ribbon and mail it to the president of the United States. Whatever I did with it, I wouldn't feel guilty. Guilt is the last thing I'd feel. In fact, I think I'd feel pretty good. I sure wouldn't regret having found the poor tot."

"I would."

"But that's just the way you are, Raine," he says contemptuously. "You regret everything. You'd regret having two eyes if you knew there was some freak of nature out there born with an extra eye in the middle of his forehead—some cyclops. You're so bored, you'd trade places with a cyclops just for the change."

"Did you know Anne Boleyn was born with three breasts?" Brent interjects. "Did you know that, Jack?"

Jack looks at Brent as though he'd like to take a razor to his perfect little face. "You buffoon, of course I knew that. And she was born in 1507 and she died in 1536, and her sister Mary was Henry's paramour before she was, and Anne had several miscarriages and one stillborn son, and Henry charged her with incest with her brother and witchcraft because she had a witch's mole in order that he could marry Jane Seymour, and he wore yellow the day she was beheaded with a sword instead of an axe be-

53

cause an axe was too messy—he allowed her that privilege—
and she had an eleventh finger as well. Did you know *that?*"
Jack gives us all the once-over one by one. "Why do y'all
always have to try to trip me up? Face it, there is *nothing* I don't
know. Nothing!"

"I know something you don't know," Brent taunts, fastening
his eyes on Jack.

"Oh yeah," Jack grins, "and what would you like to bet, my
pretty?"

"My watch," Brent says. "I'll bet my gold Rolex that you
can't guess my secret."

"Well then, hand it over."

"You have to guess first."

"I don't have to *guess* anything. I already *know* your secret."

"How do you know? How?"

"Well for one thing, Raine's making up games with The Gods
about dead babies, and for another, there's a pretty new package
under the Christmas tree, and Christmas was two days ago.
There's no way that Sheba would have waited this long to
unwrap a gift. Obviously, you've been wrapping up dead babies,
for reasons, which I must admit, escape me."

Sheba returns from the kitchen with a plate of broken
Christmas cookies left over from the party last night. She sam-
ples a reindeer. "Honeys, I don't really want to talk about this
anymore. Can't we talk about more pleasant things? New Year's
Eve, maybe? I'm sure we're all gonna have to work, but I don't
mind really. Last New Year's I made three hundred dollars before tipping out, but then that was when you could still cheat the
IRS, too. Can you even believe this eight percent crap? What do
they think gratuity *means?*" Next she grunts, "Humph, well law
or not, I am *through* declaring my hard-earned money to those
lizards. What do they expect me to live on anyway—my sal-
ary?" Sheba finishes off her reindeer and selects a frosted bell.
"Cookies anyone?"

Jack turns to me. "So, can I take a look at it?"

"The baby?" I say.

"No," he says, "the bald eagle. Yes, the baby."

"Absolutely not," Sheba says. "We're gonna bury it and never mention a word about it to anyone. And the Bald Eagle is a little pink around the gills. I think it got too much sun today. Y'all sure no one wants a cookie?"

"Well, are we gonna bury it all wrapped up like that?" asks Brent.

Jack says, "A burial is too risky. There's always a chance the bones will be unearthed someday. I vote for cremation. We could take it over to the Brookwood Hospital and throw it in their incinerator. Isn't that what they normally do with abortions and things anyway?"

"Somebody might see us," I say.

Brent says, "Well we could pretend we're delivering a present to somebody sick."

"I think we're all sick for even contemplating this," I say.

Jack says, "Maybe we ought to reconsider our prize-winners and award the baby Death of the Year instead."

"Cute, Jack, cute," I say.

"We could throw it in the Cahaba River," says Sheba. "We could wait until tonight after work and then go drivin' around, and sort of toss it out the window as we cross the overpass. Is that a good idea?"

"It's not deep enough," I say. "If we're going to sink it we need a place as deep as the ocean, someplace like . . . like . . ."

"Like the quarry!" Sheba exclaims. "We'll sink it at the quarry. What a perfect idea!"

Chapter Six

CYRA

WELL IF THAT ISN'T the stupidest idea I've ever come up with in my life. I am *such* a total mongoloid. I can only imagine what I must look like . . . And what am I going to tell Mom? . . . How am I going to explain this? People just don't get themselves in these sorts of situations. How, in God's name, after all, do you fuck up a suicide?

I'm sitting here on this fake beach under a grove of gnarly sycamore trees. Behind me is a makeshift concession stand that serves the very best hog dogs in the summertime, and next to it are two porto-potties, a turned-over life guard's chair, and some deflated inner tubes. The sand feels all sticky and grungy, probably because I'm soaked to the bone and covered in it like a marzipan pig rolled in meal. Out in the middle of the lake is an ever-expanding scum of oil and gasoline, all shiny and rainbow-colored in the sun. Mom would scream holy hell.

I've been parking my carcass here in the sand for almost an hour now, staring dumbly at that irridescent circle of sludge, watching with pure fascination the bubbles that are still rolling up from the depths somewhere. I'm counting backwards from ten, playing a game with myself in which a bubble has to break the surface before I get to zero or I lose. Now, just *what* I lose is anyone's guess, but at least it keeps me from thinking too much about the predicament I'm in. About five minutes ago a seat cushion came up, followed shortly thereafter by that infamous tin of stolen peach pies, which was supposed to have been my last meal on the drive over. Just how solid tin can float up from the fathoms is a question that might give Einstein a good day's work, but at this point it wouldn't surprise me if my Jeep itself popped up and rolled across the lake to cart my fat ass back home. My main question, however, is how the hell did *I*, the finless flubberful wonder, manage not to sink?

I remember I hit the water like a barrelful of cannonballs—that icy water—but rather than go down, down, I popped up like a champagne cork. I could see my Jeep about twenty feet away, gurgling and gargling like some bionic beast until it finally went belly-up and disappeared. I suppose I was dog-paddling, which somehow came instinctively, and after about five minutes the water didn't seem nearly so cold. In fact, if anything it felt, well, rather invigorating. I even experimented with a backstroke and a Daryl Hannah mermaid impression, accomplished by putting my legs together and flipping them like a tail. Casually, quite so casually, I stroked my way to the fake beach, as if I refreshed myself every day with a plunge off the side of a cliff.

Well, I've stalled long enough. It's time to get up and head home. Home? My God, I'm eight miles from home. How am I going to get there?

How about walking? You do have legs and feet you know. You haven't seen them in a while, granted, but they are there.

Right, Brainola, why don't you walk home and have a heart attack.

Well then, princess, what are the other options?
Hitchhiking?
*Paaalease. With the way you look? You'd have a better
chance of flying home. And by the way, Sweet Pea, how are you
going to explain what happened now that you're back with the
living?*

It was an accident. I was driving down to Pelham to . . . to fill
out a job application at . . . at the hospital, the Shelby Memorial
Hospital, as a trainee to a . . . nursing assistant . . . as a reception-
ist in the nursing trainee department—that's why I wore this
white dress, to look more nurse-ish—and I got the directions
mixed up somehow and . . . *yes, yes it might work. It's good, My
Precious, oh it's good* . . . and I got the directions mixed up, so I
was trying to read the road map and, I don't know, I guess I
must have lost control of the steering wheel. It just swerved out
of my hands somehow and . . .

"There, there honey, don't cry. It'll be okay." From the back
of the car, Sheba shouts, "Raine, turn up the heat some more.
Your sister's back here shiverin' to death." She turns her atten-
tions back to me. "Oh honey, and that pretty dress you're
wearin' is just ruined. I bet it's a dry clean only, too. Isn't it?"
She checks the label behind my neck. "Uh-huh, just like I
thought. Those are always the ones that manage to get wet. It
seems like the only times I ever fall into the pool at parties is
when I'm wearin' a dry clean only. But then, what can you do?
I'll tell you, honey, you can't do anything. Your dress is just
ruined and that's all there is to it."

"Forget the dress," I hear myself saying. "I'm just glad I
didn't get killed or anything." *Of all the miserable luck—to be
rescued by my own brother and his merry little band of barf
bags. This day couldn't get any worse.* "I can't believe you guys
came by. I mean, I might have frozen to death out there. I must
be *so* lucky." *And to have this fat-ass slut picking over me like*

some baboon at its belly. What did I ever do to deserve this? "I guess somebody up there must really like me." *Just what were they all doing out here anyway?* "Were y'all on your way to a movie or something?"

My brother's mongrel friend, Jack Roe, answers, "We were on our way to a Christmas party actually. The whole restaurant was invited to Ampersand's. He lives down this way somewhere."

"Yeah," Brent says, "that's where we were going alright."

"Uh-huh," nods Raine.

And I say, "But I thought he lived in Mountain Brook?"

Sheba says, "Oh, well, he does. But you know he has a weekend place out here. A sort of retreat."

"I see," I say, not seeing at all, but I fish around for something else just to keep the conversation going, so as to divert attention away from myself. As long as we don't have to talk about me, I won't have to make up any lies that might paint me into a corner. "Well, so, what did you end up getting him? I've always thought he was so weird. He must be hard to buy for."

"What's that?" Jack says, turning around in the front seat to face me.

"That package in your lap. What did y'all get him?"

"Ummm . . . in this package?" Jack asks.

"Well . . ." Raine says, and he sorts of darts his eyes at Jack, but then everybody looks at Brent.

"We got him a doll," says Brent.

"That's right," Jack agrees, giving Brent a weird look. "We got him a Cabbage Patch doll. You know, it's sort of a gag gift. It even looks like him, too."

"What a cute idea," I say, not believing a word of it. *Something is up. Something is up major time.* "But why is he having a Christmas party two days late?"

"Well honey," Sheba says, "he's a little like me in that he's always believed celebrations should come after the fact. Also, I think his birthday was yesterday—yeah, I believe it was, wasn't it Raine?—and so we're sort of combining it all together."

I look at my brother, who seems to want to change the subject. "Cyra, are you sure you don't want us to take you to a hospital?"

"I'm fine, I told you. I'm just a little wet, that's all."

"Well, are you sure there's no hope for the Jeep?" he asks.

"Not unless Mom wants to rent a three-hundred-foot cable, a frogman, and a crane."

"At least it was insured," my brother says. "Cyra, it was insured, wasn't it?"

"I suppose so," I sigh. "I don't know. *I* never paid any, and since when were you so interested in insurance anyhow?"

"Well, somebody's got to take an interest, not that I particularly want to, but you know as well as I do that Mom and reality aren't exactly the best of friends these days, and Dad's not around anymore."

"Well I'm sure it was insured," I say, staring out the window, watching the trees whoosh by. I'm thinking of Dad of course, and as though everyone in the car can read my mind, a silence seems to fall over the five of us. We were very close—Dad and me.

"Honey, if you don't mind my asking?" Sheba asks, brushing away some of the wet sand on my debutante's dress. "Did President Ford ever send your mother a letter of apology?"

"Of course not," Raine says. "That would have been practically an admission that he'd made a mistake. All Mom got was the money."

"Money from what?" Brent asks.

"The United States Treasury Department."

"But why did the Treasury Department send her money?"

Jack looks over the back of his seat. "You moron, didn't you know? Their dad was one of the first to get the swine flu inocu-

lation. He died three days later, and now their mother is a mil-
lionairess."

"The rhinoceros will be the first to go." Mom shakes her head
and pushes her food around her plate with a fork. "Followed by
the crocodile—maybe the caiman, its distant cousin, will sur-
vive. There still seem to be plenty of them in the Llanos wildlife
preserves of Venezuela, provided the land isn't drained by cattle
ranchers—then the green sea turtle . . . the Asian elephant . . .
pilot whales . . . the American eagle, of course . . . pandas." She
lets out all her breath. "Yes, I can see it now, and I tell you, I
can't live with it either."

Mom puts down her fork and stares me and Raine in the eyes.
"Oh, I can live with a lot of things, too. I can live with all the
acid rain and its consequences—the eutrophication, stimulated
by nitrate salts that choke all the oxygen from our coastal es-
tuaries—and I can live with our vanishing ozone layer, even
though it means that crops like rice and soybeans won't exist in
twenty-five years. What will half the world live on? And I can
even cope with these new diseases—this herpes thing and that,
that gay man's cancer—what do they call it? AIDS. Yes, I can
live with AIDS, but I can't live with the extermination of sev-
enty-four thousand acres of tropical rain forests being slashed
and burned every day of the week, three hundred sixty-five days
a year. I'm telling you, I simply cannot!"

She pounds a fist against the tablecloth. "We're going to Brazil. I'll sell the house. Pack your things, kids."

"Mom," I whine, "not again. Can't we get through just one
meal without a *National Geographic* seminar?"

"It would do you good, Cyra. Besides, if we don't do something, who will? Our government? Ha! That makes me laugh.
Look what they did to your father—and that's when they were
actually *trying* to do something right. They don't even try any-

more. They don't care. My God, kids, just think what you'll be able to tell your grandchildren—that you remember a world in its final golden days. A world where monkeys and lions and even bears could still be found in the wild, when beaches weren't littered with throwaway plastics, when the Amazon, the great Amazon basin, was more than just a reference in a history book. You don't appreciate it now. You think I'm just some kind of nut, but that's okay. You'll remember these words one day and you'll say to yourselves, 'You know, Mom wasn't half wrong. In fact, I think she was dead right.'"

"Mom," I say, a mouthful of chocolate pie stuffed in my face, "no one person can change the world." After I say this, I realize it sounds utterly stupid and clichéd.

"That's the shame of it all," she says, a tear swelling in the corner of her eye. "It's irreversible now. I realized that this afternoon, when you nearly died and barely cared."

"What? Mom, you act like I did it on purpose or something, I mean it's not like"—*why is she always so damned perceptive?*—"I meant to kill myself. What kind of person do you think I am anyhow?"

"I always thought our youth would care," she says. "That was my one last hope. They did in the sixties, you know—or maybe you don't—but they really did. Yet something's happened since then. I can't quite put my finger on it, but I think it started with Kennedy's assassination. Something more occurred that day then just the murder of a president. Something emerged from that mayhem, a worse thing than just distrust of everything and everyone. A kind of recklessness came out of it, too—a sort of nihilistic behavior, a global self-destructiveness. I can't explain it, really. It's only evident in retrospect."

Mom wipes her face with her napkin and stands. "Well, I think I'll try to do a little automatic writing, provided the powers are with me tonight, and then maybe I'll check on the trees." Me and Raine exchange looks. Raine then says something about having to call Jack, and he gets up from the table too. I notice he was preoccupied all through dinner, although he tried to disguise it by pretending to read *Charlotte's Web* at the table. Really, he just didn't want to have to make conversation. So they both leave the room, which means it's my turn to clear the table and do the dishes, I suppose, even though Mom will gripe at me in the morning because I never scrape the plates off. I just sort of throw them, grunge and all, into the dishwasher. But since I haven't helped out in the longest time, not since before the baby was born, I figure I ought to try to be sweet for once in my life and actually do a good job. Not that it would be appreciated, naturally. At least Mom didn't snipe about my Jeep. She didn't even mention it, in fact, so maybe she forgot all about it.

No such luck. Suddenly she comes back into the kitchen, a book called *The State of the World* in her hands—one of those gloomster doomster things no doubt. She sets her book down on the counter and begins helping me load the dishwasher. I try to pretend it's a harmless scene from television. "Thanks, Mom, but you don't have to help. I can do it."

"Cyra, I didn't want to say anything in front of your brother."

Oh God, here it comes.

"But I want you to know that I don't believe your story about getting lost and losing control of your Jeep. You've never lost control of anything in your life."

"Mom, I already told you . . ."

She holds a hand in front of her defiantly, as though practicing for the bulldozers in Brazil. "However," she says. "However, I won't permit myself to consider the only other logical alternative. Now, as I said this morning, if you have anything you'd like to discuss with me—*anything* at all—I'm really a very good objective listener if you'd give me just half a chance."

All of a sudden, all the things I've been keeping welled up inside me all these months—all the frustrations and humiliation and utter shame—come to a rolling boil. I sort of waver for a moment, standing there in front of her with a tea glass in my hand, then my face kind of twists down and I drop the glass and just sort of collapse into an hysterical heap next to the trash compactor. "Oh, Mom," I wail, "you wouldn't understand. Nobody's ever understood, not really, only Dad, and now . . . now I feel like I'm so hopeless. I'm fat and hateful and nobody likes me really. Mom, why can't I ever *feel* anything? What in God's name is wrong with me?"

"Oh Cyra," she says, her voice as caressingly soft as only a mother's can be, and she sits down on the floor beside me. She takes one of my hands into hers and and holds it for a long time as we both just stare in silence at the uncleared table. The broken tea glass lies in pieces on the terra cotta floor and I focus my gaze on a shiny shard next to a table leg.

"What a lie my life has become," I finally say, utter desolation in my voice. Then, turning to Mom, I squeeze her hands until they go white and, despairingly, add, "I might as well tell you. I did try to kill myself today. It seemed like such a good idea this morning, but now it just sounds crazy. *I* sound crazy. I don't know why I tried it. Well, I do know why, but I don't know why . . . you know?"

"Tell me."

"It's too awful, Mom. You'll hate me forever if I tell you."

"Of course I won't hate you, Sweetheart. Mothers never hate their children. No matter what they do, we're programmed to love them. You'll understand one day, when you have your own children."

"No, Mom," I say, "I *won't* understand." Now I turn to look her in the eyes, wondering if she's already guessed the truth, but all that I see looking back at me are pity and consolation—the two things I hate the most. I want to blurt out, "I'll never understand because I *did* have a child. I had a child and I killed it!"

But I don't, of course. All that I say is a gumptionless "I'm just so confused."

Mom smiles at me. "Well luckily, that's what mothers are best at—unconfusing their teenagers. And do you know how they go about it?" I shake my head apathetically. "The way they go about it is by asking a single question—a very important question, since it's the only one that will work. Would you like to know what the question is?"

"Sure, Mom."

"The question is—What would you like more than anything in the world? Anything at all, no matter how farfetched or inconceivable. Quickly now. If you think about it too much you won't answer truthfully."

"It's easy," I say. "Easy and impossible. I want beauty. It's what I want more than anything in the world. I don't mean pretty, either. I mean drop-dead beauty. Cover girl beauty. Brooke Shields beauty. Cheryl Tiegs beauty. Christie Brinkley beauty. I want to be able to walk into a room and have every head turn. I want marriage proposals and modeling contracts tossed at me like confetti. I want to be on the cover of magazines and have an agent, a manager, a publicist and fans, lots and lots of fans sending me letters—sacks of letters every week —all telling me how lucky I am to be so beautiful. I want to be Miss America. And that, Mom, is what I want more than anything in the world."

"But you *are* beautiful, darling. Those things mean nothing. It's what's inside. That's where the beauty comes from."

"But I already told you, I don't *have* anything inside, and what's outside is hideous. Paaleeeease, just listen to me once, would you?"

"Okay," she says, suddenly getting up off the floor. "Your wish is going to come true. No more eating between meals. No more self-pity. No more negative attitudes, or whining, or obstinacy, or lack of self-respect. Nine months from now you're walking down that runway in Atlantic City weighing one hundred twelve pounds with a scepter in your hands and a tiara on your head. Everyone in the world will envy you for all of five minutes, and when it's over you'll see what I mean and be a better person because of it. But in the meantime, fetch the scales, and while you're at it, put on some tennis shoes and something loose to jog in. I'm your manager now, and we're starting tonight!"

Chapter Seven

RAINE

"CAN'T WE DO THIS TOMORROW?"

"No. Somebody might see us. Besides, it's going to be stinking by tomorrow, and you know what a decaying corpse smells like."

"No, I don't know," I say, staring into the receiver. "Do you?"

"Naturally. Haven't you ever pulled over to the side of the road to examine a rotten dog?"

"Never."

"Well you should, and it's sure not a rose garden, believe you me, so if we don't do something with that . . . package . . . tonight, it's going to start leaking through the wrapping paper. Where did you hide it anyway?"

"The trunk of my car."

"No one drives it but you, do they?"

"Just me."

"Good," Jack says. "That's good thinking. If you'd put it in a closet somewhere somebody might have found it. Can you get away without having to answer any questions?"

"Probably. Mom never asks me where I'm going anyway."

"Good again. So just meet me out front of The Dakota in five minutes. Oh, and bring a shovel."

"What for?"

"Just do it," Jack says. "Never you mind," and he hangs up on me.

I place the phone down and check the clock on my end table. It says 8:14 P.M. The restaurant's probably packed right now, and I keep thinking we shouldn't have called in sick, Jack and me. We should have shown up, just like Brent and Sheba did. I mean, if the time ever comes that we need an alibi for tonight (although why we would need an alibi I don't know), but if we did, we wouldn't have one, except for each other, which I guess would work, assuming we're not *both* accused of . . . what *would* we be accused of? Failing to report a crime, maybe. I wonder if that's a misdemeanor or a felony? I don't suppose it's anything if they never find out there even *was* a baby. Which they won't.

So I go downstairs, careful to be really quiet so I won't have to say where I'm going. I hear Mom and Cyra in the kitchen, muffled sounds, and I lean just far enough over to see Cyra's legs. She's sitting on the floor, God knows why, but she seems to be crying, which I'm sure is just some ploy to make Mom feel sorry for her. How anyone can be so stupid as to run her Jeep off the side of a rock quarry is unimaginable. It wouldn't surprise me if she even did it on purpose. She'd probably do anything to keep from having to look for a job. I don't think I've ever seen legs like hers, not even on an elephant. I mean she looks like she has phlebitis or something.

Slowly I back away, careful to shift my weight so the floor won't creak, and silently I slip out the front door. It's getting much cooler and I should have brought a jacket, but I'm not going back inside to get one. Instead, I walk around the corner of the house and over to the garage. Cyra, the conservationist, has left every single light on in her apartment upstairs—the apartment that's supposed to be *mine*—and it casts enough light that once the garage door is open I can just make out the shape of things inside. I'm sure there's a shovel in there somewhere, because Mom is constantly gardening and tending her trees, but once when I was looking for a rake I discovered a snake coiled around a ceiling pipe, a fat black snake, which has made me hesitant about exploring the premises ever since. The damned thing nearly dropped onto my head, but instead it fell onto the hood of Cyra's Jeep—a sound like no other sound in the world . . . *Sluthump!* I get chills just thinking about it.

But at least it's winter so the snakes probably hibernating or something, unless of course it got tricked by this freak weather, in which case it's probably lurking around in here just waiting to attack me. There's only one snake I ever liked, and it's Kaa— Rudyard Kipling's python from *The Jungle Book*—which luckily isn't real. I've discovered that the less threat any person, place, or thing poses toward me, the better I seem to get along with it and that may be why I tend to avoid situations in which the outcome cannot be predetermined . . . such as the disposal of gift-wrapped infants.

In the eerie light I see the shovel gleaming greasily from the back of the garage, yet all sorts of obstacles are preventing me from getting at it without being ambushed and sucked down into some Stygian pit where, God knows, there's probably a billion of those ebony reptiles that haven't had anything to eat *all* winter. Of course, turning on the light might send them slithering back into the recesses, but then Mom and Cyra would see me and ask what I'm up to. No, the trick is just to run back there as fast as I can, grab the shovel—*the better to bury you with, my dear*—and not even think about anything else. I suck in a deep breath. Ready . . . set . . . go!

I bound over a stack of soda crates, dodge a wheelbarrow, and edge around a cord of firewood that Dad piled up here the fall before Ford murdered him—snake heaven. *So far, so good. But hurry, hurry.* I grab the shovel—*nope, no snakes back here*—edge back around the pile of firewood, dodge the wheelbarrow . . . suddenly my face brushes against something dangling from the ceiling . . . instant death! But it's only the string from a light bulb . . . I double my speed, skidding by a workbench, and leap, finally, back over the stack of old soda crates, my last obstacle before the sweet air of freedom. Inevitably, though, my head doesn't *quite* miss the bottom of a wooden cross-stud, and I feel like I've been scalped by a billy club. My feet stumble over the top soda crate, which skids off the stack, spilling out an old blanket onto the concrete floor—which, luckily, muffles the sound of the shovel dropping out of my hands. I pick myself up—*oh, I'm fine thank you, no, it doesn't hurt a bit*—wrap the blanket around the shovel, and race out the door to my getaway car just as fast and stealthily as my nimble feet and throbbing cranium will carry me.

"In a triangle with two equal sides and two equal angles, the equal angles are opposite equal sides, meaning that *you* are the hypotenuse. Do you understand the implication?"

I rub the sore spot on my head some more and again lean down to ask Jack if he sees any blood in my hair. "I told you no once already," he says, "and what's a little blood anyway? Now keep your eyes on the road. And turn on the wipers. Can't you see it's starting to rain? . . . Do you understand the implication?"

"No," I say. "I never understand *anything* you're talking about."

"You took geometry just like I did. You had Mrs. Truss three years in a row just like I did. What do you mean, you don't know?"

I turn to Jack and a boil on his neck catches my attention. It looks like a third eyeball. "I don't even remember how to use the foil method," I say, "nor, *nor* do I remember what the Pythagorean Theorem is or even what an isosceles triangle is . . . so what in the hell is a hypotenuse?" *What can't he pop the damned thing?*

"*You* are the hypotenuse, Raine—the side of a right triangle opposite the right angle. Your mother and Cyra are the other two sides, but neither one of them is as great as you."

"Oh," I say, "well that sure clears it up."

"You know, I've heard all your mother's talk about crystal workshops and Gnosticism and 'transformational values.' I know she fancies herself some sort of New Age visionary, but Raine, she's just some countercultural fringe . . . freak, and your sister's just as bad, if not worse. She's a demon. Did you ever see *The Bad Seed?* Well, that's what she is."

"Hey, it's okay for *me* to insult them. But you're not part of the family, okay? So just butt out."

"They're not good for you, I'm warning you. And remember, *you* are the hypotenuse." Jack now reaches down into his pockets. He pulls out a small glass vial, and as he unscrews the cap he says, "Vapor overexposure may cause respiratory system irritation and temporary nervous system impairment." Next, he tips the vial toward the windshield as though making a toast to self-destruction, and then holds the vial under one nostril while pressing the other nostril closed. He inhales until his whole head turns magenta. "Turn up there to the right," he says, switching to the other nostril.

I do as told, hitting a pothole, and flip the wipers on.

"Want some?" Jack says, offering the bottle to me.

"I'm driving," I say. "And where are we going anyway? I can't see a thing."

"Elmwood Cemetery," Jack says, pushing the vial back down into his pocket.

"But that's where Dad's buried."

"I know. We're going to bury the baby over his grave. It's a trick I saw in a movie once. No one ever looks for bodies where people are already buried."

"Oh," I say, as though it's a perfectly rational solution. But then I add, "Why can't we bury it over one of *your* relatives, though?"

"None of my relatives are dead yet, unless you want to go back to great-grandparents, and I don't even know who they were, much less where they're buried. Believe me, Raine, this will work out fine."

So when I get to the cemetery gates, Jack tells me to turn off the headlights. Elmwood is the largest cemetery in the city, and sometimes it takes me and Mom twenty minutes just to find Dad's grave in broad daylight, so here in the pouring rain and total darkness it's like almost impossible. Only some sparsely placed halogen streetlamps are there to guide me, but somehow I find my way to the top of a small hill with a big cedar tree on it that looks familiar. "I think it's around here somewhere."

"Well let's stop the car then," Jack says excitedly. "You know, one of my favorite games as a kid was to play 'cemetery.' It worked best at my grandmother's house because she had green shag carpeting in her living room. She also collected dolls, which I used as the bodies. I'd make coffins with my Lincoln Logs and tombstones with my ABC blocks. I was such a good preacher, too, because at church I'd memorize entire sermons. And God knows, Baptist sermons are simple-minded enough for even mongoloids to understand. My favorite of all was the one about bumblebees. I won't recite it to you now, but the crux of it was that it's okay to die, because the sting of sin has been rendered harmless by Christ's death on the cross, much in the way that a bumblebee is rendered harmless if you can catch it in a glass jar and slap a wet towel over the top—the bumblebee will sting the towel of course, thus losing its stinger. The whole thing makes absolutely no sense, but then nothing about religion ever does. It's a nice metaphor, however."

"Uh-huh," I say, beginning to feel creepy all over. "Maybe we should wait a while," I say, turning off the car, "at least until the rain slacks off some."

"Just think," says Jack, pointing to all the tombstones, "all these people are dead, yet they were once alive just like we are. Isn't it wild? And someday we'll be dead, too . . . how do you want to die? Given a choice, I mean."

"In my sleep."

"I might have known. You're the most gumptionless person on earth. Guess how I want to die? I've got it all planned, you know."

"I'm sure you do."

"Well . . ."

"I don't want to guess," I say. "I just want to bury the baby and get out of here."

"But don't you ever think about death?"

"No. To tell you the truth, no. I never think about it. I only think about pointless things like what is the point to my life? Nothing at all excites me . . . ever."

"Well, that's too bad. Everyone should get turned on by something." Jack takes out his poppers again. "You sure you don't want to try these?"

"They give me a headache," I say.

"Poor baby," he says, rolling down his window to let the rain hit him in the face. "Have you ever heard of the Chrysler Building?"

"No," I say, wrapping my arms around my waist to keep warm.

"It's in New York, and at the time it was built, in 1930, it was the tallest building in the world—a title it soon relinquished to the Empire State Building. Anyway, the building itself is art deco at its finest. All nine hundred four feet, eleven and one-half inches of it, and it's crowned with a one-hundred-forty-one-foot stainless steel spear that tapers to an absolute needle point, making the sum height of the building an impressive one thousand forty-seven feet. I'm going to die by renting a helicopter to hover over that spear, which I'll then free-fall onto. Why, I'll look just like a worm on a hook, and I'll go out on every channel in full color. What more could you ask for . . . other than a nuclear war, that is."

"The rain's slacking off," I say.

"Come on then." And opening his door, Jack gets out and walks around to the trunk. "You take the shovel," he says. "I'll take the baby."

"No way. I'm not digging up my own father's grave. You take the shovel and *I'll* carry the baby," and I throw the blanket-wrapped shovel at him. Amazingly, Jack catches it, and the two of us refuse to speak to each other, both choosing instead to huff off in opposite directions into the mist and cold darkness.

After fifteen minutes later I've lost all trace of Jack and my car. I'm just shuffling around blindly between the marble and granite—Murphy, Daly, Noe, Johnston, Cardenas, Lambert, Kearney, Moss, Phillips, Wiley, Waters—every name in the world except Freeman. I think about calling out Jack's name, but that would only prove to him that I'm the weakest, *weaker,* of the two. It starts raining again, naturally, just a sprinkle at first. Soon, though, it's like pitchforks and little nigra babies. A waterfall is cascading down my face. This, combined with the darkness, my loneliness, and the utterly macabre, once-in-a-life-time feeling associated with clutching a gift-wrapped dead baby in one's arms in the middle of a cemetery, makes me begin to panic. I wrap both arms around the package held against my chest and just start hurdling tombstones, one after another. A silhouette comes into view, backlit by a streetlamp about fifty feet behind it—a dark, humpish black silhouette . . . like a ghost holding a sickle.

"What in Christ's name are you doing?" it says. "Practicing for the Olympics?" Jack pulls the blanket off his head, letting the rain pelt his poodle's-ass haircut. "Get over here. I've found some Freemans."

The sickle turns out to be only my shovel, and Jack points the metal end of it at a slab of Carrara marble. "Is that him?"

"I don't know," I say. "It's hard to tell."

"Hard to tell? Was his name Maddox Freeman?"

"Yes."

"And did he die in seventy-six?"

"Yes."

"Then what's so hard to tell?"

"Well, I don't remember that streetlamp behind you there."

"But dummy, you wouldn't have been here at night anyhow, so you wouldn't have noticed, don't you think?"

"I guess it's his," I say, grabbing the blanket from Jack, and I wrap it around myself to keep from shivering so badly, placing the baby on the base of an obelisk. Jack sighs and starts digging, but water fills up the hole as fast as he can dig it. Suddenly, the murky light behind him catches his hair just right, and it's all red! I look at his shirt, a shirt that was yellow before we got out of the car. It's red, too. I feel my hair, scrubbing it with my hand, and then look into my palm. "Oh my God, Jack, look at this!" I whip the rain-drenched blanket off my head and wring it over the lid of a white marble tombstone. "Blood! This whole blanket is soaked in blood!"

"Let me see," Jack says cautiously, never believing anything I say. He plunges the shovel into the dirt hard enough to make it stand up on its own, then he takes the blanket and unfolds it in the light. He turns back to me. "Where did you get this from anyway?"

"The garage," I say, backing just a little bit away. I lean against the obelisk and run my fingers through my hair, hoping the rain will rinse it clean. Jack doesn't say anything. He just stares at me. "I tripped over an old crate and it fell out. I'd never seen it before then."

75

"There's something else on here besides blood," he says flatly, not taking his eyes off me. No one has eyes like Jack's. They're like lasers. A grimy smirk lifts up the corners of his mouth. "Doesn't your sister live over that garage?"

"Uh-huh."

"Your sister, who just happened to have been job-shopping in East Bumfuck today and ran her Jeep off the road into a quarry? That sister?"

"Uh-huh."

"Well, you know what this something else looks like to me?" he says, pointing to a withered purplish thing gummed into the blanket.

"Uh-uh . . . what?"

"Well," he says, scraping off the snakey thing and tossing it into the partial hole he'd dug. It floats on the surface like a rotten python. As we both stare at it, Jack reaches into his pocket and pulls out his vial again. He unscrews the lid and shoves the bottle under his nose. For a horrible second it looks like he might drink the stuff, but then he slowly lets out all the air in his lungs, and even more slowly he draws a deep, deep breath—closing his eyes in cloudy ecstasy, with a crimson flush of facial muscles that suggests he's miles away, perhaps in a place where questions don't lead to answers. "Well," he pronounces dreamily, "it looks like an umbilical cord to me."

An umbilical cord? The words don't even mean anything. The hippocampus within my brain isn't sending out the right electrical charges or something . . . the neurons aren't fusing properly . . . I can't even come up with a mental picture of what an umbilical cord is supposed to be . . . I can't cross-reference it with anything I've seen before. That *thing?* That rotten phython floating on that puddle? An umbilical cord? Is that what one looks like? Is that how it goes? It goes like that?

Chapter Eight

C Y R A

IT GOES LIKE THIS: The Miss Alabama pageant is held every year in June, but the preliminaries (which Alabama has more of than any other state) are held year-round—some as late as May, and others as early as August for the following year. The very latest qualifying preliminary for *this* year will be the Miss West Jefferson County pageant, on May 15. All the others—Miss Valhalla, Miss Birmingham Southern, Miss Mobile County, Miss East Jefferson County, etc.—have either already been held or are imminent, which means that at best I have only five months in which to lose, roughly, one hundred and fifty pounds. Think positive. It *can* be done.

There's always the hope, too, that the Miss West Jefferson County pageant won't have very many entries. Some preliminaries are lucky to get even a dozen girls, and if that's the case, I'll have a better chance than if I were entering, say, the Miss Montgomery pageant, where hundreds show up—each one looking more sheltered, anorexic, and empty-headed than the one before. Then again, the Miss West Jefferson County title is no guarantee of a Miss Alabama rhinestone tiara, which in turn is no guarantee of a solitary trot down the runway in New Jersey, but it *is* the first step. And as Mom said, I've got to take this one step at a time.

But if starving myself into looking the part is the most important goal, then *acting* the part is the next most important. I've got to start doing things like keeping up with current events. I guess I'll have to read the paper or something. There will be interviews, too, and I'll be asked lots of stupid questions, stuff like how do I feel about Reagan's foreign aid bill, or the plight of the homeless . . . or premarital sex. Ha! That'll sure test my acting abilities. As for my talent display (I refuse to sing "Climb Every Mountain" or "Send in the Clowns"), surely I must be talented at something, something other than being able to murder children without getting caught. It just seems there's a whole mentality to being a beauty queen that goes against everything natural and healthy. It's like cramming for an exam in trigonometry. Even though you have to pass, you know you'll never be able to use anything you've learned, because it has nothing to do with real life in the first place.

I smell something . . . fudge! I get up from Raine's bed (he had to work the lunch shift today and as I was snooping through his room, being the nosey slut that I am, I found something that sent me to his bed in almost a total state of shock) and thinking of how much I *love* fudge, I run downstairs to where Mom is just pulling a pan from the oven—gooey, steaming, and calorie-gorged!

"Hello, dear." Mom wipes her brow, then she reaches for a glass of water that has a chunk of obsidian in the bottom of it. It clinks as she tilts the glass to her lips. She takes a long swig. "An elixir, Cyra? I found some fresh bauxite down by the mailbox the other day, and you know what wonders it works for curbing the appetite."

"Mom, why are you making fudge? You know how I can't resist it, and I've hardly eaten anything but a grapefruit all week as it is. You're just doing this to tempt me. You don't want me to be Miss America anyway."

"Miss Crowley next door is having a levitational therapy class tonight, and I was asked to bring dessert. It has nothing at all to do with how I feel about your weight."

"Then why didn't you make something like a trifle, something I hate that wouldn't drive me insane? . . . Levitational therapy? Don't tell me she's teaching you how to float?"

"Look at the surface of this fudge, Cyra. What do you see?"

"What?"

"What do you see?"

"Pecans."

"Do you know what I see? I see desert rock formations jutting up from a sea of black sand. Or maybe I see helpless animals drowning in a quagmire of tar. Or wait, do I see the elongated heads of crocodiles floating as unobtrusively as fallen logs on the stagnant surface of a murky chocolate-colored marsh? And if we cut beneath the surface, what do you think we'll find? Why, otters of course, lots and lots of playful otters swimming through a thick bog beneath the crocodiles. We can see so many things, Cyra, if only we open our eyes."

"All I see are pecans, Mom, just pecans . . . can I have a piece?"

"No."

"Just a small piece?"

She shakes her head. "Absolutely not."

"Oh, Mom, it's New Year's Eve. It'll be my last act of decadence for the year. I won't even taste any champagne tonight. Please?"

"How much weight have you lost so far?"

"A good bit."

"How much?"

"A nice amount."

"Cyra," she says—in a voice that means "Don't play these games with me"—"you've been cheating, haven't you?"

"Never mind then, I don't want any fudge after all. I'll have an elixir, okay? I'll just have an elixir."

Mom heaves with consternation, as though torn between whether she should force the issue and pry out of me that I've only lost three pounds—*three* pounds in one week—or whether she should simply mix up a nice bauxite spritzer and leave me alone. "All right, then," she says, "don't tell me if you've been cheating on your diet. Eat the *whole* pan for all I care. Go ahead and contribute to the planting of yet more cacao trees on what was once virgin rain forest. So that soon the whole Amazon basin, all South America for that matter, will be plowed under and proliferated by the big three Cs—cacao, coffee, and cocaine. Oh, we'll be an apathetic world, but at least we'll be awake!"

"Mom, I don't understand this hang-up you have with South America."

"Then that makes us even, because I don't understand your hang-up about wanting to be the queen of North America, especially since you're not even willing to exert the minimum amount of willpower it takes to become queen, as shallow an ambition as it is!" Mom now sort of throws the pan of fudge on top of an aluminum trivet, adding, "God, it's hot in this kitchen," and then she sweeps out the back door onto the patio where the sun is already beginning to set. I pull up a chair and sit down next to her. For a few minutes we fume in silence and just stare at the two giant trees Mom planted on the days me and Raine were born. Beyond them, down the hill, is the city, our city (*which will be one of the few "safe" places during the com-*

ing global conflagration), all washed in the greeny orange glow of the last day of this year.

"Cyra," Mom says evenly and carefully, "your father's life could have been saved if it weren't for our government. Oh yes, I subscribe to the CDC's *Morbidity and Mortality Weekly Report.* I *know* what goes into the flu vaccine—all those polysorbates and mercury derivatives and lethal ethers—it's nothing you want to play around with if you don't know what you're doing. But our wonderful government feared an epidemic of swine flu and naturally took everything into their own greased hands. I told your father not to get the vaccine. I told him it was just a ploy Ford was using to win reelection—playing the keeper of the nation's good health—but you don't *know* what a hypochondriac he always was. I don't believe a day in his life went by where he didn't wake up and immediately take his temperature. Then, when the vaccine backfired and he did catch a touch of the flu, why, it had been played up so much by the press as something deadly that I don't even think he *tried* to fight it. Your father just let go."

"No wonder I hate doctors and medicine so much," I say, and then to lighten things up a bit, I add, "I must be a closet Christian Scientist."

"The reincarnation of Mary Baker Eddy. That's a very distinct possibility, you know." Naturally Mom is serious. That's one of the problems with her. She has no sense of irony or humor.

"Cyra, you'd asked me why I'm so impassioned about South America—come walking with me, dear. We need the exercise. Well, it's not the continent itself, or even the people or their culture that I think deserves preservation. It's only the vegetation. Do you have any idea how much we owe to tropical plants? Why, almost any drug you can think of has at least one tropical component—from aspirin . . . to the flu vaccine. We just owe so much to rare flora—I've always liked that word and am so happy your grandmother had the insight to bestow it upon me—we just owe so much to rare flora, and it's nothing less than a criminal offense that we're destroying these irreplaceable resources. There may have been some plant—a tree orchid or a vine or an equatorial flower—with special medicinal properties that we'll never discover because it's been destroyed to make way for 'economic growth'—the single most paradoxical set of words known to man . . . I'm sure there's something out there that could have saved your father, something that's soon to be lost forever, if it hasn't been already . . . it's going to be an ugly world your own children inhabit, Cyra, a place marching backwards."

I've learned not to interrupt Mom during these emotional blackouts of hers. She just gets so emotional over things she can't control, and instead of agreeing or disagreeing, I simply keep my big mouth shut. So we walk around the yard for a while. There's something unsettling about the tranquility of this city we live in, this state I was raised in. It feels like something sick is bubbling under the surface, and I think the fact that I'm a murderess at eighteen is a testament to this truth.

As though reading my mind, Mom takes my hand and holds it hard, and we stare at the sun, which is making its final descent this year. She says, "Everything on the outside may be corrupted, but at least the self can be pure and untainted. Why don't you come with me to the levitational this evening? It's only the beginning of our galactic transformation."

"Mom, it's not . . . for me," I say delicately. "It's not right."

"No, *everything* is permitted if it *feels* right. Ask Raskolnikov."

"Who?"

"Cyra, we have testing tools now to prove man's unlimited possibilities. We are not finite beings, and although I'm not into spiritual show-and-tell, some of us *will* be asked to demonstrate the human being's unlimited potential." Mom leads me over to my tree. Even though it's only as old as I am, it looks positively ancient. Its limbs alone are as big around as most normal-size trees. I don't know how Mom got it to grow so fast—maybe she planted crystals under its root network.

"Look at this, Cyra. Amazing growth, isn't it? If all humans could learn to tap their inner resources we could still save the planet. There's time. The chi force is within me—you've heard of tai chi—and this tree, your tree, represents the kundalina—the tree of life. Each of us is entitled to be a seer, a positive visualizer, and in harnessing the kundalina as your power center you can become aware of the energies within. There will be people put upon this earth to usher in the new millennium."

"And just when does this begin, Mom?"

"Universal time is not on my calendar. I can't pinpoint when, but it will definitely be within your lifetime. Just be aware of the duality of mind. Ancient knowings *do* return. Many people are in place for the ascension process—your father, for one, was needed on the other side. And very soon, of course, there will come a mass exodus. As for me, well, levitation is only an intermediary step toward my higher goal—teleportation. Christ already showed us this is quite possible. After all, what happened that first Easter Sunday was *no* miracle—merely a natural reality that *anyone* can summon *if* they will bypass close-mindedness and open their selves to spiritual unfoldment. Yes, the efflorescence will someday be achieved, Cyra, and even the schoolchildren—every child in the world—will proudly, as one, espouse the pledge of allegiance of this higher order:

> I pledge allegiance to the starship Earth,
> And to the universe of which we are a part,
> One world, created by God,
> To perfectly express his light and love.
> Amen."

Suddenly, I'm floored. "Well Mom, this sure sounds great and wonderful, and I'm glad it helps you accept Dad's death while compartmentalizing all the mysteries of the cosmos and everything, and I wish that *I* had such fierce convictions . . . but I don't. And the honest truth is I don't buy *any* of it. Haven't you ever heard of objective reality?"

Oddly, Mom doesn't seem the least bit perturbed by my display of insolence. "Do you believe that you are the creator of your own destiny?" she asks.

"No. Life isn't what you make of it. It's just something you're stuck with. Some enjoy it. Some don't. And some are plain indifferent. I think my time card got punched into that last one."

"Then you are lost, Cyra. I will always love you because you are my daughter, but I will never again ask you to embrace the obvious—that humanity is genetically programmed for enlightenment."

"Does this mean we don't have to move to Brazil after all?"

"Obviously, it is a pilgrimage I will have to make alone, since both you and Raine have made quite clear your unwillingness to help dispense a spiritual aura of peace around the planet. I will, however, wait until after the pageant. I made a promise to be your personal manager and trainer, and it's a promise I intend to keep. Go put on your tennis shoes, dear. It's time for our jog."

I've never been one to have problems getting to sleep, but then I've never gone to bed hungry before either. In the past, on those rare occasions when sleep would escape me, I'd just go into the kitchen and fix a nice pineapple-peanut butter sandwich, or devour a half gallon of mint chocolate chip ice cream . . . or a bag of chips (a big bag of chips, *real* big) with garlic clam dip. Just *anything!* But now, to have to endure this torture of being allowed only water after 6:00 P.M.—plain old flavorless water (*but of course, My Precious, you could always drop a rock into the glass for added flavorlessness).* So imagine what it's like now, being forced to stare at the shadows on the ceiling and count lamb chops until my pillow is slick with drool. Yet unfortunately it's not the hunger keeping me up tonight—no, I could cope with hunger. Not well, but I *could* do it—but tell me please, just what in damnation is that bloody blanket doing in Raine's closet . . . and wet at that!?

Chapter Nine

RAINE

"IT'S *NOT* WET!"

"Not wet?" Jack carps. "It's practically salivating . . . *and* it stinks!"

Sheba, who is sitting cross-legged in a ratty Queen Anne chair that she got at the DAV for six dollars, wearing only a black lace corset that she bought for two dollars at the unclaimed baggage auction in the town of Arab (pronounced AYE-RAB), which she thinks makes her look like one of those buxom voluptuaries from a Renaissance painting, shrieks, "Honey, I am *over* you boys always makin' fun of the Bald Eagle!"

"Well if you insist on parading around naked, the least you could do is cross your legs in mixed company," Jack replies.

"This is *my* apartment I'll have you know, and I'll dress any way I feel like. Besides, *you* are in the minority. Brent and Raine aren't in the least offended by a woman au naturel."

"'Cause we've been seein' you naked for years," Brent says,

86

preening at his reflection in the gilt-edged mirror across the room. "Do y'all think my feet are too big?"

Sheba glances in Brent's direction. "Honey, you do have those Appalachian toes... I've got a good one. It's the sickest joke. I saw it in one of those dirty joke books. Are you ready?"

"Is it vulgar?" Jack asks.

"Of course it's *vulgar,* honey. But no more vulgar than your crooked penis."

Jack looks mortified, a rare expression for someone as unshockable as him. "Surely I didn't actually hear what I think I heard."

"Honey," Sheba says, flipping her hair casually, "asexuality is *not* a natural state. There's always a reason behind it somewhere, and in your case, the rumor mill's been grindin' that the golden path makes a sharp curve to one side." Sheba now arches her eyebrows above her tatty chair with a sardonic grin.

Jack doesn't take it good-naturedly at all. On the contrary, he seems to be having trouble controlling himself. His face starts turning red, then purple, and he's clenching his fists. Finally, he stammers, "I think this conversation is getting just a little too meretricious for my delicate ears."

Sheba just shrugs, as if to say, "If you don't want to admit to it, then don't, but that doesn't deny the fact that it's true."

Not wanting to be a part of this, I pretend to read my book, *The Phantom Tollbooth.* However, the tension in the air is electric, and a few minutes later Sheba begins to hum a nursery rhyme that is one of my favorites: "There was a crooked man who walked a crooked mile..."

"Alright," Jack yelps, "that does it!" He stands and grabs at the zipper on his jeans. "Am I going to have to strip here in front of God and everyone just to shut you up?... It may have a slight angle to it, but..."

"A *slight* angle?" Sheba looks toward Brent and me as though this wins Understatement of the Year. "Honey, from what I've heard, a T-square doesn't have as sharp an angle as that thing. Apparently, you're the only male on earth who has to turn your back to the wind to piss into it."

God, is Sheba on a roll today. I don't know why she's in such a vicious mood, but sitting on a footstool in front of her (with a bird's-eye view of the Bald Eagle) I can't help but wonder how she gets her information. Jack, after all, does have a shy, almost Victorian streak of morality in him (at least where sex is concerned); and like I said before, unlike me and Brent, Jack never even sunbathes with the rest of us, so Sheba wouldn't have had the chance to see him undressing in the same room with her. By the same token, she would never have had the chance to point-blank ask him to lower his trunks "just a little bit so I can see what other boys' erector sets look like," her argument being, "Well honey, I have to know what's normal so that I can screen my boyfriends. There has to be some basis for comparison, something by which everything can be measured . . . you know, like Carbon 14."

In fact, I thought that *I* was the only one who knew about Jack's . . . unique structure. And even I, his confidant, only found out recently, and it was through sheer accident (even Jack doesn't know I know). The thing was, the two of us were out one night in Jack's car and it was really late and we weren't tired and we were bored with being intellectuals—a dangerous combination. (Regrettable things happen when you're too smart for your own good and have nothing to do.) Anyway, we'd already exhausted every imaginable pastime, including a rather enlightening game of "The Gods." This time, The Gods decreed that Jack had a choice of being turned into a vampire (a lifelong ambition of his), the only hitch being that he would be limited to animal blood only—cats, dogs, cows, horses, snakes, etc.—*no* humans whatsoever, or he'd die instantly . . . or, he had the choice of changing up to any five parts of his body—brown eyes to blue, pimply skin to clear, small dick to big—whatever he pleased, anything it would take to make him physically perfect . . . *but*—isn't there always one?—*but,* for every part of his body he chose to change, The Gods would whack off ten years of his general life expectancy. In essence, if he decided to take advantage of all five body alterations, being twenty-one now, he probably wouldn't get to live but another two to five years.

Well, it seemed to me The Gods were being pretty lenient that night. I mean, when it's my turn, I never get such thought-provoking choices. (Usually it's "Okay, Raine, The Gods say you get to be mangled to death in an escalator that collapses, or you get to be mauled to death by one of those psychotic polar bears at the Jimmy Morgan Zoo. Which do you choose?") Naturally, I assumed it would be a pretty clear-cut decision on Jack's part. After all, on the one hand you get to live only a few years— perfect years, granted—but on the other hand you get eternity . . . e-t-e-r-n-i-t-y . . . and what's a little dog's blood to someone who goes out of his way to run one over on the road?

So imagine my surprise when Jack chose to change five body parts, none of which he'd tell *me.* I tried to explain that The Gods didn't like secrets, that it wouldn't work unless he verbalized them, but Jack wasn't buying it. "It's *my* body, most of which you've never seen and never *will* see, and I can change it in secret if I want to."

"Fine then," I said, "be that way. But just remember, there's always a next time. And The Gods, like me, *never* forget."

Well, a few minutes later, of course, I had forgotten; and I wouldn't be reminded of the stupid game again until about two hours and a drink or four later when I was watching an ugly brown-haired girl with a diamond embedded in her nose eat six —yes, count 'em—six Krispy Kreme chocolate-covered donuts off the end of Jack's penis. Like a game of ringtoss in reverse, Jack was wearing a full erection and trying to get the end donut to fly into the girl's snapping mouth.

I had no idea whose party we were at—as I said, Jack was driving—but I'll never ever forget walking into what I thought was the bathroom and seeing him standing there, blindfolded, sporting those six donuts on his dick, the top three at a perfect right angle to the bottom three (and the way I know they were Krispy Kreme donuts is because the girl with the diamond in her nose was using the box to catch the ones that missed her mouth). Anyhow, that's the long way of explaining how I found out Jack's penis is crooked, and that he's so paranoid about it he'd even give up being a vampire to have a straight one . . . but how does Sheba know?

Suddenly, obviously bored with the subject of Jack's hidden anatomical defect, Sheba changes the subject back to herself. "Honey," she says, "speakin' of vulgarities, you won't believe what some boy said to me last night at the upside-down Plaza." (The "upside-down" Plaza is a local bar, so called because the neon sign out front reads ∀Z∀ℸd.) "I admit that I'd had a few cocktails before going out, so you know I was feelin' kind of cute. And honey, I was dressed in one of those slenderizing beaded creations, and I had on my pumps too, so I thought it might be a lucky night for the Bald Eagle, if you know what I mean, Jellybean. Well honey, things started looking up when one of those banker types sent me over two white Russians, but just about the time I pulled out my compact to check for lipstick on my teeth, this boy brushed by me and then gave me the once-over, and honey, if he didn't look me in the eye and say, 'I bet you could cut a ferocious fart.' I mean, have you ever heard anything so rude in your life? It just ruined my whole night."

The thing about hanging out with people like Sheba and Brent and Jack is that no conversation among us ever *leads* to anything. Talk is just a way to fill up time, to keep us from having to deal with the fact that life is boring and we're not doing anything about it. So, the tawdrier we can be, the less we realize we're going crazy ... or at least the less that I realize *I'm* going crazy. "Whose turn is it to change the baby?" I say, placing my book down in my lap.

For a startled second, all heads turn in my direction with looks that seem to say, "Baby ... what baby?" But then the clouds block the sun and the first voice of protest comes from Brent. "Not mine," he says, picking up Sheba's life-size mermaid doll, Miss E. Jasmine (another great find at the DAV). "I did it on New Year's, remember? And wrapped it in that nice paper with the champagne bottles on it, too. Also, I perfumed it, thank you. It was beginning to smell worse that Ms. Poodle Puss's twat over there," and he waves E. Jasmine's tail at Sheba from across the room.

"Jack?" I say.

"No," he snaps, knowing that if he storms out of the room it will more or less prove Sheba's accusation. (Come to think of it, I never did ask Jack who that girl was with the diamond in her nose.) "I've got it next week," he says. "It's Sheba's turn."

"Honey," she huffs, "it seems like it's *always* my turn."

"We'll buy you lunch today," Brent says, tempting her. (Sheba can never turn down a free lunch.)

"Well," she drawls, turning apprehensively to the big box all wrapped so festively on her kitchen table, "the Belle Sisters could use a little nourishment I guess ... and I did just buy some pretty new silver foil paper with red hearts on it that'll work nicely for a Valentine's motif, even though it's still a bit early yet. But I get to pick where we eat, okay?"

"Fine with me," Brent says.

So while Sheba changes the paper on Cyra's baby, me and Jack and Brent look over the winter course offerings at UAB. Already it's the second week of classes, and as usual we've missed at least the first session of each one, but at least the baby offers us a good excuse this time. Neither me nor Jack told Brent and Sheba that the baby we've been rewrapping these last few weeks is the child of my sister. We decided to keep it a secret between ourselves. Of course, Cyra knows I know about it because I hid her baby's blanket in my closet where she naturally went snooping. As Jack pointed out, "If only she weren't your sister we could blackmail her."

I know it's weird, since it's going on almost a month now and we *still* haven't buried that baby. Quite the opposite is true. It goes with us *everywhere*. Like common sense in reverse, we're now afraid *not* to let it out of our sight. Not for even one minute. We're afraid we'll lose it and it'll slip into the wrong hands and we'll all be imprisoned. Instead, the wrapping paper simply keeps up with the holidays. But at least the baby has a new box now; or rather, the old water-damaged box was placed inside a stronger, waterproofed box lined with Styrofoam—one that Jack stole from the UAB heart center. It's the kind they use to store organs in, which doesn't make us feel *that* bad about not giving the baby a proper burial, since its new box is the next best thing to a coffin. The only thing is, it just barely squeezes through the rabbit hole.

So there's good news and bad news. The good news is there wasn't a line at the registration terminals. We just breezed right on through. But the bad news is that everything wasn't full-up after all. Unfortunately, my "career counselor" was able to find a vacancy in Algebra 102, as well as in Supernatural Literature, which qualifies as an English elective; but at least I don't have to show up for either one except to take the exams, which pleases me enough that I might even buy the required textbooks for once.

Jack and Brent weren't as lucky. Having already fulfilled their

Mickey Mouse electives, they both got stuck with Business Law and Astronomy. But the saving grace is that both are Tuesday-Friday courses—which only squanders two days of the week instead of the four that I lose, Supernatural Lit being a Tuesday-Friday and Algebra being a Monday-Thursday. (For some strange reason, UAB doesn't have classes on Wednesday.) As for Sheba, she signed up for English 101 just to keep us company and because we were going to lunch straight from the registrar's office. (I keep thinking that if we do normal things, normalcy will follow. But it just doesn't.)

Sheba's choice for lunch was John's, one of those downtown restaurants where you can get a meat, two vegetables, bread, iced tea, and cole slaw for under five dollars. Everybody had snapper fingers with mashed potatoes and macaroni and cheese (which counts as a vegetable) except for Jack, who doesn't eat vegetables, so he ate two bowls of macaroni and cheese instead (I know, it makes no sense). For amusement, we kept dropping Brent's car keys into one another's tea glasses, and no one ever mentioned a word about germs.

"Where do we want to go now?" Brent asks, licking the tea off his keys. "Class?"

"Class?" says Jack scornfully. "But we just signed up not an hour ago. I don't ever go to class until at least three weeks into the quarter. Anytime before that is sheer plebeianism."

"A movie then," Brent says, scooting out from the booth.

"Honey, thank y'all for lunch," says Sheba, scooting out behind him, the wooden grapes in her straw hat clacking together as she leans over to take the baby. "But I feel guilty about not paying *anything*. Why don't y'all let me at least leave the tip? Here honey, take the baby a minute," and she passes it to me while she fishes through her purse, eventually pulling out seven ones which she slides under the ashtray. (Being in the business, we're all notorious overtippers.) "Okay honey, I'll take the baby again if you want," and I pass the box back to her.

"We could go to the Baskin Robbins for ice cream," I say, sort of in the mood for a sugar cone with Pralines and Cream.

"Ooooh, honey, that sounds like it's just what the doctor ordered," Sheba says, patting her stomach, the stomach that at this moment is being forced to digest its own order of snapper fingers, plus half of mine and most of Jack's, two plates of cole slaw, one macaroni and cheese, one mashed potatoes, Brent's field peas, three refills of tea, five corn fritters, two buttered rolls, and half a piece each of coconut pie and lemon pie. "But do you boys think I'm gettin' fat?" she asks as we walk out onto Twenty-first Street.

Brent unlocks the car. "I love how it's always phrased as if you're thin to begin with. It's never, 'Am I gettin' *too* fat?' It's only, 'Am I gettin' fat?'" So we slide into the car, Sheba in the front with Brent, and me and Jack in the back with the baby between us. Brent looks into his rearview mirror at me. "And speaking of weight loss, I saw your sister the other day at the Brookwood Mall with your mother, and I swear she must have lost thirty pounds since the last time I saw her. I almost didn't recognize her. She's starting to look good, Raine."

"She's dieting," I say. And then with a kind of snort, I add, "She's planning to be Miss America."

"Oh my God," Jack says, "your sister? They'll have to reinforce the stage."

"Now honey," Sheba says, putting on a fresh coat of lipstick, "don't be mean. At least it gives her a goal to strive for, something to look forward to. Can y'all think of anything we have to look forward to? Other than the Baskin Robbins, of course. Speakin' of which, I'm still havin' trouble deciding between Fudge Brownie and Pink Bubblegum."

"Well I, for one," Jack says, "am looking forward to Rose Kennedy's death—Brent, pay attention to the road. You just missed the turnoff—I mean, how much longer can she live? It seems like every year's gonna be her last, but somehow she keeps hangin' on. I will say this, though, she's a shoe-in for Death of the Year...provided somebody like Lucy or Bette Davis doesn't cheat her out of it. You know, it really would be a quandary—being forced to choose a winner among the three." Jack rubs the underside of his chin. "Just who *will* be our first nominee for eighty-four? Can y'all think of any other likely candidates...and George Burns doesn't count."

Well, Sheba finally decides on Fudge Brownie—a double scoop topped off with strawberry sauce and chopped macadamia nuts—and I get my Pralines and Cream in a sugar cone. Brent chooses Lime Sherbet and Jack gets his usual Vanilla...not even French Vanilla, just plain old Vanilla, which Sheba insists isn't a *real* flavor, "no more than the parakeets at Woolworth's are real birds, honey." Anyway, we left the baby in the car but cracked both back windows slightly because Sheba says it's a felony to leave an infant unattended in a parked car with all the windows up...don't even ask. Ten minutes later, satiated at last, we saunter back to the car with the full intention of doing good and just things the rest of the afternoon—like call our grandmothers or write checks for last month's car payments, something future-oriented like that—but The Gods are apparently in a snit (I told Jack they'd take revenge for him not playing fair, remember?) and the first to recognize our nightmarish twist of fate is Sheba. "Aaaaaaaaah!" she screeches. "Somebody swiped our baby!"

Chapter Ten

CYRA

I SWIPED THE BABY. It's *my* baby and I took it because nobody's going to make a fool out of me, and least of all my own brother. It couldn't have worked out better, actually, if I'd planned it that way. But The Gods have always been kind to me . . . *The Gods?* (I've been eavesdropping on Raine and his creep-hole friend too long.) You see, I borrowed Mom's car to go into English Village in Mountain Brook so I could check out the *chichi* boutiques for evening gowns. I figured if I saw one that I really liked, I could put it on layaway—it being sort of a dangling carrot as far as having an incentive to lose weight faster—or else I could shoplift it, depending on how expensive it was (the more expensive an item, the more likely it is I don't pay for it).

And in fact, I did find one that was just perfect—a backless midnight blue velvet one with a V-collar and long sleeves, the sleeves trimmed with lace at the wrists. I'm sure it's a little daring (no southern belle would be caught dead in either velvet or black, and midnight blue is the same thing as black anyhow), but that's just the point. Why not be original? Maybe for once in their passionless lives, the judges will reward individuality. Also, midnight blue is slenderizing.

Well, I was holding it in front of me at the mirror, this size seven dress . . . that's right, a size s-e-v-e-n (I'll get there, just don't you fret), and I was stealing glances at the frost-headed sales slut over near the door. I just knew she was thinking to herself, "Who does that cow think she's fooling?" and I was mentally ordering the phone to ring or someone else to come in, just any diversion so that I could walk out the door with my new dress, when what should I suddenly catch reflected in the mirror but those four thieves pulling up for ice cream at the Baskin Robbins across the street. Well, the dress could wait.

If there's anything I've learned in my years of merchandise-walking, it's that the secret to invisibility is *total* visibility. I mean, I've never even been *suspected,* and no one is more brazen than me. I just walk right in, pick up whatever it is that I want, and glide right out, smiling, with the object in full view. Only once has it failed me, but it's not because I was caught by the store, it's because . . . well, I'll get into that later. Ordinarily though, it works like a charm. Take that bedroom set I got last year. It was my shining hour. I simply went into the furniture store, picked out what I wanted, wrote the stock number down on a piece of paper, and took it to the greenest-looking salesman on the floor—some hick just out of high school.

"Excuse me, sir," I said, and sneaking a peek at his name tag, I very icily added, "I'm looking for a Mr. Evans . . . Oh, *you're* Mr. Evans? Well, Mr. Evans, I'm here on behalf of my employer, who also happens to be the . . . sister-in-law of your store manager. Ordinarily, of course, I would air my employer's grievances with your manager personally, them being so close to each other. But, seeing as how you're new to your job and all, I convinced my employer to give you a chance to first remedy the

problem yourself. What problem, you say? Why, Mr. Evans,"
and handing him my piece of paper with the stock number on it,
I added, "this set of bedroom furniture was supposed to have
been delivered to my employer over *two* months ago . . . by *you,*
Mr. Evans. You probably hadn't been working here very long at
the time. In any case, everyone's allowed one mistake. But I'm
sure you remember her . . . a Mrs. Freeman. Flora Freeman.
She's a very big-boned woman with silvery hair and delicate
features. She may have even tried to offer you a piece of quartz
to help clear up that complexion of yours. No? Well, just the
same, she remembers you only too well, and is extremely
disappointed . . . Yes, that's right, Freeman, just the way it
sounds. Flora Freeman. No, of course there's no shipping order.
You idiots lost it. But twice now she's called about that delivery,
only to be told it's still awaiting shipment from the warehouse
—a fact that she and I both find rather odd since there's a perfectly fine suite of it here on the showroom floor. What's that?
Well, I can only say your memory fails you. I'm sorry to have
taken up your time, Mr. Evans. If you'll just be so kind as to
point me in the direction of your manager's office . . .
Reasonable? Mr. Evans, I think *you* are the one who isn't being
reasonable, yet naturally I'm willing to make a concession, provided that the furniture is delivered by this afternoon. If you can
see to that—and the address is on the back there—if you can do
that, then I assure you it will go no further than our conversation
here today. Thank you so much, Mr. Evans. You're a fine asset
to your company, and I'll be sure to pass it along. Have a nice
day now."

*Yes, My Lily, even the boards of Broadway never saw such a
performance as you gave that day.* And what a lovely bedroom
set it was, too.

But anyway, back to my thieving brother. While those mon-
grels had their backs to me at the ice cream counter, I simply
opened Brent's car door, took my baby, and left. Not even a fly

98

gave me a second look, not that it would have mattered anyway . . . I'm the kind of person who'd deny eating a calf if its tail was hanging out of my mouth.

Well, that was about two hours ago, and thinking of which, I don't know of anything I could go for more right now than a juicy veal chop smothered in onions and mushrooms. Instead, I'm forced to chew my cud on this tasteless spinach salad. I'm back at the garage loft apartment, all alone, because Mom just took her car to go visit some architect or something. Get this, she's having a "meditational chamber" constructed in the back yard. It's to be pyramid-shaped, of course, and made entirely out of "dichroic" glass, which is some special metallic-coated crap that turns a different color depending on which angle you look at it from. Apparently, a dichroic glass pyramid is much superior to the plain glass kind because it allows you to "pursue the cosmic destiny of mankind through congeries of energy alignment." Whatever you say, Mom.

After I've finished my salad, it's time for my daily primp session, meaning I strip naked and stand on the scales in front of a mirror and ask my reflection just how much longer it intends on sticking around. At least Mom does have a point—there's nothing really *wrong* with my features. I mean, my mouth has a nice sort of Clara Bow, silent screen siren quality about it, even though the corners do have a tendency to turn downwards into a sneer more often than not—I'm going to have to work on that —and my eyes aren't too far apart and my nose is almost perfect and I have skin like a porcelain figurine of Mother Mary. Yes, my skin is my best feature. Well, my hair too. If I had to list in order all the things I like best about myself, it would go skin, hair, mouth, nose, eyes, hands—I'm certain I could be a hand model—and finally . . . my body.

What's that you say, Sugar Dumplin'? Did I hear correctly? Your body? Is that as in b-o-d-y? Dearheart, a body is something you see in a Pepsi commercial. A body is something you

99

find in a magazine wrapped in cellophane behind the counter at a U-totem. A body, my sweet cupcake, honeybunch, smoochums . . . is something you don't have.

And on this merry note, I go into my bathroom, open the medicine cabinet, and take down the carton of milk that's been in there, unrefrigerated, for about a month now. Kneeling over the toilet, I close my eyes and take a swig. Hey, what can I say? I tried the finger and it didn't work. Besides, milk's good for you.

Don't worry, I'm not adding bulimia to the growing list of all my other sociopathic offenses. But face it, it's the *only* thing that seems to work fast enough. I'm pressed for time here, after all, and that size seven velvet dress only brings home just how far I have to go. Anyway, even the normal girls rely on vomit-reduction; so in all actuality, I'm just taking one more baby step toward conformity.

Well isn't that admirable, my lovely sylph. And as long as we're on the subject of baby steps, just what steps do you plan on taking with that package on the dresser over there?

Reluctantly, and with disgust warping my pretty face, I go over to the dresser and give the box a closer inspection. Somehow, it looks a little bigger than the one I remember "the Cabbage Patch Doll" being in. Plus, the paper on this one is silver with red hearts. As I recall, the other was Christmasy—and why would they have rewrapped the thing? I lift the box. It seems heavier than a newborn ought to weigh. You know, I *could* have it all wrong. Maybe this really *is* just a present for somebody. Maybe God's giving me a second chance after all. Maybe I did get off scot-free!

Oh right, my blushing rose. Dream on. And that blanket you found in Raine's room only looked like the one you wrapped your baby bunting in.

What am I going to do? I say, pleading at the box. I'm not an evil person. Really, I'm not.

Please. Save the histrionics for the pageant.

No, deep down inside I'm really kind of sweet. And yet...
and yet somehow I've committed a murder—a murder! I've
attempted suicide—I'm counting these off on my fingers—and
now, now I've done what amounts to burglary in broad daylight.
And I'm not even considering just my everyday offenses—lying
and shoplifting and such... What kind of person am I?

*At least you can take comfort in the fact that your crimes are
getting progressively more white-collar. It is progress, my suc-
culent honeydew.*

If only I hadn't been so mean to Raine that day. That started it
all. My whole malaise and decline can be traced back to that *one*
awful day. See, there's something different about Raine. He's
gifted. Not that he'll admit it to anybody, not even himself, but
he truly is. I've seen proof. I've *destroyed* proof. And I don't
mean just talent either. I mean gifted, as in one-in-a-hundred-
million. I'm not saying this because he's my brother. In fact, it's
because he *is* my brother that I was blinded to it for such a long
time. If I had just recognized it for what it was, then maybe he
wouldn't have abandoned his calling. (Unlike me, Raine always
did place too great a store in public opinion.) But I guess I was
jealous and angry, and it's a credit to him that he never took out
revenge on me.

I remember the day perfectly. It was March twentieth of last
year, the very last day of spring break. Mom, in one of her more
flippant moods, had earlier in the year decreed that Raine and I
were not to make any plans for spring break, that instead she
wanted just the three of us to spend one final vacation together
in which she got to act out a parent role. "Next year, Cyra,
you'll be out of high school and Raine will be a junior in college, and neither one of you will need me as a mother anymore." So, we agreed on New York City—Raine and I flatly
vetoing Mom's initial suggestion of Brasília. But, as suspected,
a week of nonstop restaurants, plays, and museums only went to

prove that family togetherness didn't lend itself to harmony. Or in other words, I was starting to be a bitch.

See, Raine had brought his portfolio with him, figuring that as long as he was going to be in New York he might as well shop it around. He was hoping to get an internship for the coming summer, meaning he'd agree to work free just for the experience. (Once he got out of school, Raine wanted to be an illustrator. Wait, I mean an *animator* is what he called it—drawing purple-spotted hippos and checkerboard zebras. That sort of stuff.) So this portfolio of his had all the original artwork in it that he'd ever done in his whole life—all the good stuff anyhow—and it was nothing less than brilliant. That was the only word for it. Even *I* liked it, and I don't like anything. I mean, if he'd walked in the door at Disney Studios they'd have offered him carte blanche over the next *Bambi* or whatever. That's how good it was: so good, so perfect, that in a screaming tirade I threw it off the Empire State Building and we never saw it ever again.

It was just one of those things where, looking back on it, you wonder what kind of madness possessed you. Yet at the time it seemed perfectly rational . . . or at least called for. I really think the weather plays a big part in mood and mind-set. I think if it had only been sunny that day then none of this would have happened, but the whole morning had started off weird. The sky was all drizzly and gritty and cold, and opening the drapes in our hotel bedroom we couldn't see anything. Nothing. Just grayness. Mom, after taking a look out the window and a glance at her horoscope, announced she wasn't budging one muscle from her bed until it came time to call a taxicab for the airport. "But kids, y'all go on and do something if you want. Aquarius and Aries look just fine. It's only Capricorn that might as well roll over and die."

Well, Raine and I promptly got into an argument about how we were going to spend our last day. Mom said that whatever we did, we had to do it together, because she didn't want an innocent seventeen-year-old southern girl runnin' around loose by herself in New York City. "But Mom," I said, "I haven't even gotten one second to myself the whole time we've been up here, and you know how Raine is. He doesn't like to do anything a normal person likes to do. He's perfectly happy just sitting on a park bench watching the pigeons."

"Oh, forgive *me,* Miss Culture. And I suppose you'd rather soak up a little self-improvement—visit the Frank Lloyd Wright room at the Met perhaps? Count how many countries' flags you can name at Rockefeller Center? Eat cheesecake at the Carnegie Deli? Yeah, I bet we wouldn't have to twist your leg on that one."

"Just because you think you're *so* talented," I snipped. "You're just vain enough to think there'll be something in New York named after *you* someday." Then I threw a leg over the side of my chair and swung it up and down with frustration. "And just how many call-backs have you gotten this week, Mr. Disney? . . . Zero!"

"Cyra, that's enough," Mom said, holding an amethyst at her temples.

But right at that moment, like we were living a script from a sitcom, the telephone rang, and of course it was only one of the biggest magazines in the country asking Raine if he wouldn't mind dropping by with his portfolio for an interview in the art department around noon. I could have screamed.

But we reached a compromise. Raine, happier than a dead pig in the sun after his phone call, agreed to accompany me shopping until time for his interview. He said he needed to buy that whore, Sheba, a present anyway (he didn't call her a whore, I did)—some kind of perfume or something that they don't sell in Birmingham—so we went to Macy's because it was nearby where Raine had to be, and Raine was all dressed up in a suit with his portfolio, looking like he belonged in a window office on the penthouse floor, and there I was in my tent and industrial-strength sneakers, looking like I belonged in the employee restroom with a mop in my hands. It wasn't fair. How did Raine get all the looks and charm and talent?

"I guess I need a raincoat," he said. "It's kind of nasty outside."

"Not one of those London Fog things," I said, clomping behind him up to the second-floor men's department. "Tell me you're not going to dress like every other conformist, Jello-molded male in this city?"

"That's exactly how I'm going to dress."

"Playdough in their hands," I said. "That's your worst character flaw, Raine. You've always believed that what others do you should follow. Well hurry up. I don't want to waste all morning on *you*."

"Hold this a second," he said, handing his portfolio over to me as he pulled a raincoat off a rack. "This one looks nice, don't you think? I'm going to try it on . . . maybe a new white shirt, too."

"Just over there, sir," said a salesman, pointing Raine toward the dressing rooms. And it was at that moment, all alone for the first time that week, in the middle of Macy's with Raine's portfolio in my hands, that I saw it. It was perched there on the glass lid of a case full of pure angora sweaters—the most perfect ceramic kitten you've ever laid eyes on in your whole life. It was about four inches long with white fur and blue eyes and a tiny little pink face that turned up with a smile on it. Just a trinket really, and usually I'm not a sentimental kind of girl, but it was a dead ringer for my long lost Sugar Ball—damn that Billy Netherland—and I *had* to have it.

"How much is that ceramic kitten?" I asked.

"It's a prop," the salesman sneered. "It's not for sale."

"But how much would you take for it?"

"It's *not* for sale."

"Well thank you anyway," I said, as though I'd been planning on *buying* it, and I secretly congratulated myself for being so sweet, and I was especially pleased that he'd been so uppity about it. This way, stealing it wouldn't weigh on my conscience at all. So I swung Raine's portfolio onto the glass counter top with the open end facing the kitten. Luckily, the portfolio was plenty big enough so one little ceramic kitten wouldn't be noticeable at all. Leaning against the counter, I flexed my fingers as though carrying around such a case had made my knuckles sore. Next, I glanced irritably toward the dressing rooms, just to let the salesman know I *was* waiting on someone; and finally, giving the area a casual once-over, seeing that no one was looking at me, I deftly swept the kitten into the portfolio, picked it back up, and walked to the entrance of the dressing rooms, where I glanced at my wrist impatiently—all in one fantastic butter-smooth motion. God, was I good!

And just in time, too. Or so I thought. For at that moment Raine came out of the dressing room with the coat over his arm, but that's when I heard the cackle of laughter, a lunatic cackle. It came from a rack of marked-down slacks. Behind the rack grinned another man—a fat black one with an orange scarf wrapped around his head. I looked at him and he looked at me and then he laughed all the more loudly. He nodded and winked, and my face flushed as I turned back to Raine. I tried to sound calm. "So did the coat fit okay?" *So someone did see me. How could I have not seen him? How?*

"Well," Raine drawled undecidedly, "yeah, it fill all right, but . . ."

"Good. Get it and let's go," and I started walking toward the elevators. From the corner of my eye I could see that orange-turbaned nigra laughing at me.

"Wait a minute," Raine said, "It's kind of expensive. Maybe I ought to look around some more first, don't you think?"

"Then leave it," I practically hissed. "It's already ten-thirty and don't forget you have to buy Sheba some perfume, plus you promised Mom you'd do something *I* want to do, too. And you know we won't have time after your interview." I stabbed the elevator button for the third time.

"Well . . . but I didn't think you wanted to do anything."

"Of course I do," I said, noticing that the man had moved a little closer. He was pretendin' to be looking at some socks, but he was grinning that horrid grin and saying "meow" to himself over and over, and suddenly he snapped his fingers and leaned over and said, "Here, kitty, kitty, kitty." Two salespeople were huddled in a conference not far away, obviously discussing the best way to get rid of the crackpot without making a scene.

"Well where?"

"Where what?" I said.

"Cyra, where do you want to go?"

"Oh. Um . . . the Empire State Building." It was just the first thing that came out of my mouth. To this day I don't know where it came from. The elevator doors finally opened and I snatched the raincoat out of Raine's hands and threw it over the closest rack. "Come on. We're running out of time and it's just down the street a ways."

"Here, kitty, kitty, kitty! Here, kitty, kitty, kitty!" the man said, following us onto the elevator just before the doors slid closed. He winked again. My fists were tight white balls.

About eight other people were in the elevator with us. "But Cyra," Raine whispered, "when Mom asked if we wanted to go there the other day, you said you'd rather dive for pearls in a septic tank than resort to—how did you phrase it?—'celebrating idiocy in the clouds with a herd of morons.'"

"Well, I've changed my mind," I said, clutching the soul out of that portfolio. *Somehow, I have to get that kitten into my pocket before he asks for this back.* The elevator opened again. We got off, and I said, "I'll wait here while you look at perfume."

But by then Raine was mad. "No. You want to go to the

Empire State Building and that's where we're going. We've only got an hour as it is." He reached for the portfolio.

"I'll hold it. I like holding it."

"Suit yourself." And as I followed him out the door I looked over my shoulder, not quite convinced that we'd left "Here Kitty" behind.

The weather up there on the observation deck was just the weirdest I've seen in my whole life. The air was totally still, I mean *totally,* and it was white—white as paste. You couldn't see down or up or out in any direction. It was as if we were inside an airless, colorless vacuum staring out at the walls of a padded cell. Nothing moved beyond or penetrated the grillwork on the railing, and naturally nobody else had been stupid enough to visit the Empire State Building on a day like that except us. Only the street noises drifting up from below hinted that we were at a real place in a real time.

"What a fantastic view," said Raine. "Why I can almost make out my hand in front of my face." His voice sounded the way voices do at an indoor swimming pool, slightly echoing. "Have you seen enough?"

"We just got here," I said, still holding his portfolio and trying to think of a way to take out my kitten without him seeing. "Raine, would you mind getting me a Coke at that concession stand inside?"

"Get it yourself."

"Fine," I replied, that being just what I wanted to hear.

"Wait," he said, reaching out to get the portfolio from me. "I'll take this now. I need to double-check everything and make sure it's all organized right."

"No, I'm sure it's okay," I said, pulling the portfolio back toward me. "I'll just be a minute."

Raine looked at me like I was crazy. "Cyra, *I'll* take it now," and he reached for it again.

107

I pulled it away again. "No," I said.

"Cyra, what is wrong with you?"

"Nothing's wrong with me," I sneered. "You're the thief, not me!" My words echoed off the walls, and like sand filled up all the spaces between the invisible buildings out beyond.

"Thief?" he said, his face all screwed up. He looked at the portfolio, the slight bulge at the bottom. "Cyra, what did you steal?" and he lunged for the handles.

"Nothing!" and I started running around a corner of the deck. I knew it was insane. The whole thing was insane—for a ceramic kitten?—but it was all reflex at that point anyhow, and like Little Black Sambo trying to outrace the tigers, we just went around and around that observation platform, way up there in the motionless, gummy white sky—until I felt a hand on my shoulder, and for reasons I've never figured out, I just hurled Raine's portfolio—his whole future—over the side of the Empire State Building, where it was instantly devoured by the white walls of the padded cell beyond, and we never ever saw it or my precious ceramic Sugar Ball again.

For a few eternal, decompressed seconds, all the oxygen seemed to have been sucked out of my life with that portfolio. I pressed against the grillwork, unable to breathe, and just gaped into the whiteness. I kept expecting it to sail magically back, like a boomerang, and when I finally accepted the fact that it wouldn't, I took a deep breath and turned to face what I expected to be the numbed, expressionless stare of my brother. Instead, the hand attached to my shoulder belonged to the grinning, monkey-mouthed black-cheeked maniac with an orange babushka smeared around his head.

"Here, kitty, kitty, kitty."

Chapter Eleven

RAINE

"HONEY, THERE'S A CAT up ahead. See it? Brent, do you see it? . . . Honey, there's a cat . . . Breeeeeent!" Sheba looks over her shoulder at the bloody blob tumbling out from beneath the trunk. She turns to Brent, her face a twisted mess. "I don't believe you just killed it, just like that . . . Honey, you killed it! You purposefully ran that poor creature over and it might have had little babies and everything that'll just starve to death now because *you* killed their mama."

"It wasn't on purpose, Sheba. There was a car comin' the other way. I couldn't just swerve around the dumb thing . . . how do you know it was a female anyhow?"

"All cats on the roads are females. They're the only ones that do the huntin'. The males are too lazy, just like y'all." She takes my hand and squeezes it and glances briefly again over her shoulder, thinking maybe it had healed itself and was chasing after us. "Honey, you still could have gone around it on the shoulder side. You didn't have to just blaze right over it." She lays her white frosty head against my shoulders and it feels nice. I think to myself that I hope Brent hits another. "Why is everything dyin' all of a sudden? Honey, until I was thirty years old, the only thing that ever died on me was a lightning bug, and that's because it got stabbed by the ice pick when I was puttin' air holes in the jar lid. Now, though, I've lost two grandparents, a cousin to a fire, and this mystery baby—all in the last six months. I guess from here on, it's just like *Ten Little Indians*. No one leaves alive."

Jack now looks across me to Sheba. "I thought you were only twenty-nine."

Sheba looks startled. She raises her head off my shoulder. Two or three wild blond hairs are stuck to the skin on her forehead. "How old did I just say I was?"

"Thirty. You said you were thirty. Didn't she, everybody?" And Jack looks to me and then Brent for confirmation.

Brent speaks into his rearview mirror. "That's what you said, Sheba. I heard you."

"You didn't *hear* anything. You were too busy murdering animals. Now honeys, I may have *said* I was thirty, but I was just roundin' things off for effect, you know. Anyways, it doesn't much matter anyhow once you're past twenty-five. You boys will know what I mean in a few years . . . yeah, I think I'm gonna be twenty-nine for a good spate now. Otherwise, I'm just pushin' forty without a fur."

"Brent," I say, noticing we're heading downtown instead of away from it, "You're drivin' on the wrong side of the road again."

"Huh," mumbles Brent. "I must've made a wrong turn after we hit the cat."

"We?" Sheba says. "You're the one with the wheel in your hands."

"Brent," says Jack, "how many times have you driven us all to work? A hundred? Two hundred? And you're *still* getting lost. Doesn't say much for your intelligence quotient, does it now?"

"Doesn't say much for your intelligence quotient, does it now?" Brent mimics. "No," he adds, "and it doesn't say much for your complexion either... I wish y'all would stop makin' fun of me. One day I'm gonna be a big star in Hollywood. You'll see. Besides, I don't always get lost. Half the time it's the fault of this damn restaurant. What's it doin' out in the middle of nowhere anyhow? It's no wonder Ampersand gripes about business bein' off. Nobody can find the place... which way do I go up here, left or right?"

"Left," I say, and Brent turns onto the shaded drive. It's my favorite part of coming to work, traveling along this road running parallel to the Cahaba River, beneath the canopy of oaks and pines and magnolias—it's what you think of when you think of the Old South—but then the road suddenly empties into this glaring asphalt parking lot scraped out along the riverbank, with a huge building slung up on one end of it overlooking the river, the building designed to look like a cross between a Congo trading post and a post-modern treehouse... and you realize that no matter how much you hate the era you're living in, it only gets worse all the time.

Being employees, we're forced to park as far away from the building as we can (otherwise, it's a five-dollar fine taken out of your tips). Brent pulls into a space next to the dumpster, saying, "I hope somebody has an extra bow tie in their locker, 'cause I forgot mine again."

"So sing a new tune," Jack says, slamming his door behind him. It's amazing how quickly Jack has picked up on everyone's individual bad work habits—Brent's forgetfulness, Sheba's lethargy, my indifference—considering he's only been working with us at The Rainforest for the past month. (He got fired from being the hushpuppy maker at Captain D's. No two of them were ever the same size.)

"Hold on, y'all," Sheba says, leaning against Brent's trunk while trying to unsnag a knot in her shoelaces. "Honeys, are we all agreed here, all of us, about this baby thing?"

"Oh Jesus," says Jack. "Sheba, we've been over it a hundred times already—a thief just isn't gonna go to the police no matter what he finds. Someone stealin' that baby is the best thing that could've happened. I, personally, was gettin' tired of lugging it around everywhere myself."

Sheba jerks at the knot a few times and finally gives up. "But what if whoever stole it already *knew* it was a baby?"

Jack gives me a quick look, his eyes promising he won't give Cyra away. "Now, Sheba, how in creation would anybody *know* it was a baby? It hasn't been out of our sight since we found it. Not once."

"Come on, y'all," Brent whines. "We're already late as it is, on top of me not comin' in early to set up the stations. It was *my* day. Ampersand's gonna be mad as a cottonmouth."

"Well, Brent," I say, "no Rolex for you this month."

"Not unless he works late," Sheba adds with a sparkle in her eyes. "And I don't mean polishin' the silverware."

The Rainforest is the kind of place you might want to go for a special occasion—an anniversary or Valentine's Day or something—but for just plain dinner, well, it's a little, shall we say, tropical? I mean, it's all split-beam floors, highback wicker chairs, and potted palms. People eat off of banana leaves under wicker ceiling fans. The dining room itself is on three levels, connected by plank ramps, not stairs, and it's built around one of these basement-to-roof atriums with a glass-bottom floor so you can see the river underneath. The general feeling is of eating in a sinking jungle riverboat with a hole blown through it.

Worse still, built into the atrium (and in fact the reason for it) is "the world's largest bird cage," a roundish affair with wrought-iron bars shaped like ivy, stuffed with coconut trees, wild orchids, and every conceivable species of tropical bird that could be smuggled in—things with names like green manucodes, regent bower birds, sickle bills, green and yellow pygmy long-tailed sunbirds, plus the obligatory cockatoos, parakeets, lovebirds, flamingos, and toucans. It's no mystery why the place is losin' money. The overhead on the birds alone must be unholy; especially since most of them are half dead from concussions (they're always trying to fly through the glass-bottom floor).

We all drag to our lockers and change into our uniforms. Most of the other waiters are here already and have finished their prep work, so now they're just kind of sitting around smoking cigarettes and talking about how much they hate being waiters (it's all waiters ever talk about). The floor manager, a snarly-haired hussy named Tara (yes, they actually name girls that down here) comes in, and without even saying hello, growls, "The last ones in get the worst stations. It's a new rule I've just made up—*uh nooh ruwel ah jes maayd ihp*—because this is the second time this week you all have been late—*thu segund tam thiz wake y'all've beyun layte*—and I ain't going to put up with it no more—*uh ain't gonna puttup withit nooo mower.* The doors open in twenty minutes. Check your tables first to make sure they're set up right, then get to your preps. Raine, you've got lemons. Jack, you've got salads. Sheba, you've got the bird cage. And Brent, Ampersand wants to see *you* in his office." Then she gives us a look that says she better not catch even *one* speck of dust on our knives, *one* salt shaker only three-quarters full, or *one* crooked bow tie. It's a look that means *"Iham inna firin' mood."*

After Tara's gone, Sheba throws her pad onto the floor. "I'm over always gettin' bird cage prep! I swear I think that old dyke takes a special pleasure in seein' me sweepin' up chicken doop."

"Chickens?" Brent says. "He's got chickens in there, too?"

"Honey, you saw what happened last week," Sheba continues,

not speaking to anyone in particular. "One of those parakeets or something just dumped right in my eye. It probably held it in all afternoon, just waitin' for me to show up with the food, and honeys, you've seen what those birds can do, too." She arches her brow. "I mean they are healthy!"

Anyway, Sheba goes off to chop up a tub of oranges and sardines and sunflower seeds, Brent goes upstairs to see Ampersand (whatever that might mean), and Jack and me get stuck standing over the sink next to the Hobart dishwasher in this sizzling kitchen with almost no ventilation. At least lemons aren't as hard as salads. I can be thankful for that, but Jack now has less than fifteen minutes to get seventy-five fresh, neatly arranged salads into the walk-in; seventy five being the minimum number any weeknight shift can start with. On weekends, it's a hundred and fifty.

Each salad consists of a bed of hydroponic spinach—two ounces—topped with a ring of pineapple, a slice of papaya, overlaid with a cross of hearts of palm, a sprinkle of shredded coconut, and a pinch or two of ground nutmeg. The house dressings are Creamy Loquat and Breadfruit Vinaigrette, which have to be made up fresh by hand every day, as do the old standbys like Bleu Cheese, "Country" French and—gag— Thousand Island, too. All in all, the salads could even make a monkey retch, but they *are* colorful and exotic-looking, so everyone requests them, if just for their conversation potential.

Jack opens a can of imported loquats and drains the syrup into the sink, and I haul over a box of lemons, sigh, and grab a knife. All you do is stab it around the equator in a zig-zag pattern, in and out and in and out, until you get all the way to where you started. Then you pull the two halves apart, and what you have are "lemon crowns." Believe me, after the first one, the thrill fades quickly. "Alright," says Jack, "The Gods say you get to kill somebody and get off one hundred percent scot-free. You won't even be suspected."

"Wait," I interrupt. "Haven't we done this before?"

"Well, we're doing it again! I can't just stand here making gorilla food doing nothing."

"Well maybe we ought not to waste time with these games then. You heard Tara. She's not foolin' around tonight."

"Raine, don't you *ever* think your own thoughts? Do other people always have to put them in your head for you? Tara has about as much sense as those bottles of colored water that I'm sure she lines up along the living room window in her trailer. Do you always have to do what those who are inferior to you ask?"

"All the time," I say, stabbing the knife into another lemon. It makes the same kind of sound you'd imagine a knife going into someone's belly might make.

Jack pulls out a huge flat metal tray from a rack, sets it over the sink, and begins placing glass salad bowls on it in rows. "Don't you ever wonder why you're so impressionable? I'll bet your mother was the kind of woman who, when you challenged her authority or asked her to explain things, just responded, 'Because I said so, that's why, and because I'm older than you. You don't need a reason.'" Now Jack goes into the walk-in and returns with a bag of spinach. He opens the bag and scatters a few leaves into each bowl. Next comes the pineapple. There's a whole crate of fresh ones that just came in, but when Jack has salad prep it's canned everything all the way. In fact, *I'm* probably the only one who ever makes the salads the way you're supposed to . . . so give the boy a gold star why don't you. Jack's right. The world just doesn't have room anymore for people who go by the book. I should try to be more like him . . . he's the one who'll rise. His type always do.

Slinging the pineapple rings into bowls, Jack says, "I've been planning something lately—well, thinking about it rather—and I want *you* to tell me what you think."

For some reason, I'm afraid to ask him what it is. The tone in Jack's voice sounds, I don't know, not very lucid. "Is it somethin' about the baby?" I throw two more crowns into a ramekin.

"Forget the baby already," he says. "I told you, your sister's the one who has it, although why she'd want it back I don't know."

"Who do you think got her pregnant in the first place?" I say.

Jack throws the pineapple can into the garbage and grabs a can of papayas. "Well, I just *assumed* you did."

"Me!?"

"Come on, Raine. It's not like it's never happened before?"

"With my own sister? That fat thing?" The knife slips and a trickle of blood dribbles onto a lemon, turning it a lush shade of pink. I instinctively stick my finger in my mouth—I've always wondered why people suck their own blood—but there's nothing worse than lemon juice in a cut. Talking through my bleeding finger, I say, "You weren't even curious enough to *ask* if it was mine?" I turn the faucet on and rinse off the three crowns my finger dripped onto, then I place them back in their ramekins . . . no point in throwing away perfectly good lemons. "Damn, this stings."

"Listen, Raine, I don't care whether that baby is yours or God's, especially since it's dead and history," says Jack, opening a can of shredded, sweetened coconut and flinging it haphazardly at the salads. Some of it he eats, then he offers me the can. "Put a pinch on your cut," he says. "It'll kill the pucker." So I do and Jack just howls, saying he knew he hadn't gone wrong when he decided to cultivate my friendship, that no matter what he ever did or said, or how bad he acted, I would always be a good and faithful servant. Sometimes he says just the weirdest things, but at least he's smart. Hanging around brilliant people rubs off on you, that's my theory. I mean, *I'm* smart. I make A's and everything without trying, but I'm not a genius. And that's what I want to be.

Tara suddenly bursts through the kitchen doors, sucking in a long draw from her cigarette-sized cigar. Coughing, she shouts, "It's almost five!" Then she stares over the heads of all the nigra cooks, zeroing in on me and Jack way back here in the corner of the kitchen. A laser beam couldn't be more penetrating. "How many salads have you made up, Jack?" *Haow minny saledz 'ev yu mayde uhp, Jeeeeeck?* I feel a shudder go down my back. Jack decides to risk it.

"I'm just finishing up the last one, Tara. I made an extra twenty just in case we get an early rush. Thursdays are kind of iffy, you know." Jack winks at me. There are exactly eleven salads on the tray, eighty-four salads short of what he's just lied about. He won't get caught, though. He's lucky like that.

Sure enough, Tara takes his word for it and barrels back into the dining room, not saying a word to me. She never does. I don't know why, but I'm not complaining.

A few minutes later we're out in the dining room, stuck at the very worst stations, just like Tara promised. We're on the top floor, in a sort of windowless corner. The only view, if you're a "guest"—customers are never called customers by the staff. They're always guests—the only view if you're a guest is of the very top of the bird cage. Since we're standing up, however, we can see over the wood railing and, down below, underneath the palm fronds, we can just make out Sheba's coconut-colored hair. She's fighting off a pair of feisty scarlet macaws. They keep trying to roost on her arm while she fills the feeders. "Shoo, honey," she says, "shoo."

Jack's station is right next to mine. He's got five tables and I've got four, but one of mine is a six-top, so it evens out. Not that it matters. We'll be lucky to clear fifty dollars between us tonight, by the time we tip-out the hostess and the busboys. Jack slips behind a wall, into the cranny of a waiter station where there's a coffee machine, an ice machine, and a supply of condiments. He motions me to join him. Leaning against the fake bamboo formica counter and crunching lazily on an ice cube, he says, "So are you ready to hear what I've been planning lately?" I shrug and pour myself a cup of coffee, first making sure Tara's nowhere close to our floor. She's down below, bitching out Sheba for something or other. "What is it?" I say.

"We're going to murder somebody."

"Ha. Ha."

"You don't think I'm serious?"

"No."

"Oh but I am. Don't you think it would be exciting? Just look at your sister lately. She certainly seems to have benefitted." Jack swallows his ice and grabs another cube. My hand holding the coffee cup starts shaking. "It'll be fun, Raine. Something to share just between the two of us. You know, at first I was thinkin' it might ought to be just some nigra. But then I thought, well what's the point in that? Nobody would investigate it. The police wouldn't even care, and the whole point, after all, is the suspense of outwitting those cretins. So I thought about it and I thought about it, and just yesterday I came up with the perfect person. Do you want to know who?"

"NO!" It practically flies out of me.

"Well, I'm going to tell you anyway."

"Don't," I plead. "This mess with my sister is bad enough."

"Raine, my God, it hardly matters. Besides, it'll give you some self-esteem, which you need in a bad way." I shake my head back and forth violently. "Listen, listen," he says, holding my shoulders. "You've got to face up to things. Every day you're slipping more and more into a place you shouldn't be. Your sister doesn't see it 'cause she doesn't care, and your mother doesn't see it 'cause she's already there, but *I* do!" He lets go of my shoulders and I try to hold my coffee steady in my hands. "Half the time, Raine, you don't even hear what people say, and hell, this is at twenty. What do you think you're going to be like at forty? I shudder to think." His words start to sound like they're being shot at me through the barrel of a cannon. "Don't you see, I'm trying to make you come alive, that's what I'm trying to do, and the only way to do that is to kill somebody . . . now don't you want to hear who it is?" I shake my head a whole bunch of times, clenching my eyes shut, but he tells me anyway just like I *knew* he'd do, him knowing from the start that if I just heard it once, just once, then I'd go along with it. That's the way I've always been. Ask and I'll comply. Jack knew it, too. Jack knew it!

"That's better," he says, steadying my coffee. "You'll see, it's easy to die."

Chapter Twelve

CYRA

COULDN'T YOU JUST DIE, ANGEL?

Yes, dear God, I conceived the child of a Yankee nigra lunatic. You know, it didn't *feel* like rape. It wasn't agonizing or traumatic or even humiliating. Fear, in fact, didn't come into it at all. All I felt was disgust. My only thought was, "I hope nobody's watching." I don't have a shred of pity for these women who claim that being raped was the single worst thing that ever happened to them, that it's why they're neurotic and even suicidal. I just don't buy it. They're just lookin' for sympathy and attention, that's all, and if people would just say "Shut up about it already," they'd be fine. Like me.

I never did figure out what happened to Raine, and I sure didn't ask him later back at the hotel, not that he would have spoken to me anyway; but my assumption is that once he saw I really was throwing his portfolio to the wind, he just turned on his heels and lit off like a scalded dog to retrieve it . . . which, of course, was impossible. It's like it just vanished into that opaque sky, sucked away into the whiteness. For all we know, it could have struck somebody on the street and killed him; but more than likely it answered some lucky fool's prayers—a gift from Heaven. I'm sure some moron just picked it up off the pavement and now makes eighty thou' a year on Madison Avenue. Poor Raine. It's all my fault and I don't even care. I should though, I guess. Any normal person would.

If you ask me, though, I got the worst end of it—abused and deflowered up there on top of the world by the ugliest man that ever lived. He truly was hideous. His face looked like carved, charred wood, and that ridiculous turban only drew attention to its hideousness—the crinkly eyes, the nose as wide as my wrist, the missing teeth and the missing ear (if your first time has to be the worst, you at least want a *whole* person) and what's more, fool that I am, I made just *no* effort at all to resist. It was like . . . well, it's like one of those out-of-body experiences you read about in the *Enquirer*. There I was, pressed against the corner—the northeast corner, I think, my back to the Chrysler Building—not even feeling a part of what was happening. Maybe I was in a trance? I barely remember a thing, other than the rat-a-tat-tat of him going "Kitty, kitty, kitty" over and over and over . . . and then he was gone. Just gone. Well, I straightened my dress and just casually strolled around the observation deck a few times, my finger on my chin as though trying to remember where the car keys are, and then I left. Just like that, my mind as blank as the sky.

I wasn't dazed or in shock I don't think. I *knew* what had happened, but it didn't matter. *That* was the shocker. On my way back to the hotel, I just thought to myself, "Cyra, if getting raped by a mad Yankee nigra doesn't affect you, and ruining your own brother's life and career doesn't affect you, and feeling nothing at all except losing a cheap ceramic kitten is the only thing that inspires even a twinge of self-regret, then maybe you ought to consider the probability that you, my delicious gumdrop, are not a girl any mother could be proud of."

And so the seed of my inevitable deterioration did finally begin to germinate.

But now, oh now, it's one year later and how I *do* flourish. Like so many others who've abandoned all conscience and exist purely for themselves, I've come to the conclusion—and not a moment too soon—that most everyone else is inferior and therefore should be conquered. I can get anything I want, I've learned, if I can just *pretend* to be two things—sincere and vulnerable. It makes no difference whether my heart's in it or not. Image is everything. Image *is* reality if you can keep it up long enough—*that*'s the secret of life. It's *so* simple, so demonically simple, that I wonder why it's never taught in school. Life could be so much more comforting if you knew from the very beginning that it's only the facade that matters. Everything else can be your own. Oh, what a sweet discovery, to be able to live with myself after all, to be as perverse and abhorrent as I like— just as long as the outside glows like glass in a church window. Yes, I've no doubt it can be done. Everyone's going to see an all-new Cyra Freeman, one whose mouth *will* melt butter... even if I have to put a blowtorch against my tongue to do it.

The first thing I'm going to do is be friendlier toward my family. At the very least it'll be good practice for when I'm crowned Miss Alabama and then, ultimately, Miss America. You know, I managed to get that midnight blue velvet dress after all. What I did was stake out the shop for a few weeks until I saw they'd hired some dumb cheerleader type to help out on the weekends. Then, I sauntered in, explaining how I represented the manufacturer of that line, and unfortunately, the garment had been produced in an asbestos-insulated factory. Pulling on my rubber gloves, I then carefully folded the gown—and several others I'd had my eyes on—into a soft plastic suitcase. Walking out the door, I assured the streak-haired cheerleader that she, personally, was in no danger of contamination. Dumb da dumb dumb.

Anyway, now that I'm being friendlier to my family I've found that Mom and I *are* able to speak to each other after all, as long as we don't attempt to communicate. I just listen to her coaching and don't ever give her any back lip, because you know what? I've lost seventy-five pounds! Every day we go jogging together and then I do sit-ups, then I eat a salad and weigh myself and drink a glass of spoiled milk so I can throw the salad back up. Granted, lately I've been a little dizzy and sometimes I have headaches, but that's probably just natural when you're dieting as strenuously as I am. Also, I've started popping a few chocolate-flavored laxatives before bedtime— just two or three—which helps more than one might think. In fact, I'm doing so good that if I only lose one pound a day between now and the Miss West Jefferson County preliminary, I'll still be thin enough, and a pound a day is easy. On most days I lose at least two, and some days as much as four.

Even Raine is starting to notice. Why, just last week when I caught him snooping around the garage (obviously hunting for the baby, under the false assumption that I'd be dumb enough to hide it there a second time), he sort of mumbled something about how he was trying to find Dad's old toolbox because he needed a screwdriver—Raine always has been the very worst liar—and then, just out of the blue, he said, "Cyra, you've lost weight, haven't you?" And if Raine notices, you *know* you've done something noticeable. Yes, I just glowed and turned my profile to him there in the doorway . . . my svelte but voluptuous profile. Then, turning to go back upstairs, I said, "Good luck finding the box . . . the toolbox," and I just smiled.

He's up to something. I can just tell. Him and Jack both. They *think* I'm the one who stole back my baby, but they'll never be a hundred percent sure. I hate them both, that Jack creature especially. Why was I *so* irresponsible as to leave that blanket in the garage where just anyone could find it? Then Raine purposefully hid it in his room just to terrorize me. He knows how I am. He knew I'd go snooping, so why did he do it? Retaliation. He's never forgiven me for throwing his portfolio from the Empire State Building. Even though he never mentioned it, not once did he mention it. He even went so far as to tell Mom that the interview went well, that they were going to hold onto the portfolio awhile until they had a chance to look it over more closely, that they'd forward it back to him in Alabama—and Mom, of course, sucked it all up like coke through a straw.

Today, the first of April, April Fool's Day, marks a new beginning for me. Last night I lay awake for hours, weighing and balancing everything in my life. I came to the conclusion that it's pointless to blame myself for my past, that in any case, with the retrieval (and subsequent disposal) of my baby, it's all erased. Those four dumbbells have no proof anymore and they never will again. I've thought of the perfect solution. You see, I've wrapped the box in yet another layer of paper—this time plain brown—and I'm going to mail it (no return address) to Brazil.

Well, why not? Mom's always talking about the place as if nobody there has the sense to read or write or knows anything about the world other than what goes on in their own little village. And believe me, the place I have in mind can't be too bright either. It's called Namburi, and according to this book of Mom's that lists all the towns in Brazil—along with their populations and exports and religious beliefs and such—Namburi is little more than just a rinky-dink jungle clearing of about three hundred people, mostly Indians, whose major livelihood is cultivating a weed that, when boiled and dried and ground to a fine green powder, makes a great antidote to voodoo curses if you blow it into the cursed person's face at sunrise. If you ask me, any black magic adherents like that will probably welcome with open arms a baby wrapped in plain brown paper.

So I go to Mom to ask if she'll let me borrow her car so I can go to the post office, but I can tell right away that despite the beautiful weather and all the wisteria and dogwoods and azaleas being in full bloom and all, it's not one of Mom's *good* days. It used to be, back before she started subscribing to *The New York Times,* that Mom was only occasionally depressed about the state of the earth. But a few months ago she finally gave up altogether on ever expecting any "real" reporting from the local papers, and now she's depressed practically all the time.

It's not even noon yet, and already she's up in the top of one of the trees she planted back when me and Raine were born. I don't know what kind they are. I can't tell one from the other, but they're planted about twenty feet apart from each other in a huge circle of flowers, smack dab in the middle of the back yard with the fabulous glass meditational pyramid between them in the shade. Today the pyramid is a purplish color with splotches of blue where the sunlight hits it. Mom's perched in the crook of a limb about fifteen feet above the point of the pyramid. She's staring down at the changing colors below, slowly chewing on her lunch of chicken salad and a pomegranate (Mom's the only person I've ever heard of who actually eats pomegranates).

I go out onto the patio, with my hand over my eyes to shield the sun's glare. "Mom, can I borrow your car a little while?"

"Go ahead," she says. "Add more carbon to the atmosphere. Everybody else does," and she leans over to scrutinize a new leaf, biting simultaneously into her pomegranate. A drop of juice lands on the pyramid below.

"Mom," I say, "it's getting kind of hot out here. Why don't you come inside a while?"

"You think this is hot, do you? Well Missy, just you wait till *next* decade. You'll *see* what hot is." Rather than spitting out the seeds like a slattern, Mom removes each one from her mouth individually and delicately wraps them in her napkin. "Do you know what they're doing down there, Cyra? Do you have *any* idea?"

Uh-oh. I can tell already delicate maneuvering is going to be required here. "Mom, are you sure it's a good idea for you to be up that high? It looks dangerous."

"Oh, there's danger all right—atrocities against nature beyond all comprehension are going on. Most people don't even realize what's happening, nor would they care. No one's ever had any curiosity about South America anyway. But just you wait. States like Pará and Mato Grosso and Rondônia will roll across the lips as easily as Nagasaki and Hiroshima do today, the only difference being that *their* long-term effects shall be far more devastating. Yes, just you wait and see. They'll sure care when the world's a rainless wasteland!"

Mom wrings her hands and sort of knocks the back of her head over and over against the trunk of the tree. Her pomegranate rolls out of her lap and drops onto the pyramid—*clunk*—leaving behind a blood-colored trail as it slides down the glass. "Kiss it up to God," Mom cries. "Cyra, every year tracts of land twice the size of Alabama are literally being burned alive. The workers, they go in during the rainy season and cut down all the trees, so when the dry season comes they can just strike a match to it and up it goes—instant desert! Try to imagine the world's largest volcano—twice the size of Vesuvius, five times bigger than Mt. St. Helens, going full blast every day all year, decade after decade . . . and still you won't come close to matching the millions and millions of cubic tons of carbon and methane and nitrous oxides spewing into our atmosphere during these mindless conflagrations. Is it any wonder our ozone shield is in tatters? Is it any wonder it's been so hot lately?"

"Mom, can I borrow the car?"

"No one cares," she wails. "No one cares!" Her eyes begin to tear. I can see them sparkle even from this distance. "Only a hundred years ago," she says. "That's all. What started back then as no more than a few broiling black smutty smokestacks in the grungy part of London—in the dawn of that awe-inspiring phrase, the Industrial Revolution—that tiny pebble, having been pushed, begged, cajoled, and outright kicked to the top of the glacier, well, it's finally beginning its thunderous descent down as the biggest goddam snowball Hell ever unleashed... seals and porpoises washing up dead on the beaches, mercury and lead tainting our drinking water, lobsters with lesions, algae blooms, dead mountain tops, AIDS, skin cancer, salmonella in the poultry, three-digit temperatures in Canada, overpopulation, deforestation, babies with birth defects, and on and on and on. It used to be, a place got polluted and uninhabitable, people just moved on to the next. Well, those days are gone. There's no place left to go, Cyra. No place left in this world!"

"Mom, please get out of that tree. What if the neighbors see you?"

"What if they do!" she shrieks; but then, sighing, she shakes her head slowly. "Well, what's the difference? Just tell me please, what, after all, difference does it make now?"

Figuring it's useless to get anything sensible from her today, I turn to leave, thinking I'll just find the keys myself, when suddenly I feel her eyes on me, boring a hole through my skull. "Oh, Cyra?" she says, in the well-familiar mothers-know-more-than-you-think-they-know tone.

I don't dare turn around. "Yes?"

"Just one more thing. You can't see the future like I can. You don't *know* what's coming, and don't hear it when it's told to you... unlike your brother, who senses that whatever it is, it can't be good. That's his doom, unfortunately—his ability to see what's coming. It's what's coated him in paralysis. I've a feeling something awful happened to him, something he couldn't control... he gave up his art, you know. It was the only thing he even cared about. Now, he just tiptoes through his life, letting others make all the decisions. Like I said, that's your brother's doom."

Assuming she's finished, and still not daring to turn around, I start for the patio doors.

"Oh, and Cyra? One always has to be careful about sending anonymous packages in the mail, especially if what's inside is liable to stir up a fuss . . . the car keys are in my handbag, dear."

I swear she's psychic. The woman is psychic!

Chapter Thirteen

RAINE

"HONEY, YOU'RE ACTIN' like I'm psychic or something. How am I supposed to know if he'll be back or not?" Sheba unlatches the door on the rabbit hole and me and Jack squirm through. She's standing there with a sheet flowing around her back like Batman's cape, naked otherwise, clutching a note in one hand. "I called y'all the second I found it. Y'all know as much as I do."

"Does he sound depressed?" I ask.

"Here," Sheba says, handing me the note. "You try and figure it out."

So Jack and I follow her into the bedroom, where we all flop across Sheba's bed. It's only nine in the morning, and I'm wondering what Sheba's doing up this early in the first place. "Read it out loud," Jack says.

" 'Gone to LA, and I don't mean lower Alabama.' " I give Jack and Sheba a quizzical look but read on. " 'I didn't want to tell anybody because everyone would have just talked me out of it probly'—spelled p-r-o-b-l-y—'but this is something I had to do. I can be a waiter anywhere but I can only be a star in California'—no comma before 'but'—'and I'll miss all of you. Love and stuff, Brent.' "

"Now honeys," Sheba says, "what do y'all make of that? It's just not like Brent to up and leave without tellin' anyone."

"Where'd you find the note?" I ask.

"Crammed up under the rabbit hole door," she says. And then sitting up like an Indian with her legs crossed, her back against the headboard, Sheba takes out her Lady Remington and begins trimming the peach fuzz off the Bald Eagle. It's part of her morning ritual. "Oh, it's all my fault I guess. If I wasn't always ridin' him about how dumb he is and how he can't tell left from right, or even find his way back from the Brookwood"—the name of the nearest mall—"without getting lost when he's lived here his whole life, if I wasn't always so swift to ridicule him, maybe he wouldn't have left . . . and instead, he'd be bringin' us all some sausage biscuits and hashbrowns and chocolate milk— he always was so good about gettin' breakfast for me." Sheba scoots down lower on the bed, assuming the position women are in when they give birth. She asks Jack to hold a mirror down by her feet so she can see the bottom part of the Eagle without getting nicked. "It's gonna be pretty enough to put an Easter bonnet on."

"Did you two do anything after work last night?" I say.

"Oh honey, we walked to the Western about two in the mornin' 'cause I was famished, but then we only got into the biggest fru-ha-ha you ever saw. We were both drunker than motorcycles anyway—hold the mirror still, Jack honey—anyway, we were both drunker than motorcycles on account I had a hundred-dollar night, you know, and felt like it deserved a little celebrating—I don't know why y'all didn't join us."

"We were tired, Sheba," I say. "Jack and I had to close last night and neither of us even got out until one-thirty."

"Well, like I said, Brent and me staggered over to the Western after drinkin' a whole bottle of flower-bottle champagne—Ampersand gave it to me that night I broke the high sales record for the year, y'all remember?—and we were gonna pick up some piña colada mix and the usual snicky-snacks like chips and dips and a Sara Lee, but then Brent threw a pineapple into the buggy, a real whole one, and I said to him, 'Brent, I'm not skinnin' a whole pineapple just to make a pretty garnish on your piña colada,' and Brent said, 'Well, I will,' and I said, 'Don't be silly, honey, you don't have the sense to cut a pineapple,' and honey I swear if I'd said his mother had just died I don't think he'd 'uv looked more wounded."

"Well, what happened after that?" asks Jack, holding the mirror with both hands.

"Brent just walked out, honey, leavin' me standin' there like a fool with my Pringles and my pound cake at zero in the mornin'. That was the last I saw of him all night, too. And you know we would've had a good time 'cause 'Lifeboat' with Tallulah was comin' on at three-thirty on the cable, and it's our favorite of all time. My second cousin on Mama's side is a nephew of Eugenia Bankhead, Tallulah's sister . . . or maybe it's my first cousin once removed. It's somethin' close-blooded like that anyhow. I come from the first family of Mississippi you know . . . I mean Arkansas. Granddaddy was the governor."

Sheba tosses her Lady Remington through the bathroom door, where it splashes into the bathtub (Sheba's tub hasn't drained in months). Next, I get up and fetch her a robe. "Maybe he didn't really leave," I say. "Maybe he's just passed out in his apartment. Did anybody even try knockin'?"

"Well honey, I banged on the bathroom wall and he didn't bang back like he usually does. I'm sure he's not there."

"When did Brent get a typewriter?" I ask.

"He didn't," Sheba says, putting on her robe. "You *know* he doesn't have any hand-eye coordination. Why, he can barely print. Plus he's dyslexic to boot."

"Well, this note is typed."

"Let me see, honey." Sheba takes the note from me. "Well I'll say. I didn't even notice before. Maybe he borrowed one from somebody—the UAB librarian maybe—don't you think?" Sheba gives the note back to me and I hand it to Jack. "But honey, if that's the case, he must've been plannin' to leave for a long time now . . . and to think I loaned him eighty dollars the other day, too. He said he needed it to buy some new Neutrogena supplies—and you know me, if he'd needed it for rent I wouldn't have done it; but to run out of skin lotion . . . anyway, he promised to let me borrow it whenever I needed—the shampoo is just ambrosial—but I'll bet you he didn't buy even one bar of fragrant soap with that money. He probably used it to skip town on. The rumpless little thief. Honey, he may have a face prettier than a poodle dyed pink, but he's got no rump at all."

Jack picks up a bowling ball from a cracked aquarium tank on the floor, and tossing it back and forth in his hands, says, "From the mouth of an owner, never trust a man with no ass."

To which Sheba sagely adds, "Especially if they have a small teetee, too. That makes 'em mean. Meaner than water moccasins. Just like my boyfriend two years ago, y'all remember, Brother Davis? Well, Brother didn't have a rump or a teetee long as my thumb—honeys, you see what petite, ladylike hands I have, don't you?—and I remember on his trips up to see me every Friday—he was pastoring down in Opp, Alabama, where he had a small congregation? You know, that's where they have that rattlesnake roundup thing every year? Anyways, he was always braggin' about how he'd pick up hitchhikers on the side of the highway, especially the ones that looked like hobos, and he'd wait until they'd been drivin' a good ways and were deep in the woods and miles from nowhere, then he'd pretend to be lost and ask the hitchhiker if he'd mind handin' him a road map from the glove compartment—Have I told y'all this story before?—well honeys, the poor unsuspecting hitchhiker would go to openin' the glove compartment and out would pop a whole nest of rattlesnakes. They'd be all hot and cramped and mean as Brother Davis himself. Naturally, the hitchhiker would jump out of the car, even speedin' at seventy miles an hour, so if the snake bites didn't kill him the fall sure did."

"But didn't the snakes bite Brother Davis, too?" I say.

"He said he'd been bitten so many times he was immune to them, which I'm sure is true. There's nothin' he liked more than snakes . . . but what I'm tryin' to say is that if he'd had a bigger teetee, or a rump even, then maybe he wouldn't have been so mean."

"Yes," says Jack, "I definitely see shades of Freud there," and he tosses the bowling ball at me. "So whatever happened to this Brother Davis creature? And what does it have to do with Brent?"

"Last I heard, he'd gotten himself castrated for Jesus. Supposedly, celibacy is really in now, what with herpes and this AIDS thing going around. Honeys, maybe I ought to practice it a little myself. You know I never have been one to let a trend pass me by. Definitely, that should be my new goal," Sheba vows, holding out her hands for me to throw her the bowling ball. Catching it, she says, "Yes, show me Mel Gibson tied naked to a four-poster bed, and I'll show you a woman who can walk away. 'Please, Mel, cover yourself. Your lusty manflesh does not excite me, and your vulgarity is unbecoming.' Sheba laughs hysterically and squeezes the Belle Sisters like green cantaloupes. "Oh honey, Brent leavin' has just put me in the silliest mood this morning." She glances at the note in my hand. "But I'll never forgive him for not leavin' me at least a good-bye gift of some emollient creme or something, even if I *was* mean to him," and she throws the bowling ball in my direction, but her aim is off and it lodges in the dead Christmas tree. Two branches splinter and a shower of brown needles pellets the floor. "Should we walk over to the Bogue's Café for breakfast?"

133

"I'm sure he didn't *really* go to LA," I say. "He probably just wants some attention. He doesn't even speak to his parents, you know."

"Hey wait a minute," Sheba says, running into the kitchen. "I just thought of something," and she comes running back with a *Playgirl* calendar in her hands, pausing in front of her dresser mirror just long enough to lift her robe and make sure she didn't miss any spots on the Bald Eagle, then she jumps back into her bed, a cloud of eider feathers fluffing the air (Sheba is a staunch supporter of natural padding over foam). "What's today? Sunday?"

"It's Saturday." Jack says.

Sheba flips through her calendar until she comes across the man for April. "It's April Fool's Day! I should have known this LA thing was just some kind of joke. And here I got up early with a hangover, worried about that nincompoop! He's gonna pay for this. I want the whole line of Neutrogena, plus some new Perry Ellis sheets that I saw at Rich's the other day, *and* two whole boxes of Mrs. Field's dark chocolate chip cookies—which they don't even sell in Birmingham, so he may have to drive all the way to Atlanta to get them. Just like the rule for birthdays—if I can't eat it, wear it, or sleep with it, I don't want it. That's just how mad at him I am."

Jack, scratching at a blemish on his chin, says, "Well, I think he really did leave."

"In the middle of the school quarter?" I say.

"Oh that's right," Jack sneers, "I forgot how much he loved college—almost as much as us." The blemish starts to bleed and Jack dabs at it with the bottom of his shirttail. It leaves behind little red dots against the yellow cotton. Sheba, having accepted her notion of it all being a practical joke, is paying no attention at all. She's leafing through her calendar, spoiling all the surprise of what the men throughout the rest of the year will be like. The one thing I've always prided myself on is my ability to keep curiosity under control. True, I opened Cyra's Christmas presents early one year, but that was because she'd done something mean and deserved it; not because I was curious. If that mythical box had been entrusted to me, not Pandora, all in the world would still be well and good. We wouldn't even need hope.

Jack finishes up what he was about to say before his pimple broke. "Like I was saying, I don't think it's an April Fool's joke. In fact, I'm certain it's not because of what Brent said to me last night."

"And what's that, honey? Ummmm, September is a man after my Eagle."

"Well I had 'B' station and he had 'C,' so we were right next to each other all night anyhow—and on top of my having to pick up his slack, he got to close early because he lied to Ampersand, saying he had a big exam today—but that's neither here nor there. The point is, somehow or another we got to talking about Death of the Year."

Interrupting, I say, "How surprising."

But Jack just keeps on. "And I was saying how there's been such a miserable showing so far, that the year's a quarter gone already and the only contenders at this point are Wiliam Powell and Johnny Weismuller. Although rumor has it that Ethel Merman is on her deathbed, so maybe, just maybe, she'll be able to pull us into the black. Otherwise, if things keep on as they are, we may just have to declare eighty-four a washout. Anyway, Brent started getting all depressed, moaning about how he wasn't getting any younger himself, that people without half his looks were getting famous and qualifying for Death of the Year, while he was stuck here in Alabama waiting tables, wasting his youth and vitality—we've all heard it a hundred times before—and I tried to tell him that *some* talent is required. Looks alone don't do it, my friend. But then you know what he said? He said, 'I have always operated under the assumption that I am very special, thus I will be allowed to flourish in a field in which I am totally ignorant.' I swear, verbatim, that's what he said. It was like out of a Bette Davis movie. Then he said he'd show us all, that he even had 'connections' out there."

"Connections?" Sheba says. "Honey, the only connection he has with LA is that both of them exist on dreams. I still say it's all just an April Fool's trick."

"I don't think so. Not this time. You didn't see the look in his eyes."

"Honey, you're mistaking vapidness for ambition. Now are we going to get something to eat or not? I've got to keep my weight up."

So this time we take my car, since Sheba, in the presence of men, will only agree to be driven, and Jack drives like an old woman who forgot her glasses. But by the time Sheba's performed all her ablutions—the "number two, honey poo," the bath with Estée Lauder, and the hunt for a decent cocktail frock without too many lipstick stains on it (when Sheba *does* dress, it's always a full-scale production, never just jeans, because "only Jackie Onassis and girls without asses" can wear jeans and be chic. "Everybody else looks like country sausage.")—it's already eleven-thirty and time for lunch.

While Sheba was in her bath, Jack and I went next door to Brent's place (Brent hides his key under the cactus next to his door) but we couldn't really tell if he'd packed anything or not because Brent never uses closets, so all his clothes are just everywhere. In any case, he wasn't there. And looking out the window, we didn't see his car parked around the triangle, so who knows, maybe he *did* go to LA. Jack and I just kind of shrugged. Weirder things have happened.

"Guys," I say, "I don't feel like driving all over the world and back, so let's try to keep it in this area, okay?"

"Well honey, how about The Highlands?" Sheba says. "Although it's kind of expensive for just a fill-'er-up lunch. Maybe Clyde Houston's?"

"Whatever you want, Sheba."

"Honey, you know they have like the best chicken and avocado salad. It manages that rare trick of stuffing you full though it feels dietetic, and afterwards maybe Brent will call. He'll probably stop overnight in Dallas, don't y'all think? So we can either go back to 802-with-a-view and wait on him to call; or if you'd rather, honeys, I wouldn't mind spending a few with Meryl or Dustin." Sheba now opens the glove compartment and I half expect a rattlesnake to pop out, but she actually takes off her gloves and puts them in there. "Y'all don't let me forget these after lunch, but when I wear them to eat with they always get food on them."

"Of course there's no place to park in front," I say. "Do y'all think we'd get a ticket if I parked across the street at the post office?"

"Well it closes on Saturdays at noon anyhow," Jack says.

"Honeys, I just thought of something. Maybe Brent left a forwardin' address at the post office."

Jack says, "Oh, Sheba, he doesn't have that much foresight."

"Just the same," I say. "As long as we're here we might as well check. Closing time's not for a few more minutes yet."

"Go ahead then. Sheba and I'll save a table."

So while Sheba and Jack cross the street to Clyde Houston's, I go into the post office and am immediately greeted by name.

"Well Raine Freeman, I'll declare. I can't even throw out the dishwater today without hittin' one of you all in the face." He grins and holds out his hand. It's Morton somebody—I don't recall his last name—but he's a regular-looking kind of pudgy sort of guy, totally average and exactly the post office type. I mean, if somebody pointed to him on the street and told you they'd kill you if you didn't guess what he did for a living on the first try, then you'd live.

"What?" I say.

"Why your sister was just in here not just five minutes ago, and lookin' p-r-e-t-t-y, too,"—Morton winks—"and I tell you what's the truth, that girl has lost *some* more weight, I tell *you* she has," he says.

The reason this Morton guy feels like he's my best friend is because last fall I did this whole big direct mail project for some marketing class I signed up for in a fit of career fear. I had to come up with a national sweepstakes gimmick for "my favorite brand of toothpaste," so Morton helped with the forms I needed to fill out to get a direct mail license, throwing in a few free tidbits of advice on how I should arrange all the zip codes in order, that sort of stuff. He really thought he was doing his part for higher education. God only knows how he knows Cyra.

"Yeah," he says, "I don't recall you mentionin' you havin' relatives down in South Amurica." Just like we're old friends, me and Mort.

"Uh, well," I say, trying to figure out what she's been up to this time, but old Mort, fortunately, runs with his own string.

"Just a few dollars short she was, for the postage, on account she wanted to send it first class, but I told her not to worry about it, it bein' a birthday present after all. I said to her, I did, we can't have people not gettin' their birthday gifts just 'cause some types of mail is slower than others, now can we now?"

Suddenly, Cyra's "birthday present" starts making sense, if sense is what you want to call it. "She just now left?" I say.

"I swear I don't know how y'all didn't bump smack into each other."

"Then it's still here? It hasn't gone out yet?"

"I'm tellin' you, the ink'll still smear from the rubber stamp."

"Well thank God I caught you in time then."

"Don't tell me," he beams. "Don't tell me. Let me guess. I'll bet you forgot the card."

I try to look amazed. "Why, how'd you know?"

Morton lifts up his knee to slap it, then snaps his finger. "I knew it, I just knew it. Everybody *always* forgets to wrap up the card. Is it somebody close to you?"

"An aunt... she married a Latin American after our uncle died. I'll just take it with me and bring it back on Monday if that's okay. I know you're about to close and all."

"Oh it's no problem a'tall," he says. "Shoot, it don't take but a minute to rewrap it."

"Well... I... it's the card. The one we have's not quite right, and you know how older relatives are. They take everything personal, so we need to find a different one. Yeah, I'll just bring it back on Monday and pay the difference in what Cyra still owes, if that's okay."

"I understand," he says, "I understand perfectly. You're right. It's all in the card. Why, the gift don't mean nothin'."

"Nothin' at all," I say, watching him go into the back; and sure as sunrise, here he returns carrying the baby. That fat bitch. Well, as long as she thinks it's safe and gone, then let her... but she's crazy if she believes I'm just lettin' slide what she did to me last year in New York. No, not hardly.

Chapter Fourteen

CYRA

YES, HARDLY AT ALL. That's how little it matters down here, Cyra. Why, what's murdering a baby? It's nothing. Nothing compared to what some of these other gals have done . . . I'll bet you thought this place didn't really exist, didn't you? Well I must admit this particular chamber is a little . . . different. We're more of a private club than, oh how shall I say it, open to the public? You understand. All of the girls here are volunteers. They *asked* for the bars and locks and the rooms with no windows—there's nothing to see anyhow. But don't get the wrong idea. We don't enforce anything here. When a girl asks to leave, she's more than welcome. Just keep in mind though, this here's the good room.

Now, that girl over there? The one pulling the needle through her ear lobe? That's Zinnia Fledge. She absolutely refuses to eat cockroaches, though she'll be the first to steal your crickets if you turn your head . . . fed her twin sons the mercury from a thermometer, she did. Just broke off the tip and let them suck it

140

like a straw. And that woman with the cherry-colored hair is Jerri Love. She attempts suicide on the sixth of every month, increasing her aspirin intake by one each time. She's been with us now, oh, eighteen months I guess. So this month, with nineteen aspirin, it'll be even money. Last time she went into a coma. Baked her daughter in the microwave. Can you stand the excitement?

Of course, those girls over there holding hands are the Lambert sisters. They don't believe in necrophilia, or drawing and quartering, or self-mutilation, or flagellation . . . tied cinder blocks around some three-year-old's feet, put him on the tracks in front of a train and told him to run. The hunchback making faces at that girl suckin' her toes is Miss Sylvia Laverly. Ain't it such a pretty name for such an ugly woman?—lye in the formula. And the girl doin' the toe-suckin' is Cissy Ochre. Isn't she beautiful, and only twenty-two. Like you, she used to weigh about a hundred and fifty pounds more than she does now but that was when she first got here, before she cut her stomach out. I don't know whose toes those are she has in her mouth. Do you see anyone around with a foot missin'?

The girl layin' board-stiff in the corner is Libby Floy Hook. She says she's a razor blade, except on Tuesdays, when she stands up straight and says she's a broom handle. Used to be a kindergarten teacher, but beat more kids to death than you can shake a stick at. Julia Flaherty, the woman drawin' pictures on the wall, spray-painted all three of her kids with six coats each of lime green just because the Ides of March is only two days before St. Patrick's Day. Peyton Dill is the short woman with blue hair, and Mrs. Bloodworm is the woman combing it. She loves icicles. She used to be a sculptor before she roasted her hands, and her kids' faces, over a gas stove . . . and such pretty fingernails, too. The woman with clothes on is Mae, laughing at Ginger G. Whit—a half-dozen kids she had, and ain't it strange how all six of 'em were playin' just a little too close to that open window on the sixteenth floor—and there's Mrs. Araby Feld-spar, and the Darla Girls with matching armbands and ankle weights. Old Miss Rumple is scared of light; and Georgia Foxe, the one moaning on the floor without her foot—I guess hers is the one Cissy chopped off—doesn't think she's really dead. She screams anytime the chain saws start up. On the other hand, Babe thinks we ought to order more. She always wants you to guess her age, which is at least a month older than air. Speakin' of which, Babe tied plastic bags around her three children's necks.

Cornelia Bean is that woman holding the two pencils in her hands. She never lets loose of them and screams like a banshee if one gets broken. When she's sleepin', she keeps them in a "special place." Stabbed her brother's son to death with one. Don't look now, but Billie Sue is staring at you. Her last name is Kitchens, appropriately. Hands like a meat cleaver. She'll chop you to pieces if you get too close, just like she did the neigh-bor's kids. And that wispy little beauty painting Zinnia's picture over there—Valara is her name—she dances and reads palms as well . . . blind as a butcher's cat though; she cut out her eyes after she did the same to her ten-year-old. That silver-haired woman is Millie Spoon. She claims she's been back in time and says she's even spoken with Mary Magdalene and Empress Car-lota of Mexico, but I don't believe her. How can you talk to foreigners?

The girls at the door are twin sisters. Don't look it, do they? They can't speak a word of English. Their names are Xandiada, or some such nonsense. Hell only knows where they're from, or how they ended up here. They sure don't . . . so polite though, always smiling, as though they're only here temporarily. You'd never guess in a billion years they boiled runaway kids alive. Next to you, I think I like Valara the best, I guess because she's blind. But she's got something extra in its place—imagination, you might say. I love imagination. You can think of some pretty horrible things when you have imagination—things like babies on skewers, roasted over red coals, eaten by South American Indians deep in the Amazonian jungle—things like that. I guess you're beginning to get the picture now, aren't you, Cyra? You're in Hell's special sector—the room for baby killers... for women who murder their children and let the dogs eat them, especially mothers who mail their babies to Brazil...

MOTHERS WHO MAIL THEIR BABIES TO BRAZIL!

I go bolting upright. It's zero in the morning, and as usual these last few days, more sweat than Saudi Arabia is dripping down my face. The clock says 4:47 A.M., so there's no point in trying to get back to sleep. It's Easter Sunday, after all, and even though we're fervent pagans the rest of the year, nobody misses sunrise service—not psychotic brothers, not crystal-carrying mothers, not baby-killer sisters—*nobody!* It's just what you do. You make reservations at the Sheraton in Mountain Brook for Easter brunch, which follows a special morning church service at Mountain Brook Baptist, which in turn follows the hellaciously early sunrise service. Easily, it's the worst day of the year.

Grandmother comes with us, Dad's mother, even though her bones are rotten. What do they call it? Osteoporosis? Just the same, she can still roll the windows down and hear the preacher from the car. They hold the service on this grassy knoll of the cemetery, where three big wooden crosses are stuck into the ground; and I guess some engineer must have really been on the ball, 'cause just like out of the Bible or something, as we're standing there, sure enough, the sun comes rolling up from under the knoll, bright as you please, in direct alignment with the middle cross—just like the aura of Jesus himself. It cer-

tainly does—you'd never think it happened every single day—
and me and the dogwoods at our absolute peak!

How glorious and untroublesome dawn feels in comparison to
just a couple of hours ago. The nightmare seems just that, a bad
dream, and now there's no babies to worry about or anything.
All there is is me, standing here in the fresh new sun in a flow-
ery dress weighing only a paltry hundred and thirty-seven
pounds. Just twenty more to go, *twenty measly pounds,* with a
full three weeks yet before the Miss West Jefferson County pageant—*you can do it, My angel.* I can surely do it. I'll double up
on the laxatives, jog an extra mile, eat a few ounces less of
salad. A cinch!

In total happiness I squeeze Mom's hand, pretending to listen
to the preacher, and I even smile at Raine. He's looking hand-
some in his creamy linen suit and bucks. If I weren't his sister I
might even be inclined to flirt with him. Just wait till I win Miss
Alabama though. Raine will look as ugly as a mud fence compared to all the boys who'll be after me then. Let *him* see how it
feels to be the ugly one for a while. Yeah, let him just see.
Pulling my hair haughtily behind my ears, I turn my chin upwards, looking so pious, you'd think I was the one being wor-
shipped here today.

Later, over brunch, Mom starts dishin' me and Raine this sap
about how lucky she is to have raised such respectable, good-
looking children, how fine and decent we are and all. I notice
Raine just sort of becomes real interested in his bacon omelet all
of a sudden. The wimp. "And I think both of you should make
more of an effort to get along," she says. "Don't you agree,
Mrs. Freeman?" (That's what Mom calls Grandmother: Mrs.
Freeman.)

Grandmother says: "You'd think a city the size of Birmingham could provide these things for its senior citizens, but I guess
they think we can get by just nicely on nothin' but our Social
Security." She never hears anything right. "And me needin'

driveway reflectors so bad," she continues. "I can't hardly see where the turnoff is even in daylight as it is."

"Would you like something else to eat, Mrs. Freeman?" Mom holds her coffee cup to her bottom lip and stares at Grandmother, waiting for an answer which doesn't come. Raine pushes back his omelet plate and takes *Charlotte's Web* from his lap, opening it on the table. Please, how many times can someone read that damned thing?

"Two," Grandmother says. Just out of the blue like that. "Two."

"Two what, Mrs. Freeman?"

"What?" And Grandmother gives Mom a look like she's lost her mind.

Mom leans over real close to her. "You just said two."

"Alright," Grandmother says.

I look at Mom and shrug. Raine doesn't even bother. It's like the two of us are terrified of making eye contact. But I don't care anymore if he knows the baby is mine. He's so weird-acting these days anyhow, that even if he did squawk, a person would only think he was lying. And naturally I'd deny it to the bitter end. Everybody would be forced to believe me, too. Even if deep down they had doubts. After all, *where's* the proof?

"Is there a restroom in this den of heathens?" Grandmother says.

Den of heathens? Where does the old bat think she is?

"I'll take you," Mom says. She gets up from her chair and helps Grandmother into her walker. Raine's color starts to fade. He's thinkin' the same thing as me. We'll be left alone at the table together, just the two of us, and Raine unfortunately visited the restroom himself about five minutes ago. So there goes that excuse.

"I'll take her, Mom," he says. What a saint my brother is.

"Don't be silly. I'm going to have to help her *inside* the room, too."

"Oh." Raine swallows hard. I can just tell he's thinking that if I were even a halfway decent sister I'd volunteer myself. But I'm not and I don't. I want to see him squirm. I fact, this should be quite interesting. I don't think we've actually been alone together, I mean without a buffer of some kind since, well, probably since the Empire State Building.

"Be back in a few minutes," Mom says.

"Chickens I guess," Grandmother says, lifting her walker a few inches in front of her. "Or ducks maybe."

Raine grabs his book for dear life. I lean back in my chair, staring at him, just swirling my water around lazily in my glass. The waiter comes by offering more coffee. "Refill, sir?" But Raine doesn't even look up. He shakes his head and turns the page. Old Charlotte must really be up to something interesting.

"I'd love a refill," I say. "Raine, are you sure you don't want more?"

He purses his lips and stops pretending to read, like he might be debating whether or not he should just walk out. But no, that would go against Raine's character. He doesn't make scenes. He only takes them. That's our major difference. Raine always does the right thing, or whatever will please the most people (if there's a distinction). He looks to the waiter, narrowly avoiding my smile. "No thanks."

After the waiter's gone, I decide I'll really get under Raine's skin. So I lean on the table with my elbows, propping my chin in my palms, and just stare him straight in the face. At first he acts like he's really reading, smiling at the funny parts and everything, but it doesn't take long before he's turning the pages just a little too fast. I can hear his legs jiggling under the table. Finally, he can't take anymore. "You really are a sociopath, aren't you?"

To this, I blow Raine a kiss. He goes back to Wilbur.

"Raine," I say languidly, "do you think I'm getting more

beautiful every day, that I'm fine-tuning a certain, oh, *je ne sais quoi?*"

No answer.

"Do you think I'll win Miss Alabama?"

Still no answer.

"Well I do. There aren't but twelve girls in all entering my preliminary—the Miss West Jefferson County—and I've seen four of them." I turn my thumbs down. "So ugly, they could stand behind a tombstone and hatch a haunt. Oh, I'll win it alright, which'll still give me another month of lead-time to polish up all my rough edges for the biggie at the Civic Center. I'll be competing with nearly sixty other preliminary winners there —all beautiful, all thin. You're going to come, aren't you? It's four nights long. The first three nights—Sigma, Alpha, and Mu —are for choosing a finalist in swimsuit, evening gown, and talent. Then, on the fourth night, Saturday, they crown the final winner; althought the thing is, the winner isn't always, necessarily, one of the Sigma Alpha Mu finalists. Realistically, I doubt I'll win the swimsuit competition—you know, there could still be stretch marks from my dieting, which I plan on having *fixed* sometime over the summer before Atlantic City in September— but I've a good chance to win evening gown, and even a better one at talent... aren't you going to ask what my talent is? Raine, come on Raine, don't you want to know what my talent is?"

My brother looks up from his book and stares at me, or over me rather. Our eyes don't meet. I know what he's thinking, and he knows I know. Go ahead, I'm thinking, smiling at him— daring him to say it—say it, damn you. Say it... *ba-by kil-ler.* But he just pushes his nose back down in that book. Reaching across the table, I snatch it from his hands and throw it on the floor. "Did you hear me? Ask me what my talent is?!"

The people at the table next to us start whispering to one

another and shaking their heads. Raine, with all the politeness of an undertaker, closes his eyes and braces himself. "Okay, what is it?"

Suddenly I smile. I really never thought he'd ask. I give him credit. I bow my head. God, I'm a bitch. But what is this crap? He's trembling. For Christ's sake, he's literally shaking. He *really* would rather us just keep on pretending. Then, for the first time I get this feeling that maybe it's not just a matter of keeping up appearances. Maybe he *has* to pretend things are normal just to keep his grip. One explanation for this children's book fetish of his. Maybe make-believe is the only thing that works for him. In a way, I guess, that's Mom's defense, too. All her crystals and pyramids and things. But is it also mine? Am I just make-believing I'm pretty underneath the fat? What if even after I'm thin I still don't win Miss Alabama? What if the judges and everybody all laugh? Oh my God, are all three of us just staking out different plots of the same fantasy land?

"The tuba," I say suddenly. "I'm going to play *Hotcakes* on the tuba. You know, Carly Simon's old song?" Do I see Raine breathe a sigh of relief? Continuing, I say, "I figure no one's ever done it before. A tuba's not exactly feminine, you know, but I think I can pull it off. Besides, they only have three buttons. There's no way I could learn to play a flute or the sax in time, and singing's out of the question. You know how tone-deaf I am . . . Raine, hello! Why do I feel like I'm talking to myself?" I take the butter knife and start tapping it on top of my uneaten cinnamon roll. I think I could eat a hundred of them and still have room for an ox. "I'm going to make you talk to me whether you like it or not," I tell him. "Do you hear me? So . . . so what's your friend Brent been up to lately? I haven't seen him around."

"Cyra," he says finally, slowly, evenly, and obviously planned, "didn't one of our aunts have a birthday a few weeks ago?"

"What?"

"Oh nothing. Nothing."

The butter knife I'm holding goes squishing into the top of the cinnamon roll. "What did you say?"

"Nothing, I said," he says. "It's just that I thought one of our aunts in Brazil had a birthday recently, but then I remembered we don't have an aunt in Brazil. Nothing. Well look here, Mom and Grandmother are back."

You bastard!!! The accusation wants to fly out of me, wants to dive across the table and wrap its claws around Raine's holier-than-thou neck, to strangle him until he's azure. *Don't show anything, My precious. Don't even blink. Stay cool, collected, serene—you know nothing of what he's saying* . . . what *is* he saying, though? What's the bastard saying? . . . He saw you go into the post office—an aunt in Brazil—more than that, he . . . he saw the label on the box? No, no he . . . he's got the goddam baby back!

Chapter Fifteen

RAINE

"BACK HERE, BABY!" *Baaaack heah, baybee!*

Tara, or Terror, as everybody at The Rainforest has taken to calling her lately, is standing in the little alcove in the back of the kitchen where the garbage cans are, urgently motioning me to come see what she's discovered. Uh-oh. It's twelve-thirty, and whatever it is this late at night, it can't be good. Nothing to do with Tara is ever good.

Of course I'm right in the middle of punching in my checkout sequence at the order terminal. It's a very complicated process that every waiter at the end of his shift must do; the management's way of counterchecking everybody's total sales just to make sure a waiter didn't *accidentally* exclude a tab or two. Or three. Still, cheating is as rampant here as it is anywhere I've ever worked. In theory, every order, down to the last tea or coffee refill, must be logged in on your own personal waiter code (mine's number "8"), at the register of your assigned waiter station, where it is then simultaneously printed out here in the kitchen for the cooks to read. This way, the management keeps tally of what and how much food has been served on any given night by any particular server. It's computerized itemization is what it is, for cost control and all that crap.

But—and it's a biggie—*but* the cooks are only responsible for the actual meal itself. The hot stuff. They don't have anything to do with salads or desserts or drinks, and this is where the "forgetfulness" comes in. What you do is you present to whoever is paying a slip of paper with only the grand total on it; the *accurate* grand total—never cheat the customer, only the restaurant. This way, if the customer is a suspicious or chintzy sort and requests an itemization, you can say "Certainly sir," and race back to the terminal to add in those things that, as far as the management knows, went unsold.

There's only one cardinal rule about cheating this way: *Don't get greedy!* Tara's gonna *know* there's a nigra in the woodpile somewhere if, at the end of the night, she decides to punch in your waiter code and finds out you didn't sell one single salad or cup of coffee or dessert. Personally, I've only cheated twice (and both times I felt I'd been given a bum station unfairly and knew I wouldn't make my quota of fifty dollars any other way), but some waiters make as much as seventy to a hundred extra under-the-counter bucks a night! Jack for instance. It's like he almost dares Tara to ask him how it is that his printout shows no desserts sold at all, when she *knows* she saw guests in his station sampling the kumquat mousse on more than one occasion. (Tara, however, has a pretty hefty sweet tooth herself, and the one time she did make an issue over Jack's printout discrepancies, he only threw it back at her. "I think you must be hallucinating, Terror, dearie. Just as I'm certain that I was when I saw you hiding in the back of the walk-in scarfing a mocha roulage.")

Anyway, tonight was the third time in my history here that I blatantly cheated: the old We'll-Just-Have-A-Salad scam. It was the classic setup. Four women, all wanting separate checks and only ordering tropical salads and tea. Well, they all paid for what they got, but somehow it just slipped my mind to enter the order. Imagine that. And now having Tara screeching "Back here, baby!" like one of those caged birds in the dining room; well, it's like I may be looking for new employment tomorrow.

The alcove she's in is a sort of waiting room for the garbage before it's hauled out to the dumpster at the end of the night. The reason it just sits there, hours on end, stinking up the kitchen, is because lately Ampersand's been complainin' that the busboys and waiters are clearing tables too carelessly, that he's had to reorder silverware time and time again because it's getting thrown away. So now Tara's taken it upon herself to sift through every single can, every single night. It's no secret she wants a promotion.

"Is there a problem, Tara?"

She's rolling in sweat, holding a buspan like a baby on her hips, and the pan is loaded with an assortment of filthy forks and knives, even a few cups and slimy saucers dripping all kinds of coffee grounds and salad dressing and little flecks of food. (Tara won't wear gloves because it tarnishes her martyrdom.) Maybe she just wants me to help, I'm thinking. With her free arm she points the end of a knife toward a shape slumped on top of the garbage in a half-emptied can. "Baby, do you see that? What is it?" *Whutizit?*

Bravely, I peer over the edge of the can, half expecting to see a full place setting for twelve or something. Instead, what she's pointing at is like the weirdest thing I've ever seen. It's about as big as my fist, sort of roundish, like a blob of raw meat, sort of not though, and all covered with goop and shreds of lettuce and soggy scraps of bloody paper napkins. "Your guess is as good as mine," I say.

"What was the special tonight?" she asks. *Whut wuz thu spay-shul tunayht?*

"Mahi mahi a la orange," I tell her. "Dolphin meat."

"Maybe this is a burned one?" she says.

"No, it's served raw. Only the orange sauce is hot. Besides, fish doesn't look bloody like this."

"Uh-huh," she says, setting down her pan of silverware. "Have all the cooks left already?"

"About half an hour ago."

"Is anybody left besides us?" *Iz innybuddy layaft busudz uzz?*

"Only Jack. But he did his checkout over an hour ago. He's waiting for me in the bar so I can give him a ride home. Isn't Ampersand upstairs in his office?"

"No, baby. One of those dumb birds got sick and he rushed it over to the vet people—had to wake the animal doctor up and everything. But you know, maybe this could be a bird somebody plucked all the feathers off of. Last week I overheard the sous-chef complainin' he was tired of working nigra wages—*tarred 'u wuhkin' nigra wajuz*—that he hadn't gotten a raise in over a year. Maybe he did it?"

"Maybe," I say, unconvinced. I nod to Tara to hand me her knife, and then I jab the thing softly. "But birds have bones in them. This thing gives."

Tara pulls my hand away from the thing and we both take a step back from the garbage can. "I tell you what," I say, not wanting to look like a sissy, "I tell you what. If you'll tilt the garbage can downwards, I'll get a plate and sort of scoop it onto it." Tara says okay, and straddling the can she tilts it forward, holding it steady with both hands. The angle is just right for me to wedge the plate up under the thing, and tap it onto it.

"Oh holy God, baby." Tara's whole face scrunches into a prune, as the thing kind of rolls around on the plate a moment. "What in the hell is it?" *Whutinthuhayleizit?*

Just at this moment though, both of us staring horrified at this thing, Jack's voice comes echoing in from the dining room. The birds let out a screech and I can hear them ruffling to one side of the cage as he comes through the swinging doors into the kitchen. "Anybody still here?"

Call it fear, call it reflex, call it guilt. Whatever you want to call it, Tara and me suddenly jump, and I hurl the whatever-it-is back into the trash—it slithers off the plate, leaving a smear of blood behind—and both of us kind of leap out from behind the floor-to-ceiling embankment of ovens and stainless steel shelves, looking more guilty, I'm sure, than if we'd been having sex in the linen closet.

"I'm still here," I say. "Tara was just checking out the kitchen. All that's left is the trash."

"Don't worry about it," Tara says, turning to me, her manner nervous and overly professional. "Y'all go on home now. I'll take care of what's left."

Jack casts a glance first to me and then to Tara. I'm sure he's wondering whatever has gotten into this woman. She *never* offers to do anyone else's job. "Thanks, Tara," I say, handing her my leftover tickets and charge card vouchers. I untie the apron around my waist and chuck it toward the hamper. "We'll see you tomorrow. Ready, Jack?"

"Yeah," he says, still looking at Tara as he follows me into the dining room, all silent and dark. (Nothing's weirder than a deserted restaurant after hours.) Jack grabs hold of my arm. "What were y'all doin' back there?"

"Just lookin' for silverware," I say casually. Something inside me, some subterranean instinct, tells me not to mention the thing in the garbage can. I don't know what it is about Jack lately, but he seems to have turned from just a pretentious intellect into a malicious one. I mean all this stuff about murder, like him askin' me to kill myself the other day . . . and being serious about it, too. But it'll be so *easy*, he said. And then you'll know what's on the other side. You'll have solved the great mystery. Yeah, like it's on my list of top priorities. It's just that Jack can be *so* convincing, and then I start getting all confused and thinking I'm not really even alive, that I'm in Hell, and I start getting this urge to cut myself just so the blood will prove that I'm real. I mean, is this normal?

Sheba told us the other day that the problem we both have is that we're just too smart. She said, "Honeys, all the really, really bright people I know are constantly depressed, all gaggin' on an ant and swallowin' a camel. I think it's just modern living that does it. This complexity starts overloadin' the brain, and before you know it, fuses blow."

I remember Jack countered that his brain was *not* overloaded. "For anyone's information," he said, "I scored a thirty-one on my ACT. Raine only scored a twenty-eight."

"Twenty-nine!" I said. "It was twenty-nine. Besides, there's a two-point margin of error in either direction, so we'll never know for sure if I was only having a bad day or not. I *could* have gotten a thirty-one myself, you know."

"Yes," he said, "and I'm sure I was having a *good* day, that in truth, you're the more intelligent. That's what you'd like me to believe, isn't it, Raine? Isn't it?" So then Jack took out his bottle of poppers and took a long snort and started querying me and Sheba on like how many inches are in a mile, and who won the best actress Oscar in 1942, what's the depth of Lake Victoria, and why does August have thirty-one days? Shit like that, you know, and anytime we missed one he'd roll down the window and holler out, "Another moron blights the planet!"

"Just lookin' for silverware?" Jack repeats. "Is that why you both leaped higher than four feet up a bull's ass when I came in?"

"You startled us. That's all. Tara didn't know anyone else was still here." Jack follows me into where the lockers are, adjacent to the restrooms on the ground floor. As I'm changing into my jeans, he leans against the Pepsi machine and says, "But that doesn't explain *your* reaction."

"Hmmm," I say evasively, as though absorbed in the mechanics of tightening the laces on my tennis shoes. The door to the dressing room here is open, and from where I'm sitting I've got a view that lines up straight through the bird cage and through the two square panes of light on the swing doors to the kitchen. I can see Tara in there, pulling the breaker switches. The pin lights over the bird cage are the first to go out, followed by the recessed lights on the three levels surrounding it. The only remaining lights at all are the ones in here and the kitchen lights. The glass panes in the kitchen doors and the vertical crack betwen them seem to be floating forms of iridescence unto themselves.

"What does it feel like to you when the restaurant's all dark like this?" I say. "To me, it feels like I'm in a horror movie, especially with that big bird cage and the river water reflecting up through the glass bottom and onto the walls like it does. See how they seem to sway like that, all the way up to the third floor? It like distorts your sense of spatial depth and distance, don't you think?"

"Are you going to tell me what y'all were doin' back there?"

"I thought you were watching Johnny Carson at the bar," I say.

Jack says, "What is this? A question for your thoughts? What in the hell were ya'll doing?"

"We were screwin' in the walk-in. Is that what you want to hear?"

Jack gets this smirk on his face, this don't-even-*think*-you'll-fool-me smirk. "If you don't tell me," he says, "then I will." He picks my lock up off the bench and tosses it to me. I put it through the hole, close it, and give the wheel a quick spin. "If you *really* want to know, I'll tell you."

"Well I don't," I say, following him out of the room.

"Don't forget to hit the light," he says.

So closing the door behind me, I flick the light off, and we both stop at the cage on the way out. It's something I like to do—hold onto the iron ivy bars and gaze down at the river. Sometimes you can see raccoons or even beavers when it's real late like this. "There," Jack says, pointing to the edge of the bank near a clump of cane. "See it? What does that look like?"

"A bear?" I say. "My God, it looks like a bear!"

"A bear?" he laughs. "There aren't any bears anymore, you idiot. Look again."

Yet my eyes are still adjusting from the glare of the locker room and the glass is all spotted with bird droppings, so it's hard to make out. "Hell, I don't know. A person?"

"Could be," Jack shrugs, "I don't know," and he starts walking away. "G'night, Tara!" he yells, cupping his hands around his mouth. Like in a cave, the words reverberate about the room. The birds, all in a great whoosh, flock up to the top of their cage, squawking and cawing. Jack loves to do this every night. "Come on, Raine," he says, but I linger a moment longer, still trying to focus in on the shape beneath the glass. It doesn't budge. Yet it has to be a bear, I'm thinking. There's just nothing else it could be.

"Leopold and Loeb," Jack sneers. "Those stupid, pompous boys. If only they'd stayed with their original victim it would have worked. They shouldn't have compromised on Bobby Frank. But don't worry, Raine. We'll do much better. We'll get it right. We'll be the bee's knees."

"What in God's name are you talking about now?"

"Just nothing," he says, drawing penises in the moisture on the inside of the windshield. "I should have known you'd be totally ignorant of one of the most famous murder cases this century. Where would you be without me?"

Instead of dropping Jack off at The Dakota, we've decided to go to Denny's at Eastwood for a grilled cheese, it being the only place open this time of night. We do this lots of times after work, sometimes taking Sheba (who always makes us walk across the street to the Krispy Kreme afterwards), and even Brent before he moved—he still hasn't called—but I've got a paper due tomorrow in Supernatural Lit, so it's going to have to be a fast one. At first I was planning to write about unicorn myths, but then I figured everyone would do either unicorns or vampires, so finally I decided on pyramid power, it literally being a back yard family project. (Mom now says she's mastered the trick of levitation, finally, if only within the supercharged ion-aligned sanctity of her pyramid, and only when she's totally alone, of course, and usually late at night, like now, when decent souls are asleep and "the protean energies of internal balance can be laterally unified.") I guess it's like that age-old question of whether a falling tree in the woods makes sound. How do you dispute it if you're not there?

"We're going to kill your sister," Jack says evenly. "You get to pick the method."

"Just stop it already, okay? I'm tired of all your talk about death and murder."

"But that's the future, Raine. The past is the consequences. Don't you see?"

"No."

"Raine, everything's going to go. It's already started. *Everything*. Just like a line of dominoes down a hill. Force equals mass times acceleration . . . murder won't matter at all."

"How can you say that?"

"Because laws will become unenforceable. With the elite it's always been the case, with the impoverished it's becoming the case, and by next decade it'll be the same with the middle classes too."

"You and my mother ought to get together. Take a trip to Brazil."

"Hey," Jack says, "isn't that Beowulf up ahead?"

"Should I stop and let him in? He's probably hungry."

"No juicy babies around lately I suppose . . . I still don't think you should've told your sister we got it back. It just wasn't smart."

"I didn't *tell* her . . . I only hinted a little."

"She's not sane, Raine. I mean, she killed that kid. She might try to do the same to you."

"No, I think if anyone's crazy it's probably you and me. Not her."

"Slow down. There he is."

I brake the car to a halt, open the door, and Beowulf leaps in, tongue and tail just a-waggin'. Happily, he lies down between the two of us as though we're his best friends in the whole world, then falls almost instantly asleep. Jack strokes his back with one hand, and with the other continues to draw porno graffiti on my windshield. "Does she know where we hid the baby this time?" He points at the glass, smiling. "Look at this one. Uncut."

" 'Course she doesn't know. How could she? She's got no reason to go to The Rainforest . . . but I still say we'd be safer just puttin' it in my trunk, or your apartment or something. *Anywhere* else!"

"Your car is where she found it last time. It'd be the first place she looked. Then she'd cover your bedroom, then the whole house, then my place, then Sheba's . . . if she hasn't done it already. Raine, I'm warnin' you. She's not gonna let anyone or anything fuck up her chances at that damned beauty pageant."

"But in the bird cage? What if somebody else finds it?"

"Who? Me, you, and Sheba are the only ones who ever go in there. Even Tara, as big an ass-licker as she is, won't wipe up after those shittin' vultures."

"What if somebody sees it though?"

"That brown paper blends right in with the twigs and bushes. Nobody's going to see it."

"But why does everything have to be so risky? Why can't we

just once and for all get rid of the damned thing? . . . I should have let her mail it. I knew we should have just left well enough alone."

"And then what would we have to occupy our time, huh? UAB? That's a farce. Our jobs? Our career goals? Raine, we don't have any ambitions. Games are all we've got . . . maybe I'll try Swiss instead of American this time. Some cheese soup, too. Denny's does have the best cheese soup, doesn't it?"

"The best."

"You just missed the exit ramp. Relax, Raine. Okay? Go on up to the Montevallo Road exit. I think it's the next one." Jack takes his sleeve and erases all the graffiti, then blows on the windshield for a fresh slate. "We'll lure her to the restaurant after closing one night. That's where we'll do it . . . remember, *you're* the one who mentioned revenge in the first place. Although why you won't tell me what it is she did, I don't know." He gives Beowulf a loving pat. "All that matters is that we do it quick, before she has a chance to do it to you first."

"I really don't think I care," I say, pulling into the parking lot. It's the time of night that's too late for the early crowd and too early for the late one, so I'm able to get a space right near the door. A glitter from the lights reflects off Jack's wrist, the one he's petting Beowulf with. "When did you get that watch? It looks just like the one Ampersand gave Brent."

"It is Brent's," he says, getting out of the car. "I guess Beowulf will be fine out here. Let's make sure to bring him something."

"You bought it from him? Is that where he got the money for LA?"

Jack shuts his door and stretches. "You are just so dense sometimes. Who do you think that was you saw on the river-bank tonight? Whose heart do you think you and Miss Terror were playing with in the kitchen? Brent never went to LA. *I'm* the one who typed that note. Me." Jack shrugs lightly. "He wanted to be Death of the Year. We needed one. You wouldn't agree to it . . . so I seduced him and murdered him. The logic is clear."

Chapter Sixteen

C Y R A

CLEARLY, THERE'S NO LOGIC HERE. First off, you have to literally crawl into the dumb thing and next be built like a linebacker just so your shoulder bone doesn't crack in two; but even then, after you're holding it steady and everything, you can't get over this creepy feeling that it, not you, is the one in possession here— something like having a bronzed anaconda wrapped around your head—plus you need a pearl diver's lungs to get just one miserable burp out of it, but never does it actually deign to make what even a tin-ear like me might call *music,* just these sick flatulent honks, like a dinosaur with gas. I mean, what kind of pervert conceived this thing?

But I go ahead and rent it anyway, even though the sheet music has to be, like, specially ordered from Electra Asylum and won't be here for a week, which'll at least give me time to practice some; 'cause God knows that by the time I go prancin' out onstage in my cutesy little fake admiral costume with the gold epaulets on the shoulders I'd dang well better look like my tuba and I—excuse me, my *sousaphone*—practically even go to the bathroom together. I tell the guy I'll drop back by to get it before leaving the mall, which still gives me two hours to kill, as Mom came with me. She said she'd need at least that long to get enough names for her petition; so I guess I'll just wander around and check out the cookies I can't have, the ice cream I can't eat, the dresses I can't afford, and some laxatives I need to steal.

I know it's a stretch mentally, and maybe it's Mom's relentless social conscience seeping in, but every time I go "shopping" I'm in total awe. I mean, to think this *one* mall is just the teensiest microcosm of all the stuff there is in the world, and like, *where* does it all come from? Take just one thing. Take the Orange Julius over there. How many oranges must this one little store use in a single day? Five hundred? A thousand? And then you multiply that by all the grocery stores around the world, all the restaurants, and every single person in the U.S. alone drinking a glass of orange juice for breakfast; why mathematically, wouldn't every single inch of land on this planet have to be planted in orange trees just to keep up?

Then take something as simple and common as, say, eggs. How many people are there in the world? Six billion? And let's be conservative here and say that only, oh, four billion of those people use just one egg a day—boiled, fried, scrambled, mixed into a cake, frozen into ice cream, melted into chocolate, thrown at a politician, or whatever—and eggs come from chickens, right? But has anyone ever actually *seen* a chicken? The only logical conclusion is that chickens are the horniest creatures alive, and that they're roosting in all the orange trees. It really just blows my mind.

"Cyra honeeeeey!" I hear it like a shotgun blast. Suddenly coming at me, grinning and gnawing a sandwich, is that rhino, Sheba Eagles. Of all the people to have to run into.

"Hey," I say, trying to smile. *Don't give an inch, Sweetness, even if she's catty enough to bring up the baby here in public. Be all purity, ignorance, and light. Remember, it's the new and charitable you.* "It's so nice to see you again," I add, bending over to kiss the air next to her cheek.

"Holy motorcycle, honey! Raine mentioned you'd lost weight, but I had no idea! Spin around. What is it? You've got to tell me. The Scarsdale? Beverly Hills? I know—Optifast? No, I know, it's the rice diet, isn't it? Whatever it is, I'll start right this second," she says, cramming three-quarters of her sandwich down her throat.

How dare that rude hog eat that right here in front of my face, me being so starved I could wrestle her to the floor for the crumbs. "Just healthy dieting," I say—*you know, starvation, bulimia, forced diarrhea*—"and lots of exercise. Mom's been jogging with me every day."

"You look fantastic. You don't even look like the same person from when I saw you last. When was that, too? I guess back when you had that accident at the quarry? Remember?"

Don't you dare, Miss Accordian Ass, get self-righteous with me. I've heard those rumors about you having a charter membership at the abortion clinic. So don't even pretend you haven't dipped into the wading pool a few times.

"Oh honey, I'm sorry," she says, noticing my tightened lips. "I guess it's something you'd just as soon not think about, isn't it? I don't know what it is with me, but seems no matter what I say, I'm always mixin' a little pepper with the sugar . . . I was in a car wreck once myself."

Car wreck? Is that what she's talking about? "You buy anything special?" I say, peering in her bag, steering away from the subject.

She smiles. "Only the things every full-blooded girl needs to live: scented floating candles, a bucket of amaretto popcorn, a remaindered two-pound solid Easter bunny at the Chocolate Chocolatier, and some Icarus angel wings from a display they were taking down at the Hallmark . . . real feathers, too. You know me, always thinkin' about Halloween." She lets out this great wheezing, sucking roar of a laugh. "Honey, how is your mother? Wanna walk with me down to Rich's?"

Stepping in stride with her, I say, "She's fine. She's down at the pet store trying to get people to sign a petition against importing tropical birds." *Why am I walking with this sow when I hate her guts?* "She says most of them are smuggled in illegally."

"Oh honey, that's so sweet. She's a real dynamo, your mother is."

After this, neither of us can seem to think of anything else to say to each other, and I get the feeling that Sheba regrets having been so neighborly. She starts glancing at her wrist, like she wishes there was a watch there. "So you're just stuck here killin' time?"

"Well I just finished rentin' a tuba for the Miss Alabama pageant, but I kind of need to go to the drugstore."

"A tuba? Honey, that's so inventive!"

"You think so?"

"Oh, you'll be the hit of the show."

"Really? You really think it's a good idea? I've never played one in my life."

"Well don't you worry. My brother used to play one in the marching band back in high school, and honey, if he can do it . . ."

"You don't think it'll look dumb, do you? Overpowering, I mean. The thing's as big as I am."

"Don't you worry about that. Take it from an expert, honey. Size makes no difference. If it did, a cow could catch a rabbit. Talent's what matters." Sheba pauses a moment, looks a little perturbed, then says, "And that's what worries me about Brent all alone out there in LA. He still hasn't called or anything. I even asked his parents, but they haven't heard from him either. I

just hope he's okay. That boy doesn't have any street smarts."
She leads me to a window to drool over an ostrich boa. It's
almost embarrassing to be seen with Sheba. Here it is, two in
the afternoon, and she's dressed in this beaded flapper thing with
pearls and an emerald-colored hat with like a foot-wide floppy
brim that might have been chic at a garden party fifty years ago.
She reminds me of *Really Rosie* for some reason. "Oh but
honey, it's two hundred and I haven't paid April's rent. Well,
I'm sure there's something just as nice waitin' for me at the
unclaimed baggage sale. Do you have your evening gown
picked out yet?"

"Uh-huh. It's blue velvet...a size seven. I still have a few
more pounds to go."

"Oh, you'll make it. Who designed it?"

"Dior."

"Oh honey, he's my favorite. Him and Halston and Perry
Ellis. Although I hope those rumors about him and Way Bandy
aren't true. You know, about having that AIDS thing? It scares
me sometimes, too, 'cause I haven't exactly been Donna Reed
in the kitchen these last few years." She heaves a sigh. "But
then again, I guess we all gotta go. And if that ends up bein' my
exit ticket, well, I'll be there in Heaven with Way to do my face
and Perry to dress me." She smiles one of her smirky smiles
again. "I'll be the most sought-after angel in Paradise."

"What do you need at Rich's?" I say, not wanting to get any
deeper into the subject of death or anything even remotely connected with the baby. I'm beginning to wonder if, in fact, Sheba
doesn't know it's mine after all. And if she does, just how
up-to-date is she? Does she know Raine stole it back again from
the post office? Does she know where it is now? She's not acting
a bit apprehensive. Maybe only the other three know—and
Brent's out of the picture 'cause he's in LA—which only leaves
Raine and that pimpled Hitler, Jack. There's got to be a way of

finding out how much she knows without bringing up the subject.

"Some new shoes for work, honey. Something with crepe soles if I can find it. I'm tired of wastin' perfectly good loafers just in the name of lookin' cute. They're too expensive and they wear out too fast. Plus I've nearly killed myself twice already, what with traipsin' up and down those ramps all night and waiters trackin' all that grease around the kitchen. Not to mention the bird doop! It seems like I *always* get that bird cage prep. It's that Tara woman. She hates me... or loves me. I don't know which."

The restaurant! Of course, Turtle Dove, of course that's where they've hidden it! You've checked everywhere else. You've turned that whole house inside out, you've found an excuse every day to borrow Raine's car just to check the trunk, you've even managed to case Jack's place—the door wasn't even locked—where else could it be?

"Honey, you won't die if we wander over here to the Cookie Connection, will you? I can't help myself, though. Me and junk food go way back." So she orders this two-level double fudge chocolate chip cookie with creme in between, and switching her bag to the other arm, she bites into it, goop squeezing out the edges. "So where's Raine today, honey?"

"I'm not sure," I say. Quickly. Absently. My mind going double-time. "Probably off with that Jack doing whatever it is they do." *I don't think she knows. She's been disqualified for some reason, probably after I stole it from under their noses at the ice cream parlor. Maybe she accepts that as just some random happening—a blessing in disguise. Maybe you should take a gamble, Lollipop, and just point-blank ask her whatever happened with that baby they found back at Christmas. If she's ignorant, she'll only assume Raine told you about it, figuring it no longer mattered since it had been stolen anyhow; and if she knows it's*

167

yours she'll just assume the obvious—that you have no soul or shame. In either case, you've not much to lose . . . except the pageant if she tattles.

"Honey, I'm tellin' you, that Jack is too much for TV, isn't he?" She shoves the last of her cookie into her mouth and then slurps the crumbs off each finger one by one. "You promise not to say anything if I tell you a secret? . . . I mean aside from him walkin' the crooked mile." She rolls her eyes, giving that technicolored hair of hers a saucy, mysterious toss. "If you know what I mean, Jellybean."

"I won't tell, hope to die."

She leans close to me, her voice a whisper. "Well, I don't know how much you've hung around him, but if it's any length of time at all then you'd know he's obsessed with dead things. Ob-sessed." She tilts her head down. "It's all he talks and thinks about. Especially celebrities. He's really into dead celebrities. Anyway, and I guess I'm going to have to backpedal for this to make any sense—come on over here and let's sit on that bench —anyway, right after my Christmas party we found something . . . I shouldn't be telling you this but it's gone now, so what-the-hell. We found . . . we found a baby. It was dead. Now, I don't know whose it is or where it came from, but the point is, we didn't go to the police. We didn't do anything. Honey, I know it doesn't make any sense and I hope you're not too scandalized, but I've been wantin' to tell somebody this for the longest, and, well, I don't usually like women but I feel close to you somehow because I know Raine so well. Plus, we've both been overweight, you know, so there's some common ground around us, and if I'd told a man, he'd have only been judgmental about it all, which wouldn't have reflected well on me, not that I have any boyfriend I could have told anyhow . . . oh honey, I'm talkin' too fast and not makin' any sense at all, am I?"

"No, no, go on," I say, so relieved she's ignorant of this web that it's almost touching.

"I knew you'd understand, honey. Only a woman would. But like I was sayin', we were too afraid to do anything with it, so we just wrapped it up in a box and carried it around everywhere until one day it was stolen, just out of the blue like that, and at first I was scared but then I was relieved. Then I got scared again. Honey, I think Jack did it. Not literally, I mean, 'cause he was with us, but I think he had somebody do it. He just passed it off too easily. It didn't bother him at all. Not a bit." She licks her fingers some more. "And honey, even though *I'm* the one who suggested ice cream, let's face it, I am a creature of predictable habits."

"That's the last time you saw it?"

She nods. "But honey, it gets stranger. Brent left a typewritten note when he took off—Brent, who wouldn't even know how to turn a typewriter on—and even though Jack's denied it, he *owns* a typewriter. The reason I know is because he lives right above me and sometimes I hear typing through my window at night."

She's right there. You saw a typewriter in Jack's closet, didn't you, Sherlock . . . and just what was his apartment door doing open anyhow? Could he have been expecting you?

"Plus, honey, Jack's been wearin' Brent's watch. But the other night at work I asked him about it and he said it was a fake. Right. Like I don't know the real wheel when I see it. Then I mentioned it to Raine, but he only turned white and rambled something about having to check his tables. It's like he couldn't get away fast enough. You know what I think, honey? I think Brent fathered that baby and I think Jack found out about it somehow—he never has liked Brent—and I think he bought his watch from him and blackmailed him to leave town. That's the only explanation for Brent not callin' me. 'Cause we were close, you know, and it's just not like him not to tell me he was leavin', even if we did have a squabble."

"But Sheba, isn't Brent gay?"

"A little, but no more than any other boy that cute. Honey, all the eights and over make fair game for both sides. You'll start realizing that when you've danced around the campfire as many times as I have."

"Well," I say, using all the abandon of a bystander, "what do you think Jack wants to do with that baby?"

"How would I know? He's just crazy, that's all. But lately Raine eats, sleeps, and breathes every word he says. I think they're cookin' something up, Heaven knows what, but I've seen them having conferences in the waiter stations. We never do things together anymore either, not since Brent left. They don't even come thriftin' with me to the DAV. It's just weird, honey. And you wanna hear what Jack did to me the other night after work?"

"What?"

"It was after we'd all finished our checkouts and everything. I'd made fifty dollars exactly—a decent night but not a great one—and I'd asked Tara if she'd change it in for a fifty-dollar bill, as how I wouldn't be tempted to break it quite so fast, you know. Well, Jack swiped it out of my apron up on the third floor where I was clearin' my tables, then he walked over to the railing and held it over the bird cage and said I had three guesses to name which president was on it. Well, naturally honey, I missed. So Jack dropped it, and I had to walk all the way downstairs to get it, but Jack, he followed me down. Then, when I got inside the cage he slammed the gate, locking me in. It's a door, really, with steel bars shaped like ivy and all; and honey, as I found out for the first time, the bars are too close to reach your hand through to the doorknob, and I didn't have the key on me. So guess what Jack did then?"

"I'm afraid to ask."

"He said he'd go to Amerpsand for the key only after I named a five-letter word that couldn't be broken down into anagrams."

"Wait. What's an anagram?"

"You know, like using the letters from one word to make another."

"Oh, okay—sounds like something Jack and Raine would get into."

"So picture this, honey. There I was, standin' there in that cage goin' 'fluff,' 'table,' 'grand,' 'blimp,' 'dream,' just any five-letter word that came to mind, having to keep a lookout above for bird droppings; and Jack, like some computer, rattling off anagrams just as fast as I could come up with words. In the meantime, too, one of those buzzards had swooped down on my fifty and taken it up to her nest, but finally I thought I had him with 'civic,' but even that wasn't acceptable. He said the letter 'i' is also a word, which of course ruled out anything with an 'i' or an 'a' in it. I'm tellin' you, if Ampersand himself hadn't come down when he did, I would have been there all night, stuck in that cage, shit dropping on me, saying five-letter words till I dropped."

"Did Ampersand say anything to Jack?"

"Oh honey, he's so out of touch with what's going on he just thought it was an accident. When he unlocked the door, Jack stood behind him, though, with hate in his eyes, leering at me, and snarled, 'Lynch.' I never got my fifty back either."

"Where was everybody else during this?"

"They'd all gone home already, even Raine. See, only the closin' waiters have to stay past eleven usually. Listen, you won't tell Raine I told you any of this, will you? I still love him and all."

"You don't have to worry about that."

"Cyra, I can't tell you how much better I feel to have somebody to confide in. I knew when I ran into you it was fate. Really, honey, I was about to bust." She leans over and gives me a squeeze. "Now, you've got to tell me where I can get tickets to the pageant."

"I think Mom may have some extra ones... about Brent, you've no idea who the mother is?"

"None. Honey, you don't think I'm just bein' paranoid, do you? 'Cause I do come from a good family. Granddaddy was governor of Missouri, you know."

"I don't think you're being paranoid. I always suspected Jack was somewhat of a back number." *Please, Saint Joan, spare us the sanctimony.* "You haven't noticed any other strange things going on, have you? At work I mean." *No dead babies lying around, for instance?*

"Only that everyone seems to be havin' these bizarre obsessions lately. That Tara creature can't tear herself away from the garbage cans. Jack's all but having an affair with the walk-in freezer. He's *always* in there, and every day this past week your brother's been bringin' in new plants for the bird cage, arrangin' them all just so, like it's not already a jungle in there as it is."

"Plants in the bird cage? What kind of plants?"

"*Plant* plants. You know, bushes. Trees. Expensive stuff with lots of leaves. It must be costin' him a fortune, unless Ampersand's underwriting it all. Still, I don't know why Raine's doin' it. He's never cared about those birds before."

Oh, My Sweetness, what a stroke of luck you've had today ... the bird cage. Of course that's where it is. Poor dumb Sheba, though—outside the triangle, not knowing what to make of it—the ignorant, fat, unsuspecting wretch.

Standing, I glance around, acting as though I suddenly remembered I don't have time to go shoe shopping after all. "Sheba, it looks like Mom's finished at the pet store. It was so nice runnin' into you. I'm sure Brent'll call soon. I'll have Mom send you a pair of tickets, too, assumin' I take my preliminary. Bye now."

Sheba waves at me. "Which you will, Sugar Booger, I just know it."

Chapter Seventeen

RAINE

"I KNEW IT! He snaps his hands together and holds them up, quickly tilting his head—Dick Nixon doing his victory salute. "Didn't I tell you, Raine? Didn't I?" He turns back to Sheba. "And you're absolutely sure she's coming?"

Sheba throws out her arms, palms up. "Honey, how many times do I have to say it? *She'll* be here. You should've watched the way her eyes lit up when I told her Raine was totin' plants in every day. I'm tellin' you, she took off faster than a weevil from a cotton fire. I don't see how she's stood it to wait as long as she has."

"She's probably waiting to see if she wins the preliminary first," I say. "That Miss Jefferson County thing, or whatever it's called."

"A genius," Jack says. "I'm a despotic genius!"

"All right people—*awraht peepul*—no congregatin' in the kitchen unless you're runnin' food out. Herd those tables. The hostess just went into a wait!" *Hurred doze taybulls. Thu hoze-*

dez jes whint entah uh wayte! Tara fixes her attention on Jack. "Did you know one of your tables was sat a full ten minutes ago and they still don't have menus?" *An' dey steel dohan hev mihnuze?* "Does a green grasshopper have a red asshole? Of course I knew. They're waiting on somebody else to join them." He cocks his head and, leaving Tara to eat her dust, meanders blissfully toward the freezer where he's been keeping Brent's body stashed in a plastic drum marked "TROPICAL BIRD FEED. DO NOT OPEN." The cooks don't question it and Ampersand never goes in there, so I'm the only other person who knows what it really is. Lucky me, again.

"Order up twice," calls out the chef, wiping his brow. Sheba and I grab a serving tray apiece. She whispers, "Honey, I still don't like what y'all made me do. Now she thinks I'm her best friend."

"Hey, wait. I don't have anything to do with this. It's all Jack."

"Raine, she's *your* sister . . . and just how are y'all so sure it's hers anyhow?"

" 'Cause I found a bloody blanket in the garage with some of the umbilical cord still in it."

"You didn't," Sheba says, screwing her face into a road map. She slings a lemon crown onto each plate. "Why didn't y'all tell me this before?"

"I was ashamed of her I guess. I don't know."

"It's just incomprehensible, honey. She seemed so . . . pleasant."

"Yeah, well, there's a lot around here that defies imagination."

She hoists her tray onto her shoulder. "When's Jack gonna tell me where Brent's stayin'? He promised he'd tell me soon as I got back from the mall. Now it's been nearly a week already. Also, I don't understand why, just because Brent's payin' Jack installments to get his watch back again, that Jack gets to be the only one of us privileged to know Brent's whereabouts. I mean, he didn't even *like* Jack. What could he possibly be doin' out there that requires such secrecy?"

I hold the door open for her and shrug. "I don't know either, Sheba."

"She's asking lots of questions," I say, plowing an ice cream scoop through a gallon of mango jubilee. My breath is a cloud of frost, blurring the image of Jack, sitting on the "bird feed" drum in the far corner. The only light is a thick glass bulb suspended within a steel cage from the plated aluminum ceiling. It's dim and coolly eerie.

"I expected she would."

"But I can't keep evading everything forever."

"And you won't have to. I told you the plan."

"But I don't want to go through with *the plan.*" The scoop isn't working right; the freezer's set too low. So I'm having to help it into the dish, leaving finger-holes behind in the ice cream.

Jack leans forward, pulling his head back from the frozen wall. A clot of hair doesn't make it. "Listen, Raine."

"No, you listen to me a second. There's one dead body in the bird cage and now one in the freezer. Hell, pretty soon they'll be all over the place. Don't you know what we're doing?"

He jumps down. "Sure I do. Want to see it?" He pulls off the lid. "Voilà!"

"Put it back!" I whip around, facing the shelves of ice cream and frozen fish wrapped in waxed paper. "Please, put it back."

"Oh, come on, Raine. He's dressed."

I shake my head, smoothing over the holes with my thumb. "I've got dessert to serve," I say, backing toward the door. "You've been in here too long, too. Sheba and Tara both are getting suspicious."

175

Placing the lid back on the drum, Jack says, "You're right. It's getting too cold in here anyhow." He gives me a reassuring smile. "We'll talk about this more after work." Then he pats me on the back like Beowulf and follows me out the door. "Just remember, Raine—the plan."

"Queer as a football bat," clucks one of the nigra dishwashers, watching us come out of the freezer. He grins—fat white teeth—turns up his radio, adjusts his cap, and goes back to the groove of shoving fish bones down the garbage disposal. Jack salutes him.

It's not that I'm disgusted to find out Jack murdered Brent or even that he went about it in such an emotionless way—playing upon Brent's self-pity late one night after Brent had a spat with Sheba, telling him how he'd always lusted for him, knowing it was just what Brent needed to hear. Then, rendezvousing with him on the river bank, tying him up, gagging him, and slowly cutting his heart out just to watch his facial expressions—no, that isn't what keeps me wondering if I'm alive or not. It's not the gruesome things at all. It's the placid, calm, even way in which the day-to-day parts of my life keep flowing by unchanged: shaving in the morning, being careful not to nick myself; drinking my tea unsweetened because the sugar isn't good for me; calling my grandmother once a week because she's very old and doesn't have much longer to live; covering over the finger-holes in the ice-cream so as not to offend a customer. These are the things driving me over the edge. These, these . . . social expectations. And, of course, not being able to trust anyone. Even my own mother.

See, she straggled in from the mall the other day (the same day Jack pistol-whipped Sheba into "bumping into" Cyra) depressed as all get-out. She'd been hoping to get at least five hundred people to sign her petition banning the sale of tropical birds but had persuaded only nine. I was in the kitchen when she came in. Cyra, I saw, hightailed it instantly across the driveway to her own apartment; in order, no doubt, to scheme up some cockamamie strategy for stealing back her child—a plan that, whatever it required, would certainly end up playing right into Jack's own. He's a master at that; being able to second-guess his opponent's next move . . . yet he hates chess. I can't guess why. The game was invented for him.

In one fluid motion, Mom pulled out a chair, ripped up her petition, tossed the pieces into the air, and skittered two airline tickets across the table. "I stopped off at the travel agent on the way home. One for you. One for me." A flake of petition settled in her hair. She brushed it away.

"Where are we going?"

"São Paulo."

Well surprise, surprise. "Mom," I say deliberately, "I don't think that would be a rational move."

"Don't give me rational, Raine Freeman. I've *tried* being rational before. But nothing rational, nothing real, nothing of substance and cause has any place anymore . . . nine people. Nine miserable people. And four of them only signed it because they remembered me from that levitational therapy group. The other five were kids. It made them feel grown-up. Not a single one of them had the tiniest inkling of what I'm fighting for here. A beautiful world for the future. Not that they would have cared."

"Mom, I can't go to Brazil. I don't know anyone there. I don't speak the language." Standing, I crossed around to the other side of the table and sat next to her. "We just wouldn't make a difference."

"You have to come with me, son. We *can* make a difference. We can stop the slaughter. The madness . . . we can at least stall it awhile and pray *somebody* wakes up."

"But . . . but what about Cyra?"

"She won't come. Won't even consider it. She's inspired only by her vanity . . . please, Raine. It's the only hope for saving us.

If we don't go, if we don't act now, then we'll only unravel when things start going wrong."

"Things? What things? Nothing's going to go wrong. We'll be okay. You're just a little tired. You should try to relax more."

"That's not true! There's going to be a war soon—for a dozen years maybe. Could be a little more. Probably less. It'll be the end of life as we know it now."

"How are you so sure?"

"I *just* know. I don't pretend to understand it all, but a new era is being ushered in. Can't you feel it? Can't you? The accelerating energies? The mass consciousness? We can no longer exist just for ego alone. We must submit ourselves to a greater purpose, for we're entering a perfect position to bring new order to our gentle earth. Man *can* coexist harmoniously with nature, but there's too much resistance. Raine, our *true* identity is not material. It's spiritual. God never established karma, we did, with our own free will. Of course I have my astrological chart, but I know about my free-will options and am not bound by choices in an interlife before I came here." She opened her purse and took out some weird-looking stone object. It looked like a cat. "Raine, we must have alternatives to this Judeo-Christian myth because there is simply no trusting rational thought anymore." She pushed the object toward me. "A sphinx," she said. "Looted from burial grounds in Peru. It's of the ancient Moche Indian culture. They preceded the Incas by a thousand years. It's a very important tool. The sphinx and the pyramid are the two most powerful symbols on earth. They are eternal. This sphinx is a four-dimensional expression of the new reality. It represents the full power of man—the female's breasts, the male's face, the wings of an eagle, and the lion's body. You should carry it with you always."

"Mom, where did you get this?"

She pushed away from the table and went over to the range where she turned on a flame beneath the tea kettle. "I could feel you slipping away, son . . . so I bought it when we were in New York last spring. It's why we went."

"Slipping away? Wait just a minute here, who's slipping from whom? *I'm* not the one roosting in the trees out back!"

"Listen to me," she said, ignoring my outburst. "We'll only stay a little while. We'll just ride it out and come back when it's over, whatever there is to come back to. You could start your painting again. There are still beautiful parts of Brazil. You could preserve it, son. *You* can show them how it's supposed to be."

"Mom . . . Mom, I could paint here if I wanted to."

"But you're not! You're *not* doing it here and I don't understand why. It's your gift, Raine. It's what you're *supposed* to do."

"I'm sorry. You just have to go without me. Maybe I am floundering a little right now, but at least it's familiar . . . it's not that I don't think what you want to accomplish isn't worth anything. It is. But I just can't handle change. I don't think I've ever been able to."

"So, just like that, huh? My own children turning their backs on the single most crucial age in human history. One out of vanity and one out of fear." The kettle started whistling, and she carried it to the sink where she held out her hand and began pouring the scalding water over the back of it.

"Mom, what are you doing? . . . Mom!"

"Oh, I know what you're both thinking—that your old mother has gone denser than a box of rocks. Her battleship mouth's finally overloaded her rowboat mind. Am I right?"

I kicked back my chair and grabbed the kettle away from her. She only smiled and held out her hand for me to see. It wasn't pink or blistered or puffy. It was perfectly normal. "See what you can do when you can overcome fear, son? You can do anything. You can change the world for the better, or you can change it for the worse. Stay behind, and the easier of the two will win out. I'll let you guess which one that is."

So now, in addition to *my* life, I can no longer even trust my mother to keep her own out of danger. There's no telling what stunt she might pull next—jumping out of her trees? Setting herself on fire in front of the pet shop? God knows! But at least I can keep an eye on her here. What if she really goes through with this Brazil thing, though? I shudder to think what might happen to her down there.

"Okay," I say, "here's the thing. The Gods say your whole family's finally fallen over the brink. They've gone totally schizoid. Your mother, well, she's about to move to South America where she can pour boiling water on herself and ride out World War III, leaving you in the mansion alone with your kleptomaniac sister to play hide-and-seek over her dead baby— your sister, Miss America. But this, you can handle. This, you're used to by now. No, the trouble is your best friend, whom you've practically grown up with; the one who saved you from the narrow-minded jaws of southern conventionalism, who opened your mind to real thoughts, advised you to be your own person and not to wallow in the shellacked morass of any collective mentality—never considering that perhaps you weren't cut out to be a revolutionary—well, maybe considering but certainly not caring. But that's neither here nor there. The point is, there is the very distinct possibility that something has, oh how shall I phrase it, 'happened' to this friend, that maybe he's grown too bored along the way and, consequently, is now more stark raving mad than all the others combined. Furthermore, either consciously or unconsciously, he's sucked you down with him—be it for companionship, a feeling of superiority, whatever—the end result being that you... me... *I* no longer even have the capacities to tell the real from the unreal. So, given that all has become just a numb, colorless wash, the question The

Gods are just dying to know is: of the aforementioned people and circumstances, *who,* when all's said and done, gets out alive?"

"You do," says Jack, sitting next to me, Indian-style, here in the middle of the triangle out front of The Dakota. It's three in the morning, and Sheba's window, way up on the eighth floor, is the only one in the building with a light still burning. Either she went out and hasn't come home yet or she's reading and eating. It's still way early for her bedtime. "Only you," he says, passing the bottle of red wine back to me.

"You're drunk," I say, swigging it.

"Than a nine-eyed nigra on payday." He unscrews the cap on another. "But I always have my facilities . . . my faculties about me, even as we speak."

"What about you?"

"Me?" He looks around, as though to confirm the question was meant for him. "What about me?"

"What's going to happen to you?"

"You think I know?"

"I'm sure you do."

"You're right, Raine." He takes another gulp. "Right as rain," he says, chuckling humorlessly at the pun. He leans back, wavering, and squints up to Sheba's window. "You see her in there?"

"No. She's out I guess."

"Out of what?" he says.

"What?"

He hiccups three times real fast. "What's she out of? Her mind? Luck? Onion dip? All of the above?" Next, he aims his newly opened wine bottle toward Sheba's window. It makes a wobbly arc a few feet higher than our heads, then shatters on the street behind my car. Jack always did have the most pitiful throwing arm. "Just you wait 'til all the scores are tallied. She's the one who'll end up doin' better than any of us. It's always the lazy, happy ones who do the best."

"You think she suspects about Brent?"

"Hell no. Death doesn't enter the thoughts of a sybarite."

"So maybe you won't kill her after all?"

"That's not what I said."

Chapter Eighteen

CYRA

"WELL, THAT'S WHAT I heard. And if she hasn't had a boob job I'm a natural honey blonde."

"The one over there with that missing-link-monkey look? What's she plannin' to do for her talent, chew Milk Bones?"

"Pardon me, Sweetness. I can't help but wonder though, is that Clairol or Chlorox?"

"Such a pretty white beaded gown, dear. Be careful you don't sit in any lipstick now, you hear?"

"She didn't? That old roadwhore? Why, if she had as many pricks stickin' out of her as she's had stuck in her, she'd be a porcupine."

"Taped them? Well isn't that just the difference between chicken shit and chicken salad."

"She calls *that* an evening gown? It looks like she flew around all the pretty buttercups and landed on a cowpile."

"Big hair. Biiiiiiiig hair . . . Miss Helium Head."

"Oh my God! Is she in the pageant again? If I have to hear one more rendition of 'Buttons and Bows' in A-flat, and I *mean* flat . . ."

"And who's been frostin' your hair, Sugah? Duncan Hines?"

"Look at Lady Sumo over there, the one with the tuba. She's not actually going to *play* that monstrosity?"

Lady Sumo indeed . . . just you wait, you little snit. You and your dainty little waist with your dainty little clarinet. We'll see who ends up at the Miss Alabama pageant next month, and it sure won't be any dime-a-dozen clarinet player. I'll guarantee you that!

Just take a deep breath, My Beauty. Hold it for five seconds and then let it out slowly. Don't be nervous. The secret lies in appearing calm. It's only a beauty pageant and your chances are every bit as good as any of these cackling shrews. After all, you made it, didn't you—a size seven? True, you're hungry enough right now to eat the makeup off your face and wash it down with nail polish, but I doubt you're alone. (Produce so much as a soda cracker in here and you're risking a riot.)

"Well, there you are," Mom calls from across the dressing room. "We've been lookin' all over for you." She pushes her way toward me, smushed into the corner back here all alone.

Oh Dear God, and look who's behind her!

"Hey, honey!" Sheba, dressed for a luau, smiles and hugs me. "Honey, you won't believe it, but Jack agreed to take my shift tonight just so I could come watch you win. My, but if you don't look prettier than *Life Goes to the Movies,* doesn't she, Mrs. Freeman?"

Mom agrees and says, "I'm so proud of your new confidence, Cyra."

Sheba brushes at a piece of lint on my shoulder, then takes some hairspray off the counter and touches up a loose spot behind my ears. She looks up as the lights start blinking. "You need anything before we take our seats?"

"I'm all set."

"Well come on then, Sheba," Mom says. "Let's don't make her any more nervous than she already is."

Sheba starts to follow Mom through the crowd but then, like an afterthought, she says, "Mrs. Freeman? You go on, I'll be right there. I just need to give Cyra one last piece of lucky advice."

Oh, just what you need.

She turns to me conspiratorially, hand over her mouth. "Will you meet me after the pageant? I have to talk with you."

Great. Another stupid theory about why Brent left town?
"Well, I have to at least make an appearance at the party, even if I lose. Plus, well"—*think, Cyra*—"plus Mom asked me if I'd help her pack; she's leaving for Brazil soon, you know."

"But I have to tell you something." Her voice goes serious. "It's *really* important."

Why me, Lord? "It'll have to be late."

"The later the better, honey. I've got to drop back by work after the pageant anyhow. That Tara woman, our 'manager,' took vacation this week to go hiking with her girlfriend in Wyoming or some such place, so Ampersand's entrusting me with the keys to lock up every night."

I add an extra dab of eye shadow. "Around twelve then?"

"Perfect."

"I'll meet you at your apartment. It's the eighth floor, isn't it?"

"No, not there. Anywhere else but there." She smooths down the zipper in the back of my gown and scans the room as though afraid somebody might be listening. "Something's wrong, I . . . I feel like I'm being watched there. Oh honey, I know it sounds crazy but I'll explain it all later. How about just at the restaurant?"

Where those swine have my baby stashed? "But won't there still be people there?"

"Well, you pick a place then."

Wait just a minute, Precious, what are you doing? Don't you realize this is your golden opportunity to check out that birdcage? Like, how often do these chances come along? You may not like her, but she sure has a way of popping in when you need her the most. So don't blow it!

"No, no the restaurant's fine. Twelve o'clock."

She seems relieved somehow, and smiling at me she holds up her hands, fingers crossed. "I'll be the one clappin' the loudest."

I don't know, the closest thing I can compare it to is sleep-walking. It's like for two hours of your life you're going through these animated motions—smiling and striding and parroting lies about yourself—your only conscious thought being, *Please dear God don't let me trip.* Miraculously, everything goes okay. At least from your perspective (even your tuba recital) and then, suddenly, you realize you're standing alone onstage with just one other bimbo; she's got blonde hair for days and a klieg light smile (if you had to guess her name, you'd say "Sunshine"). The brightness around you is blinding—all the flashbulbs and spotlights and cameras—so all you can see is some groomed-to-the-gills master of ceremonies in front of you, a card in his hands, bathed in a white aura like Jesus himself. Dimly, you realize that he does, after all, hold your salvation in his hands.

It occurs to you that if he personally favored Sunshine over you then he could easily lie and you'd never be the wiser. The judges wouldn't dare make a scene. They'd have to go along with anything he said, but you're holding Sunshine's hand nevertheless. She's your best friend in the world.

"And the first alternate, winner of a one-thousand-dollar scholarship to the college of her choice is ... Cyra Freeman! You, Daphne Baker, will be the next West Jefferson County representative at the Miss Alabama pageant next month! How do you feel, Daphne?"

It doesn't immediately hit me. Kind of like if you touch a pan just out of the oven it doesn't immediately feel hot. But then suddenly the burn sets in, and my hand just sort of slips limply from Sunshine's grasp as she brings her own up to her face, her teeth chattering and her eyes tearing. Flashbulbs magically begin popping yet I feel my own body imploding upon itself. A giant hibernating claw has sprung to life in the center of my stomach, seizing the organs closest to it, and is now wrenching and twisting them, pulling all my bones, muscles, tissues, and blood toward it. The outside of me begins buckling. A supportive arm grabs me by the elbow. I'm being led offstage ... a dozen red roses? That's it? Six months of starvation for twelve fucking roses? It can't be ... it just can't be. "Liar!" I hear someone scream. "He's a liar!" *My God, it's me screaming.* "I see the card! He's lying!"

At first no one seems eager to take responsibility for this outburst, certainly not me. There's a murmur in the audience and a few outright guffaws from the other girls. One of the judges comes onstage, pressing his palms to the air in an embarrassed effort to quiet the commotion. By now I'm panting, obviously delirious, probably as much from hunger as from losing. But the judge is shamed into double-checking the card just the same.

Arching his eyebrows with disbelief, he clears his throat and says, "Well, there does seem to have been a mistake." He flashes the master of ceremonies a look that says it might be wise of him not to plan on hosting this affair next year. "I'm sorry, Miss Baker . . . but if in any event Miss Freeman can't fulfill her obligations as Miss West Jefferson County between now and the Miss Alabama pageant, then you . . . ."

I don't even hear the rest of it. Me? My hands fly to my cheeks. There really was a mix-up? *I'm* Miss West Jefferson County after all? Suddenly that claw in my stomach lets go and the first thing that pops to mind is, *The baby! Now's the time to get rid of that baby once and for all!*

It's nearly midnight before we finally get home from the party. Everyone there congratulated me, even Sunshine, and in turn I graciously confided to her that come next year she'll be the one to beat. But despite my happiness, all I could really think about the whole time was how much higher the stakes have suddenly been raised; that from here on out, the higher I rise within the pageant circuit, the more important it is no one *ever* finds out about the baby.

Pulling into the driveway, I say, "Mom, I need to borrow the car."

"This late at night?"

"Sheba asked me if I could meet her. She's at the restaurant."

"Is that where she took off to so fast?"

"Well, the manager's on vacation this week so she's havin' to close."

"Well when did you two become so chummy? She's a nice girl, sweet as she can be, but a little . . . oh, unusual. Don't you think?"

"Mom, you're really one to talk."

She says nothing, but leaves the keys in the ignition as she gets out. "Don't you at least want to change out of that dress?

You don't want to ruin it before the real pageant."

"I don't have time. I told her I'd meet her at twelve. I'll be careful though."

So Mom nods and heads up the sidewalk, stroking the amethyst around her neck, but before I've even turned around in the driveway she's motioning me to wait. "Cyra, I just remembered there's a present for you in the trunk."

I roll down my window. "Present?"

"Hand me the keys and I'll take it out. That friend of Raine's —you know, Jack—he brought it by earlier while you were getting ready and asked that I give it to you after you won." She walks with the keys around to the back of the car. "I don't know why I didn't think about it sooner, 'cause he specifically said I should hand it to you on the stage . . . I guess my mind's just been so preoccupied with my pilgrimage."

In the rearview mirror I see the trunk pop open. *This can't be happening to you, My Pet. You've come too far for this.*

"It was so nice of him to just *assume* you'd win . . . not that I had any doubts myself—you are such a pretty young lady, Cyra —and that tuba recital was nothing less than inspired." She pushes the trunk lid back down.

You could kill her right here and now . . . you . . . you could say she left early for Brazil, that she decided her guidance just couldn't be postponed any longer . . . Raine's not here—his car's gone. It's midnight for Christ's sake. Who would see you?

"I just wish your brother had taken off work, too. Oh well, he'll be sure to catch you next month at the state level." She comes back around to my window.

Just as you suspected, even down to the wrapping—brown paper and all.

"Cyra? Dear, are you okay? Don't you want to open Jack's gift? He'll be just heartbroken if you run into him at the restaurant and he finds out you haven't even opened it yet."

"I . . . I don't have time, Mom." *Girl, just throw the door*

open, knock her down, then run her over. It's not that hard.
"Just give it to me and I'll open it at the restaurant in front of him. He'll like that."

"But he specifically said for you . . ."

"Mom, just *give* me the box!"

"There's no call for that tone of voice, young lady. You may be grown but I'm still your mother, and I still expect you to respect that. When you get to be my age you might be able to stand with the Devil's grandmother, too. But in the meantime, how you're perceived is reflected in the company you keep, and Jack's one of the nicest young men I know. I can't care if he does look like he needs to sharpen his pencils, I won't have you bein' rude to him; a reaction that comes all too easily for you as it is. You must keep in mind, Cyra, that in being a pageant representative you're a role model for many young girls. It's what you wanted and I expect you to live up to it, regardless of your natural inclinations. Do I make myself clear?"

"Yes ma'am."

"It's even more important now that I'll be leaving soon. I can't go down to South America havin' to worry about you all the time. I have to feel you're on a proper course."

"Mom, I wasn't being rude. I'm just in a hurry, that's all."

"Fine then," she says, opening the back car door. She slides the box gently onto the seat, closes the door, and backs slightly away from my window. She smiles at me now, woman to woman. "I always did suspect that Jack had a soft spot for you . . . you could do worse." She crosses her arms. "My daughter —the beauty queen. Oh well, have a good time, dear, and don't stay out too late. Remember, you promised to help me disassemble the pyramid tomorrow. I want to make sure it's on the same flight I am."

I nod at her and surge out of the driveway, turning left onto Argyle. A thin, straggly fog has settled in beneath the trees, but luckily I'm the only one on the street, 'cause automobile safety is about the last thing on my mind. Steering left again, I switch onto Niazuma and then down to Highland Avenue. I pull up to a well-lit curb, shut off my headlights, and reach around to grab the box. Surprisingly, it's lighter than I expected it would be. Much lighter. I shake it, but hear nothing.

It's just a trick, it can't be the baby. Can it?

A car passes by and for some reason I duck. Lying down in the seat, I hold the box against the floorboard on the passenger side and yank at the string, then, I break a nail clawing at the paper (my nails took like two months to get into condition). I curse Jack's name and rip open the box flaps ... *a bird cage?* But sure enough, it's just one of those domed wire things with a single little swing in it, something like what Tweety lives in. Perched on the swing is a folded card. I open the cage door and pull it out, sitting up in the light to read it. It says:

A box in a cage or a cage in a box?
Which one is it?
P.S. Scared you, didn't I?

Chapter Nineteen

RAINE

"NO, NOT AT ALL."

"But how can you say that? Sheba's one of the best friends we have . . . the *only* friend you have, besides me that is. And I'm not even so sure about that anymore."

"A little late for self-reckoning, don't you think?"

"You *can't* stand there and honestly tell me you won't feel any regrets about this."

"I just did."

"But . . . but what about me? I *like* Sheba."

He shrugs unconcernedly. "She knows too much, Raine."

"She does not. All she knows, or thinks she knows, is that Brent told you where he is and you're not tellin' her. She doesn't realize he's dead. She doesn't know you killed him."

"You forget we had to tell her who the baby belongs to."

"We didn't *have* to. We didn't *have* to do any of this. What does it matter if she knows anyhow? She was there when we found it. She has a vested interested in keeping mum. Why would she tell?"

"Because I told you before. Your sister's plannin' to murder you tonight and Sheba knows that."

"Who told you this? Cyra herself?"

"Sheba told me. She dropped by my apartment this afternoon, all in a fluster, and said she'd just gotten off the phone with Cyra. Apparently, your sweet sister confided in Sheba that if she won tonight she'd murder you."

"I don't believe it. You're just makin' this up."

He does a scout's honor salute. "Swear on your grave that's what she said. Raine, I've been tellin' you she'd resort to this all along, but you're so afraid of the truth you won't listen. If you'd had any sense, you'd have just let her go ahead and mail it to Brazil, or at least not have hinted you'd gotten it back."

"But *you're* the one who *made* me keep it. I was all for returnin' it to the post office that following Monday."

"Wouldn't have made any difference. A crow doesn't care what kind of ammunition the farmer's using."

The things Jack says never follow any natural, A-to-B order of thought. He's always gettin' me confused, like now, talkin' about crows. He sidetracks me, he purposefully does it, just to make it seem like *I'm* the one out of focus. "Wait a minute," I say. "Even...even if Cyra was plannin' to kill me, she wouldn't be blabbermouthin' it off to Sheba. I *know* my own sister and she doesn't operate that way. She's a loner."

"Go ahead then. Choose denial if it helps you cope any better, but don't expect me to help you when she comes barrelin' through those doors in a few minutes aimin' a shotgun at your face."

"Oh really? And where in sam hill is she going to get a shotgun? A minor just out of high school."

"Sheba told me this afternoon that Cyra had been outright

braggin' about how she'd just shoplifted one—just waltzed right into Sears, took it off a shelf, and waltzed right out. Of course, now I suppose you're gonna tell me your sister would never shoplift either."

He's got me there.

"She knows the baby's here, Raine. Knows beyond the shadow of a doubt . . . trust me. Hell, she's looked everywhere else, even my own apartment. In fact, I left the door open just to save her the trouble of havin' to make up a lie to the super for the key. I didn't want her making a copy of it and feelin' like she's welcome any time . . . and I know she's been there 'cause the thread I tied to the doorknob on the closet was snapped. She's a creature without ethics, Raine, and she's coming here tonight to kill you."

Somehow, in some deluded, ghastly way this makes sense. Cyra's vindictive by nature, plus she's obsessed with this petty beauty pageant stuff. Not to mention that she's never even liked me. God only knows where she's headed in a few years, undoubtedly either prison or the presidency. She's an extremist like that. "I just can't believe it. And Sheba's known all about it but isn't even doing anything?"

Jack, looking momentarily startled, says, "Raine . . . where's your mind? . . . Sheba's helping her."

"What?"

"Do I have to spell everything out with a crayon?" He puts his hands on my shoulders and leans me against the cold, stainless steel doors of the freezer, real coach-to-athlete-like. Slowly, very patronizingly, he says, "I had to tell her that you killed Brent."

"Me? Me! You goddamned liar!"

"Hold on a minute, just hold on. Get your eyes back in your skull. It was the only line of tactics that would work. The only way to make your sister's vengeance against you appear to have even a threadbare rationale behind it . . . Sheba's visit caught me off guard. I had to think of something fast."

"Oh God, this isn't happening. It can't be real. It can't be." I try to come up with some logical argument, something to clear my head, but everything's like one of those jumble squares where you have to find the right words, either backwards or diagonally or upside down, and it's just been too scratched over too many times. "But I'm so mixed up. Why was it so important that Sheba believe Cyra's acting rational? Why didn't you try to convince her of just the opposite?"

"Because Cyra's going to attempt to kill you regardless. If not here, then somewhere else. She's liable to try it anywhere, any time. You'll never know. The only way I can protect you is if we can control the environment it takes place in . . . but in doing so we have to have Sheba's cooperation, and the only way to get that is to convince her that you're a threat to the safety of all of us. Don't you see?" Now he looks to the floor, feigning embarrassment. "Sheba asked me to help her, Raine. What could I do? I had to say I'd keep you here tonight after everyone else is gone. When she comes back to lock up, she'll be bringin' your sister with her. We can take them both at the same time."

I start laughing in spite of myself, but it's a laughter with no humor in it at all. "Let me see if I've got this straight: The three of you are supposed to kill *me* tonight—the only one of us who's even halfway normal—but all for different reasons? Cyra because I'm jeopardizing her chance at being Miss America by keeping her baby stashed in the bird cage, which *you* did; Sheba because I supposedly murdered Brent, and you because the location's good and it's all such a hoot?"

"No, not me. Raine, I'm here to help *you.*"

"And what a charitable act it is, too."

"Raine Freeman, I never thought I'd live to see sarcasm pass your lips. It buttresses my long-held opinion that beneath that polyurethaned exterior lurks something living after all."

For a fleeting lucid cut-glass second it occurs to me that if I just opened the freezer door and pushed Jack in, locking it behind me, my troubles would be over. *You could turn down the temperature, and by the time they found him tomorrow he'd be as solid as Brent!* Yet Jack would find some way to incriminate me—he'd scratch my name into the frost or something. He could probably get me for Brent's murder as well. They'd surely find both bodies. Also, worse, there's the chance he's actually telling the truth . . . God in Heaven, what if he is?

Who'd go to prison? Not Jack. He could lie his way out of Hell. Not Cyra. She's in the running for Miss Alabama and might as well be Caesar's wife. And certainly not Sheba. She's barely a bystander. No, I'd be the one leaning on steel. All the evidence points to me alone, thanks to my best friend here. No one else but me . . . *but not without a body it doesn't.*

"What time is it?"

Jack checks Brent's watch. "Eleven-forty."

"And what time are they getting here?"

"Sheba and I agreed on midnight."

"Then we've still got twenty minutes."

"For what?"

I fling open the freezer door, run inside, and begin dragging out the "birdseed" barrel. "You're sure all the other waiters and cooks are gone?"

"The last one left about half an hour ago . . . what are you doing?"

"And what about Ampersand?"

"He left for the Galápagos Islands yesterday afternoon. Penguin hunting or something. Where are you taking Brent?"

"Help me drag this toward the dishwasher."

"You don't want to open that lid, Raine. It's not pretty."

"And grab me a knife. A big one. Like the kind you used on his heart."

"The dishwasher? Raine, that's mine. It belongs to me."

"No way am I going to prison."

"Prison? Who mentioned anything about prison? Everything's taken care of, Raine. Just stick to the plan."

"Push dammit!"

"The plan, Raine."

"Fuck the plan, I'm not killing Sheba."

He pushes his face up under my own, resting his hands on the barrel lid, while I strain to pull it across the rubber-matted kitchen floor. "She'll tell," he glowers. "I know she will."

"Let her. It'll be nothing but hearsay without a body. We've got the note you typed. I'll just say Sheba's been acting a little manic depressive lately because he hasn't called her. They can't prove he's not in LA."

"And what about your sister?" He presses down harder on the lid, his face a boiling beet.

"I'll take my chances . . . where are the damned knives?" I'm jerking randomly at the drawers beneath the cutting-board surface of an island the head chef uses for slicing meat.

Jack's mouth drops open as I snatch out a meat cleaver. He jumps onto the barrel, curling his fingers under the lip as though fearing the top could blow at any second. "Raine, you know how squeamish you are. Remember how . . . remember when you threw up last year when I took you through the animal research lab at UAB after hours one night, and remember when you fainted that time in ninth grade after I broke my leg at Six Flags and the bone came through?"

"Get off there and help me lift the barrel up to this island."

"No, Raine. It's mine!"

"Okay then," and I throw the meat cleaver at him. He dives to the floor and it narrowly misses his forehead, clattering into the steel sink behind him instead.

He jumps to his feet, incomprehension engraved in his eyes. "You could've killed me, you know that!"

I go back to the sink and grab the cleaver. "I'm putting his body down this garbage disposal, be it in one piece or twenty."

"Have you lost your mind?"

"Possibly."

"No, I'm sorry," he says, "but I just can't let you do that."

"You can't stop me."

"Yes I could...but it won't work anyhow. He's frozen solid."

"It'll work. I've seen that dishwasher guy shove tin cans down the thing. There's nothing it can't turn into soup."

"You're not going to do it."

"Watch me," I say, daring him, brandishing the meat cleaver in front of me like something out of a horror film. I go over to the barrel, pull off the lid, and with a Herculean surge of adrenaline, tilt the barrel up to the chopping block. Brent's body, naked, thunks onto the table—a pasty bluish unrecognizable thing—just a chunk of matter, a piece of frozen mass, resembling nothing like the person I once knew. I can no more imagine that it previously breathed oxygen or spoke to me or ate popcorn with me at the movies than I can imagine myself in prison. I take a mindless, vapid whack at what was formerly an ankle, thinking to myself that the instinct of self-preservation has to be the most powerful force in nature.

The separation is as clean as if I'd sliced through an apple.

"Raine," Jack pleads, trying to connect the foot back to the shin bone, like the parts are magnetized or something, "think about what you're doing. This isn't a side of beef here, it's Brent...Brent, our friend."

"Was, Jack. He *was* our friend. Now he's nothing...turn on the spigot and flip the disposal switch on. I'll cut, you grind. Toss that foot into it. Here's the other."

But before the cleaver comes down again, while it's poised for a microsecond above my shoulder, Jack grabs it—grips it around the blade—and snaps it out of my clutches. The red starts trickling onto his palm even before he's pulled it to him; it's at this moment, seeing his blood, that the situation's grave clarity spins into sharp focus. I take a step back, staring first at Jack's hemorrhaging hand and then to the frozen, crumpled heap on the island. "This isn't what youth is supposed to be about," I say. I turn to run, to get just anywhere away from this kitchen. But The Gods are still in a playful mood.

"Honeys," the voice comes reverberating in from the dining room, "is anybody still here?"

Chapter Twenty

CYRA

WHERE DID EVERYBODY GO? I drive into the lot but there's not a car in sight. Even the street lights have been turned off. The windows in the restaurant are pitch dark. Am I that late? The only other time I was here was several years ago when the place first opened, back before Raine was hired. Mom brought us for a celebration of sorts, another straight-A report card for Raine or something (it seems we were always congratulating *his* achievements). The place was like *the* hot spot at the time and the lot was full. Nothing like this. I don't remember the woods being so close or it feeling so . . . isolated.

Maybe Sheba hasn't gotten here yet. A little bit of a moon is up and the river in front of me is glowing quietly and gurgling as happily as a baby . . . *don't forget what you came here for, Sweet Pea.* As long as I'm waiting I might as well take advantage of the river. I step out of the car, closing my door softly, then reach back through the window for Jack's little gift; the bastard. I walk to the edge of the lot, my high heels making a light clickity-clack against the pavement, and fling the cage as far as I can. It lands about midstream, and for just an instant it appears to float, but then it vanishes. Already I feel triumphant. What's Sheba got to say that's so hushy-hush anyhow? Whatever it is, I'm sure I couldn't give a flying cat's back. *Then why don't you just go ahead, sneak into the bird cage, find your baby, and get the hell out?*

I pull off my shoes and, very skulky-like, walk up the series of crisscrossing wooden ramps to the entrance, it being on the top level where a verandah with a thatched overhang wraps all the way around the building. When the weather's nice, people can take drinks out here or eat dinner while they watch the river. It's a great place for parties. Eerie isn't the word though if no one's around, but maybe this'll work out better than I'd hoped. I mean, it's not like somebody might come passing by and see me. It'd be so easy to just, rather casually, break in through a window.

I glance around for something heavy. Down at the other end of the verandah is a hanging clay pot with a fern in it. But as I go to remove it from its hook, I spot the three cars—Jack's and Raine's and Sheba's—way at the end of the lot, lined up all nice and neat, almost hidden behind a dumpster under the trees. A chill goes down my back, knowing they've surely been listening to me clomping around out here, are probably snickering among themselves, just waiting to see what I'll do. Damn them.

Well, so what? Sheba asked you to come by. It's not like you're trespassing or anything. You're expected.

Suddenly though, it hits me. How could I be so dumb? No wonder the lights aren't on—it's a surprise party! Oh God I feel stupid, and slipping my shoes back on I walk back to the door. Covering the sides of my eyes, I press my face to the glass and can just make out the top of the bird cage beyond the hostess stand and the coat room behind that. Just how many people, I wonder, are in there? "Hello," I call.

Somewhere, down on a floor below, a light snaps on. It flashes up through the cage as though from the bottom of a well. All the birds go shrieking to the top like somebody's just fired a shotgun or something... and that's when it happens: the scream. A woman's scream. *Sheba?* God, it's awful. Even worse than Sugar Ball's. Like the loudest, most hair-raising sound I've ever heard. Lurching backwards, I catch myself against a post. Just as mysteriously though, the screaming suddenly stops and the light goes out again. All's as still and quiet as before, but for the racket from the cage.

What is this, some kind of joke? Scare the wits out of the beauty queen—is that what it is?

Trembling, I go back to the door but see nothing. The birds still won't shut up, however, and from their background I can faintly pick out some kind of machine just turned on in the kitchen. It's making a slow, gurgling sort of noise... no, not gurgling, grinding. Grinding? *Run, girl. Just jump in your car and leave!*

But there's one part of me too curious to tear myself away, a part of me that wants to know exactly what *is* going on down there—the same part that makes me go snooping in places I ought never snoop, the part that makes me take things without paying for them and throw objects over sides of buildings that aren't mine; the very part that kept me denying pregnancy in the face of all obviousness—a part I tend to submit to rather than submerge, to ignore rather than intimidate; a part that'll probably be the death of me... *but hot damn, didn't she look good!* I grab the fern pot and smash it through a window.

Jack screams, "I told you, Raine! And there she is now, coming to get you!"

I run over to the railing next to the domed top of the cage. In the filmy river light reflecting up from its glass bottom, I can just make out my brother, shaking all over, as he comes charging out of the kitchen. Jack's right behind him, blood smeared all over his hand.

"My God, what happened to you?" I say, gripping the rail. Terror fills my brother's eyes.

"Don't come near me!" he yells, retreating back toward the kitchen door. "I didn't have anything to do with . . . with . . ." He points to a spot in the cage beneath a bush.

So it is in there after all.

I look to Jack, who only embraces me with the wickedest grin ever. "And what are you smiling at?" I say. "Who screamed a second ago? Sheba? Is she here?"

"In the freezer," says Jack, nonchalantly.

"The freezer?"

"Oh, it's a big one. She's plenty of room. Unfortunately, you see, she walked in on a—he turns to Raine—help me out here, will you? . . . A rather grisly experiment, you might say."

Experiment? Not with my baby?

I start running across the catwalk and down a ramp to the second landing. "But what's she doing in there? She's all right, isn't she?" Raine backs further away the closer I get. He's got this dazed, myopic look on his face, like someone in shock. Something feels awfully wrong here. I hesitate, slowing down my stride, as I get closer to the two of them. "Why aren't any lights on?"

"Why, the better to flatter your rare beauty, Miss Freeman," says Jack, bowing cavalierly as I reach the bottom. "And how fetching in velvet you look, too. We did win, I hope?"

At this point, Raine scurries back into the kitchen and a moment later I hear this heavy, grating noise—like a battleship being dragged across concrete. Then, through the door's porthole windows, I see him straining to position a case of metal shelves in front of the kitchen doors. A barricade? Flying pots, a cacophony of silver, plastic jars, utensils, and dishes go clattering out all over the place. Next come these muffled banging sounds as though from someone locked in a closet. *Sheba in the freezer?*

"What the hell's going on here?"

"Oh you know," Jack shrugs, "just our usual Saturday night at the asylum . . . you wouldn't happen to have heard any good palindromes lately, would you?"

"What?"

"Able was I ere I saw Elba?"

"You're crazy. You are fucking crazy."

"Well no, that one doesn't quite work. It has to read the same backwards as forwards: 'Lewd did I live and evil I did dwel' . . . a special favorite of mine."

More muffled bangs over the crashing cutlery. "Is that Sheba?"

"Probably . . . Raine, can you hold the noise level down just a little in there? I'm trying to have an intelligent game with your sister!" He turns back to me. "Now then . . . 'step on no pets?' "

I take a step backwards, just a tiny one, suddenly recalling the advice of some naturalist on one of those nature programs Mom used to make us sit through. "If you're in the woods and happen across a grizzly bear, never ever run from it. Stand your ground and he won't attack." Why does this spring to mind now?

"Can't think of any?" Jack says, making a move toward me. "Tell you what, you being a novice and all, I'll even give you credit if the words don't break the same in reverse—if you can just get the letters themselves in sequence. 'Never odd or even' for instance. It doesn't even have to be a complete sentence, just a phrase will do."

I look over my shoulder to the kitchen. "Raine," I call, "whatever's happening here, I don't want anything to do with it. I only came by because Sheba asked me to."

"Don't get near me!" he yells, as though in trench warfare. "I've got knives!"

Jack moves a little closer. "Only because Sheba asked you to, huh? Well isn't that what girlfriends are for, you both being so close like you are."

"What is *wrong* with everybody!?"

"You wouldn't be telling us a little white fib now, would you? It wouldn't be for any other reason, would it?" He spreads his arms out like a game show mannequin. "Like for the surprises we might have here in cage number one?"

"Fuck off!"

He lurches toward me, grabbing me by the elbow. "Miss America, what a crude tongue you have . . . I hope no one takes a notion to cut it out."

"Let go of me!" But he twists my arm behind my back and kicks me in the back of the knees, shoving me against the cage. "Stop it . . . Raine!"

"I'm trying to play a game here," he says, clenching his teeth, "and you're not being a very cooperative opponent." With his free hand he fishes a big set of keys from his apron pocket, deftly inserts one of the keys into the cage door, and then rams the door with his foot. "But maybe you'll get better as the night wears on."

"What are you doing? You're hurting my arm!" All of a sudden I feel a kick in my side, like from a baseball bat—the birds go screeching into their tree—and before I even realize it, I'm inside the cage with the door locked. *This can't be happening to you.* I jump to my feet, staggering from the blow, and yank at the bars. "Let me out!" I look to the kitchen again. "Raine, come out here. Talk some sense into this person!"

Jack steps away from the door, grinning. He drops the keys back into his apron. "So nice of Sheba to get here before you did. I guess it's just my lucky night . . . Did you get my gift?"

"Oh God," I'm saying, "Oh God." I begin pacing in little circles on the glass floor. Stay calm here, Cyra. Stay calm. Raine will come to his senses. He will.

Jack goes over to a table and drags a chair up next to the cage door. "Now then," he says, sighing happily, "Bob, did Anna peep? Anna, did Bob?" He looks at his watch. "Your turn. You've got one minute. When the minute is up, if you still don't have a palindrome, it doubles. Which then gives you two minutes." He holds up two fingers, like a teacher explaining addition to a kindergartener. "And when your two are up it doubles again, and so forth and so on. We could easily be here all night."

Furiously, I yank the cage door, rattling the iron lock back and forth in its catch so fast it sounds like a machine gun. *This can't really be happening . . . it's too much like one of your nightmares in Hell.*

"Oh, and by the way. You'll find baby Jesus underneath that rubber plant next to the waterfall. You've been a neglectful parent, Cyra. A mother and child shouldn't be separated such great periods of time. It thwarts the child's emotional development, inducing defiant and aggressive behavior—just ask my own mother, if you can find out where she's living . . . I never could." He crosses his legs, checking his watch again. "Now it's two minutes."

"Raine! Raine, please!"

His response, tinny and thin, comes echoing back. "You said you'd help me, Jack. Remember? Remember? . . . Did you get her gun?"

Gun? I turn to Jack. "What have you been telling him?"

Snickering to himself, he casually reaches into his apron again and pulls out a small bottle. He unscrews the cap, pushing it under his nose, and inhales. Even from this distance in the dark, I can still see his face flush. Now he wads up a cloth napkin and douses it with the rest of the bottle's contents. Next, taking a pack of matches from an ashtray, he lights a candle in the center of the table. A single pink tulip, overhanging the flame in a vase next to it, immediately begins to crinkle and turn an ashy color. In fascination, Jack watches the flower sink lower and lower until finally it drops completely limp against the glass, charred and unrecognizable. "Isn't it amazing how much heat one tiny candle flame can produce? Don't you find that amazing, Cyra?" He picks up the candle, wraps the saturated napkin around its base, and begins walking in a slow circle around the outside of the cage. Round and round and round. A few laps later he says, "I just figured out why it is I respect you so much, Cyra: we can both kill without remorse—a useful trait. . . . May a moody baby doom a yam? Four minutes."

"Raine!"

Jack pauses for a moment, allowing the flame to catch its breath. Suddenly, he snaps his fingers. "Damn, I knew I forgot something." He looks at me almost apologetically. "I'm sorry, but here we have wasted all this time and I've completely failed to mention the most important rule of all."

Carefully, he places the candle down in the center of a cleared table, bunching the doused napkin around it. Then he goes to all the other tables, gathering up more napkins, which he piles in a circle around the doused one. He stands back, clasping his hands together, admiring his cleverness. "Now, the longer it takes you, the shorter this candle gets, and the shorter the candle gets, well, you're a clever girl, Cyra. I'm sure you understand the consequences of dallying too long."

I run to the part of the cage closest to the kitchen, nearly tripping over a peacock. "Listen to me, Raine. I don't have a gun. I never had one. Whatever Jack's been telling you, it's just a lie!"

"Oh yeah!" he shouts. "So what about that phone call you made to Sheba this afternoon?"

"What phone call? Raine, I've never called Sheba in my life. I don't even know her number. All I know is that if you don't do something soon, this whole place is going to burn down over our heads!"

"Eight minutes," says Jack.

"Raine, get the keys and unlock this door!"

Jack smiles at me, as though to say, *it's my finger he's wrapped around, baby, not yours.* Suddenly though, he whips around toward the kitchen as the light snaps on. That grinding noise I'd heard before has started again.

The garbage disposal? At this point, with the candle flame a mere quarter inch above the folds of the napkin, I start screaming; less out of desperation and futility than from what I see in the kitchen as Jack rams against the doors. They swing inwards, causing the barricade to go screeching onto its side—any remaining bottles and jars spinning out in all directions like firebursts. But one of the doors doesn't swing back into place; it catches against the handle of a heavy black skillet, which acts as a doorstop. There in front of me, as though I'm looking through the yawning, fluorescent-lit gates of my Hell, lies Brent Brantley—blue and naked and minus his feet—the roar of the disposal's motor burying every other sound around me . . . *Billy Netherland, Billy Netherland, Billy Netherland!*

The birds are going crazy. They're flying all over the place, directionless and disoriented—crashing into the glass floor, into my head, squawking and cawing, feathers swirling everywhere. The fire's caught! The doused napkin has burst into flames, instantly igniting all the others around it . . . a bonfire on the table!

"Somebody!"

"I told you not to touch him," barks Jack. He shoves Raine away from the sink, knocking him against a wall. A cork bulletin board goes sideways. Both of their faces look all greenish under the harsh kitchen lights. Raine's breathing hard, shaking his head.

"We've got to let her out," he says, wiping his hands on his pants.

Oh thank God. He's finally come around.

"She'll freeze to death," he adds.

"Hey!" I scream. "Hey! What about me?" I grab the door again, rattling it back and forth. A few of the burning napkins waft onto the floor. One of them singes the draped edge of a tablecloth a few feet away. The corner of it smolders a moment, then catches. In no time, the flame is climbing aboard the table-top, lapping at the wicker underliners. *Come on sprinklers. Turn on, dammit. Turn on!*

Jack presses Raine against the tilted bulletin board, scratching his fingernails into the cork. "Don't be ridiculous, Raine. She's *seen* the body already."

"But she knew anyhow! I thought you told her I did it?"

"Well, well maybe I was exaggerating a little."

"What?"

Jack takes a step back, smiles, and matter-of-factly says, "It's all part of the plan, Raine. Everything's been factored in from the very beginning, even from the first day the baby was found. Every mathematical and psychological detail. Each little decep-tion; just a cog of an intricate whole . . . all the way down to the conversation we're having now. You've only been in on the parts you needed to know. I could even tell you who'll still be alive when the sun comes up tomorrow and, of course, who won't."

Raine stares at Jack as if out of all the people in the world he expected such a thing from, Jack's the last. "You mean until she got here tonight, Sheba really thought Brent had been in LA all along? She didn't come here to kill me?"

Abruptly, the fire alarm sounds, a blaring horn that fades in and out like the wail of a doomed ocean liner. Raine looks first at Jack, not quite comprehending what the noise is. Then he turns to me. I'm screaming my lungs out. Fires have blazed up on several tables by now, with napkins—flaming tumbleweeds —scuttling from one to another. An acrid cloud of purply brown smoke is beginning to blot out the top branches of the tree inside the cage. All the birds are now scurrying around my feet like psychotic rats. "The keys, Raine! Jack's got the keys!"

"And Cyra didn't come here to kill me either?"

"You're mumbling under your breath, Raine. Maybe you just need to lie down a few minutes and sort things out. Let's go upstairs to Ampersand's office." He holds out his arm for Raine to take it.

"Don't listen to him! My God, can't you see the building's on fire! . . . The keys! Get the keys!" All around me, in every direction, the fires are finding more and more to feed on—rattan chairs, osier paneling, thatched alcoves, raffia mats, and buri screens—why, the whole damned place might as well have been built of newspaper! "Hurry!"

"The keys?" he repeats, like it's a word he's never heard before.

The alarm seems to be getting louder and the smoke getting denser by the second. I grab at the hem of my dress and pull it up to breathe through the fabric. Panic is setting in. I mean the *real* stuff. *I'm not going to make it. Dear God, I'm just going to burn to death in a fucking bird cage.* My eyes are tearing from the fumes, but rubbing them only makes it worse. I kneel down at the fake rock waterfall and splash water into them. "Don't let me die, Lord. Not this way. I know what I did wasn't right and I'm sorry for it. Really, I am. I'll even go to Brazil with Mom if you'll just let me live through this. I promise I will. I'll make up for all the bad things I ever did. I'll be so good. I'll help save the rain forests and care for starving people and educate people about pollution—all that stuff, if you'll just let Raine get the keys. I won't ever shoplift anything again. I won't be rude to my brother. And I won't even think about beauty pageants. Not ever again. I'll even let Sunshine be the new Miss West Jefferson County. Please, please just let me live."

I glance up for a moment, but the smoke's too thick now to see any more than a rectangle of murky light where the kitchen door is. Jack and Raine appear to be grappling with each other in silhouette. Only a few of the birds are still making any noises; and way in the distance, through the dark clouds, is a whole wall of flickering orange. My hair suddenly feels hot. It smells funny. Instinctively, I duck my head into the water, bringing it back up again to wipe my eyes. From somewhere comes the sound of splintering wood. Upstairs, a beam crashes. Now I jump completely into the small pool, counting the seconds, concentrating on making a palindrome, listening with all I've got for the rattle of keys in an iron cage door. Suddenly, I feel a bump against the back of my head . . .

Chapter Twenty-one

RAINE, 2003

"AND I DON'T REMEMBER anything after that. My last recollection—just a fragment really—is some smoky, hallucinatory scene of me and Jack fighting in the kitchen with butcher knives, Brent dead on a slab between us with no feet, Cyra locked in the bird cage, Sheba in the freezer, and the entire building burning down around us. I mean, it wasn't exactly a situation that inspires perfect recall, you know. Also, it *was* twenty years ago. Sometimes I think you forget that."

Scratching at the whisper of his mustache, Dr. Rivenbark shrugs placidly and glances at his watch. "I've offered hypnosis, Raine, many times. I really think it would help you with the gaps." His voice is gravelly yet without hard edges, like polished stones pumped through a padded cylinder. He shrugs again. "But you seem to have some ungrounded aversion to it that I can't understand."

"No, it's not the technique I'm opposed to . . . I just don't want to know. That's all."

"Not even if it's for your own good?"

"Not even."

He looks at me, attempting to make eye contact, but I just sigh and bring an ankle up to my knee. "Raine," he says, "there are some things we do in our past that, despite all evidence to the contrary, never seem real in retrospect. Just last night, for instance, I watched a movie about the Holocaust. It's hard to believe it ended only four years ago, yet our systematic 'relocation' of *every* single Japanese-American citizen seems no more believable to me than I'm sure Auschwitz did to the Germans after World War II. I know it happened, but what came over us?"

"So what are you saying?"

"What I'm saying is that as hard as it is for you to examine those lost months in your life—specifically between December 1983 and May 1984—you're going to have to try. Those six months are your own personal Auschwitz. Your personal San Jose. They *did* happen, Raine. And until you force yourself to sift back through the rubble, you'll never get over this feeling of being somehow responsible for it all." He scratches at his mustache again, then lightly pats his peppery hair. A single, tiny gold bead of an earring catches the dim light and sparkles for a split second. "Just relax, Raine. Don't get flustered. Try to remember."

"Look, how many times have we been over this? A million? Two? All they ever found were bones. Just a few charred bones is all, and I can't offer any more pieces of the puzzle than that."

"Yes, but you said yourself they found enough to positively identify both Brent *and* Jack."

"*So* what? We all stuck by our story—Brent came in from LA hoping to get his old job back . . . someone had left a burner on in the kitchen, there was some grease on the stove . . . they didn't make it out in time—happens somewhere every day."

He brings the tips of all ten fingers against his chest. "Raine,

I'm not accusing you, but obviously you're uncomfortable with such a simple, sweeping generalization, even if the police are not. I'm only trying to help you." Next, he leans slowly back in his chair, clicking a pen spasmodically. He adjusts the vertical blinds a fraction. "Now what about all these little unsolved *details?* Tell me how you feel about them."

"Details?"

"Brent's foot bones, for instance . . . never found a trace of them. No clothing remains either. Not a shred." He clicks his pen again. "Can you shed any light on that?"

"Nothing. It's just a blank."

"Well how about Jack's broken ribs?"

"Excuse me," I say, "not broken—sliced. That's what you meant to say, isn't it? At least that's how the inquiry phrased it: 'as though with a knife of some sort' . . . a meat cleaver, perhaps?"

"Yes," he repeats evenly, *"sliced* is what I meant."

"Well," I add, tossing my arms into the air, "as long as we're on the subject, why don't we bring up those teensy-tiny unidentified bones found *inside* the cage—the bones not anything like the other birds' at all. Certainly, too, we can't leave out that partially burned body discovered in the freezer—the one with the missing heart . . . poor Tara. Hide nor hair was never heard from Ampersand again either. I'm sure if they'd 'sifted the rubble' a little more thoroughly they might have found him, too. No telling who else." I turn a fierce look on the doctor and his glittering ear. "Do you want me to admit to killing them all? Is that what you want?"

"You're pitying yourself again, Raine. I've told you before, *no one* is accusing you. We both know who the guilty party is."

"Well, if *we* know, why is it the police were so willing to accept our feeble alibi? Especially in light of all these mysterious little 'details'?" I give him a pleading look, noticing for the first time the polished rhino horn on his desk. In Asia, it would fetch two hundred grand, easy.

"I can't answer that, Raine." He brushes at the sleeve on his jacket, then licks the ends of both index fingers and pushes up his eyebrow hairs.

"Well why is it I always feel like I've gotten away with something that no one else could've pulled off, even though deep down I *know* I never did anything? Does my sister feel the same way?"

"Raine, I've repeatedly told you that's privileged information." He leans over his desk, places his pen down, and picks up the rhino horn. The man cannot sit still. He strokes the jade base, then taps the tip of his pinky against the dulled point. "Now, if you'd both like to start coming to group—"

Shaking my head, staring at that manicured finger tapping the point of an extinct animal's face, a sudden mental ticker tape of all the other recent fatalities begins clicketing by: *the African elephant, the Asian elephant, the dolphin, all whales, all reptiles, the Russian bear, the American bald eagle* ... "No thank you," I hear myself telling Dr. Rivenbark above the racket ... *the panda, all owls, the whooping crane, the reindeer, the koala, bluebirds* ... "No, I'd rather we keep it one-on-one for the time being."

"Something bothering you, Raine? We still have fifteen minutes."

"No," I say, unable to take my eyes off that horn. *Manatees, sea anemones, the salmon, the oyster, snail darters, all woodpeckers, clams*—something's happening here, it's like I can't shut the damned thing off—*elm trees, abalone, coral reefs, the platypus, chestnuts, coconuts, toucans* ... "Doctor Rivenbark, have you ever been to Brazil?"

"Brazil?" he says, startled but trying not to show it. Undoubtedly, he assumes I'm suffering a setback. Reluctantly, though, he takes the ball. "Well no, but my son was there last summer as part of that environmental reconstruction program all the colleges have started. For three months he did nothing but plant trees in the desert . . . most useful thing he ever did in his life." He places the horn back on his desk and again picks up the pen. "Your mother's the one who initiated that, isn't she? How long's she been the ambassador now? Ten years?"

"Twelve."

He chuckles and resumes the clicking. "What's that nickname the papers are always calling her? Mother Theresa of the Amazon? You must be very proud."

. . . *Ebony, mahogany, teak, cacao* . . . "I've been thinking about joining her, in fact."

He arches his slicked-back eyebrows suavely. "But your latest showing was such a success. You sold them all, didn't you?" He swivels around and smiles at the painting behind him. "Even I got suckered in."

"Yeah, but I need to try a new setting."

"The juices here beginning to stagnate?"

I squinch my eyes together so tightly I can feel the crow's feet. I'm trying to ignore that damned horn, but the racket is only growing more and more torturous and deafening . . . *clickety-clackety, clickety-clackety, clickety-clackety . . . krill, crayfish, goldfish, all marsupials, kapok trees, snow leopards, Siberian tigers, birds of paradise, belladonna, all sharks, starfishes, seals, capybaras, cardinals, ducks, egrets, lovebirds, partridges, peacocks, puffins, parakeets* . . . "It was Mom. It was Mom!"

"Pardon?"

"Of course. I don't know why it never occurred to me before! But she'd come for the birds that night—all those tropical, caged birds that Ampersand used to smuggle in. Their natural, God-given rights to freedom were being violated or something of the sort—at least that's what she told us afterwards—but you know, that couldn't have been the real reason she was there."

"No?"

"Well, why did she pick that night? Why not the night before, or five years before for that matter?"

"Are you saying she knew what was going on?"

"I don't know," I say, "I don't know. But she always had an uncanny intuition about things. I remember she gave me a sphinx once—a miniature one from the Aztecs or something— that supposedly has this great power. Well, she went to make some tea, but she burned her hand somehow . . . no, wait. She, I know, she poured the boiling tea water on her hand, and it *didn't* burn her. Apparently, this was proof enough to give me some weird mind trip about overcoming fear. It was her ploy to make me agree to come to Brazil with her. But I guess when she saw it wasn't going to work, she set her sights on Cyra, even though she knew Cyra would probably be twice as hard to convince . . . but then Jack came by with that box on pageant day, the one with the bird cage in it—which Cyra, remember, thought was the baby—well, Mom must have seen an opportunity. I'll bet she knew about Cyra's baby all along!"

Fondling the gold stud behind his ear, Dr. Rivenbark says, "What makes you think that?"

"Because I switched out that box at one point earlier in the week—the week of the fire? Things were getting kind of hairy, you know. Jack was acting crazier than ever and I was convinced I'd be the one going to prison if anything slipped up, so on his off day I replaced the baby with a box that only had a block of wood in it . . . Those little bones shouldn't have been found in there at all."

"Well, what did you do with the baby?"

"I destroyed it. It went the same way as Brent's feet, box and everything, which I suppose means those bones really were just some sort of strange tropical bird."

Dr. Rivenbark runs his fingers along the crease of his lapel.

"Tell me this," he says. "Do you remember whether you destroyed the box and baby separately, or together?"

"Well I sure didn't open it, if that's what you mean. Hell, it'd been dead for six months."

"So when was the last time any of you actually *saw* the baby?"

"Well let me think. You know, I guess only the first day we found it. None of us looked at it after that. We just kept rewrapping it all the time."

"So then you can't say for sure that the baby wasn't switched out months before by someone else?"

"No, no," I say, not quite realizing his implication. "We never even let it out of our sight."

Smiling, Dr. Rivenbark holds up one spindly finger. "Not once?"

"Well . . . only in the very beginning I guess. It kept being rotated from one car to another. It's hard to remember now."

Like a rhino himself, the good doctor snorts happily, sending the tips of his mustache into a flutter. "You know what I think? I think your mother is the one having the last laugh here. I think she took that baby away right from the very start. Call it the maternal instinct to protect one's own, but I do believe she thought that one or all of you would've ended up bungling it, left to your own devices, and then somehow incriminated the rest of you. Think about it. She sure couldn't have her pride and joys in jail, now could she? No matter what kind of crazy, post-adolescent hormones were producing such behavior. No, she's a woman of vision, your mother. A woman with foresight and plans to protect the future." The doctor leans his elbows onto his desk and lets his hands flop back, palms upward. "Who's to say she simply didn't stash the poor child away somewhere until an opportunity presented itself—like the fire, for instance. By that time, she was bound to have known all fingers would end up pointing to Jack anyhow, and that in the end, her two precious babies would be the true free birds."

"Three precious babies. You left out Sheba. Mom and Sheba are very close these days. Although I have to say, I've never been a hundred percent convinced it's the environment that keeps Sheba down there so much as how popular she's become with those Latin types. Apparently, she's the toast of Brasília."

"Oops!" croaks Dr. Rivenbark, "I'm afraid we've gone three minutes over." He stands and extends his hand. "Inform your sister if you will, that I'll be on vacation next week—goin' to Antarctica. Never been before, but the beaches are supposed to be gorgeous! Eighty-two degrees year round, so they say. My travel agent told me a group of tourists last month even spotted a penguin. A penguin! Can you imagine?—Uh, well anyway, she can call me anytime before Friday to reschedule. Damn good pediatrician, your sister. I heard she delivered her two-thousandth baby the other day. My, my." He takes the door and slides it back for me. "And I suppose I'll see you again in three weeks, the same time?"

"No," I say, staring him straight in the eyes, "I don't think I'll be back again."

The doctor looks momentarily disjointed. His mustache begins to twitch from the middle.

"I'm joining my mother and Sheba. There are still some beautiful things left out there, and I think it's time I did my part. I suppose it's something I should have done long ago, but then who ever dreamed things would come to this point . . . the world I mean."

"Your mother did."

"Yeah, you're right," I say distantly, thinking back to all those years ago when everybody thought she was crazy. "Mom was the first."

The doctor holds out his hand again, and turning my attention back to him, I say, "But anyway, maybe when I return we can pick up where we left off."

Gripping my fist, Dr. Rivenbark salutes me with the closest thing to a genuine smile I believe I've ever seen him wear, and with a wink of his eye, he says, "Hopefully not, Raine. Hopefully."

Exit

THE PAST

YET PLANKTON, poplar trees, honey bees, all crustaceans, kiwis, polar bears, the leech, the lynx, finches, the sea slug, the screech owl, the ass, the katydid, the newt, marijuana, ginseng, the coca plant, the karakul, the buffalo, date palms, free-range chickens, natural gas, coffee beans, uranium, sturgeons, gnats, mites, the yak, the okapi, the ibex, the iris, the ibis, mistletoe, Queen Anne's lace, Drosophila flies, algae blooms, tomatoes, terbium, tungsten, the mud dauber, lice, rice, green and yellow pygmy long-tailed sunbirds, black widow spiders, the bluebon-net, the coelacanth, cranberries, loganberries, leather, flint, Fa-bergé eggs, Hare Krishnas, the krona, The Volga River, apples, rayon, nylon, Neptune, pablum, pigs' knuckles, India ink, color wheels, manila envelopes, banana pudding, mezuzahs, March, hay, claustrophobia, the White Album, Ash Wednesday, the col-lected novels of Edith Wharton, gerbils, ersatz, sugar cubes, sunburns, sinkholes, quarks, victory gardens, yellow ribbons, words without vowels, the color roan, Rumania, Ramtha, Van

Gogh's "Sunflowers," Warhol's cookie jars, acne, ficus trees, aplastic anemia, menorahs, The Du Pont Corporation, nursery rhymes, rumours, The National Bone Marrow Donor Registry, things that start with the letter 'H,' pumpernickel bread, plastic pink flamingos, neurons, cotton, chop sticks, IBM, opals, okra, gerunds, WIN buttons, tapeworms, the paintings of Grandma Moses, chicken McNuggets, hungry children, Spago, pooper scoopers, Disney World, dentists' chairs, the films of Kim Novak, raisins, snips and snails and puppy dogs' tails, saturated fats, comic books, corn, Kentucky—a man, a plan, a canal, Panama—Polaroid, croquet mallets, scrap iron, hors d'oeuvres, silver nitrate, the poetry of Ezra Pound, peaches, petunias, depression, the Maldives, ground chuck, woodchucks, tombstones, The Beverly Hills Hotel, steroids, faux marble, FAX machines, Yosemite Sam, Stonehenge, bird's nest soup, shoplifters, oboes, envy, varicose veins, that extra five pounds, ivy, umbilical cords, forks, passion fruit, the Pentagon, hashish, pec decks, silos, Glasnost, golden parachutes, paintings on black velvet, hummingbirds, vinegar, temper tantrums, polyester, company picnics, fair weather friendships, weather, Saki stories, Arkansas, protest marches, Goo Goo Clusters, Christmas presents, *Huckleberry Finn,* The Falkland Islands, white chocolate, barbed wire, Velcro, garden-fresh salad bars, bones, football jerseys, tin cans, astro-turf, porno movies, cough drops, Haight Ashbury, moonlight, Bigfoot, dumbwaiters, dumb waiters, cirrhosis of the liver, pomegranates, Lincoln's birthday, acrylics, artificial intelligence, wicker, disinformation, self-cleaning ovens, Homer, herb gardens, right-to-lifers, pollywogs, flax, urine, spaghetti westerns, the songs of Goffin and King, thermodynamics, Third World nations, Alfred J. Prufrock, Jello-brand gelatin, things that start with the letter 'U,' blow-jobs, trumpeter swans, lace, baby's breath, sin, things that glow in the dark, gigolos, interstate highways, Hepatitis B, pineapple upside-down cake, prefixes, denim, oregano, hippies, cysta-

scopes, arboretums, the West Bank, the man on the flying tra-
peze, dypthongs, hydrothermal vents, fast cars in slow-motion,
grief, better mousetraps, Meryl Streep movies, the six o'clock
evening news, gravity, egg plant casserole, Scottish moors, the
capital of Sri Lanka, turkey pot pie, all things considered, teta-
nus, the Commonwealth of the Bahamas, Wimbledon, zig-
gurats, the Fiores, Lyme disease, beach balls, *Green Acres*
reruns, lady wrestlers, tofu, isotopes, Columbus Day, self-ad-
dressed stamped envelopes, Yale, turnip greens, the sand
grouse, things that end before the fat lady sings, wall-to-wall
carpet, lapis lazuli, the lap of luxury, mountain laurel, opaque
glass, chromium, refrigerator magnets, cabbage, the cogno-
scenti, preferred stock, all the ways to skin a cat, hold buttons,
automatic sprinkler systems, dope, anagrams, acronyms, Fuji
film, the Parthenon, voodoo, Saturdays, imitation vanilla ex-
tract, Hells Canyon, toothpicks, toxic waste, Halloween, edel-
weiss, newsreels, a quilt like the kind your grandmother gave
you, cough drops, pleated skirts, flamenco dancing, The Eman-
cipation Proclamation, The Fifth Amendment, chess, The River
Thames, metallic balloons, lye, lazy susans, gurgling brooks,
crystal springs, the month of May, guitar chords, all things that
rhyme with 'cook,' The World Trade Center, fire and ice, Mo-
nopoly, Grey Poupon mustard, drug tests, shoulder blades, padded cells, suicide, genocide, all photographs of Grover
Cleveland, secular humanism, search warrants, ground zero,
Less Than Zero, disinformation, eczema, ivory towers, the second door from the end on the west side of the eighty-ninth floor
of the Sears Tower in Chicago, Chicago, sea salt, testicular
cancer, Bic lighters, dictionaries, daily horoscopes, periscopes,
The Wizard of Id, factory outlets, brie, gorgeous naked women,
Egyptian scarabs, gorgeous naked men, the caffeine high, petri
dishes, magma, chromosomes, involuntary manslaughter, tie-
dying, yucca, calculus, amino acids, string, pollen, semi-
quavers, Istanbul, judicial power, trimorphism, RNA, fool's

paradise, magnetic domain, *Go Dog Go,* family planning, boring dinners, pogo sticks, rudderfish, colloids, the peritoneum, Tokyo, things that defy gravity, Angola, the AFL, beginner's luck, campfire girls, myxoma, weaverbirds, books on Watergate, wash & wear, slaughterhouses, opinions, immunology, brown-nosing, The Euxine Sea, golden jubilees, kidneywort, quotation marks, Crayola crayons, fire-and-brimstone, the stoney end, weekends at the Hamptons, orthography, whiplash, parsley, sage, rosemary and thyme, Tinkerbell, trophy rooms, rapier wit, gunnery sergeants, thc G.O.P., ozone sickness, kaffiyehs, the usual suspects, Rotterdam, music you can dance to, the Hunt family, merry widows, lady's-slipper, seals, neoromanticism, elderberries, muscatel, scuppernongs, The Holy Land, bar stools, gender-benders, race riots, cornbread, fluff, sweet bippies, potato-potahto, tomato-tomahto, grandstands, memories of the Holocaust, farm-fresh milk, megatheres, brook trout, pantaloons, helium, Nostradamus's fifteenth quatrain, sodomy, sodium, gas chandaliers, unicorns, Latin, rubidium, rubies, wolfhounds, vicious book reviewers, marzipan pigs, gravy trains with biscuit wheels, red number 19, mink coats, undertakers, nitrous oxide, dog whistles—this little piggie had roast beef, this little piggie had none, and this little piggie cried, "Wee, wee, wee!" all the way home—roast beef, eye sockets, insane asylums, revenge, grapefruit, shamelessness, YUPPIES, Johnson & Johnson, wimpering puppies, blueprints, limestone, five-star restaurants, nit-picking, death wishes, insomnia, the narwhal, supercalifragilisticexpialidocious, human beings, everything you ever wanted out of life, less and more, in the end, no longer existed.